Freedom's Ring

...powerful journey into past and present...
and uplift. Prepare to indulge in this ma...
country that both haunts and heals long...

JULIE LESSMAN
award-winning author of the Daughters ... ...hange,
and Heart of San Francisco series

"Heidi Chiavaroli's poignant exploration of the deeply broken and very human hearts of two Boston women, separated by centuries but connected through a mysterious gold signet ring, captured my heart and fired my imagination. *Freedom's Ring* paints a stunning portrait of the healing power of love and forgiveness through divine strength. Days after reading, I'm still caught up in the rich historical detail, in the intrigue and mystery that brought three centuries together, and still pondering the difficult choices made by each character. Beautifully written, a riveting debut novel."

CATHY GOHLKE
Christy Award–winning author of *Secrets She Kept* and *Saving Amelie*

"In *Freedom's Ring*, Heidi Chiavaroli masterfully weaves together a moving story about the complexity of love and forgiveness, a novel rich with truth that transcends the barrier of time. Her writing captured me from page one, the strength of her words reflecting the journey of her main characters—past and present—as they sought courage to overcome their fears. A brilliant debut!"

MELANIE DOBSON
award-winning author of *Chateau of Secrets* and *Catching the Wind*

"Heidi has penned an intriguing tale of two women separated by time connected through their search for a strength they desperately need. History and the present are so deftly entwined, readers will be turning pages to keep up with the story tugging on their hearts."

MELISSA JAGEARS
author of *A Heart Most Certain*

"In her debut novel, *Freedom's Ring*, Heidi Chiavaroli skillfully blends two equally compelling stories, set in two different eras. With fresh writing and a richness of detail, the author does a brilliant job of drawing us into each world. From courage in the face of tragedy to the healing power of forgiveness, this book will leave you with a wonderful message of faith, hope, and second chances."

SUSAN ANNE MASON
award-winning author of the Courage to Dream series

Visit Tyndale online at www.tyndale.com.

Visit Heidi Chiavaroli at heidichiavaroli.com.

TYNDALE and Tyndale's quill logo are registered trademarks of Tyndale House Publishers, Inc.

Freedom's Ring

Designed by Nicole Grimes

Edited by Caleb Sjogren

Published in association with the literary agency of Natasha Kern Literary Agency, Inc., P.O. Box 1069, White Salmon, WA 98672.

Freedom's Ring is a work of fiction. Where real people, events, establishments, organizations, or locales appear, they are used fictitiously. All other elements of the novel are drawn from the author's imagination.

For information about special discounts for bulk purchases, please contact Tyndale House Publishers at csresponse@tyndale.com or call 800-323-9400.

Library of Congress Cataloging-in-Publication Data

Names: Chiavaroli, Heidi, author.
Title: Freedom's ring / Heidi Chiavaroli.
Description: Carol Stream, Illinois : Tyndale House Publishers, Inc., 2017.
Identifiers: LCCN 2017001854 | ISBN 9781496423122 (sc)
Subjects: LCSH: Victims of terrorism—Fiction. | Boston Marathon Bombing, Boston, Mass., 2013—Fiction. | War victims—Fiction. | Boston Massacre, 1770—Fiction. | Loss (Psychology)—Fiction. | Faith—Fiction. | GSAFD: Christian fiction.
Classification: LCC PS3603.H542 F74 2017 | DDC 813/.6—dc23 LC record available at https://lccn.loc.gov/2017001854

Printed in the United States of America

23	22	21	20	19	18	17
7	6	5	4	3	2	1

a novel

FREEDOM'S RING

Heidi Chiavaroli

Tyndale House Publishers, Inc.
Carol Stream, Illinois

To Daniel,
my husband, hero, and best friend

ACKNOWLEDGMENTS

IN THINKING ABOUT the people who have supported me in this crazy writing journey, I am overcome with gratitude for all of your love and support.

Thank you to my agent, Natasha Kern, for believing in this book, and for your encouragement and patience with my many newbie author questions. I'd be lost without you.

Thank you to all the wonderful people at Tyndale. Jan Stob, thank you for taking this book on, for smoothing the many aspects of the publication road for me, and for extending grace during our brainstorming sessions. You are awesome. Caleb Sjogren, you've done so much to make this book all it could be. I'm so appreciative of your brilliant insight. Thank you for helping me dig deeper into these characters and for your positive spirit of encouragement. I love working with you. Nicole Grimes, thank you for this beautiful cover. And to Karen Watson, Cheryl Kerwin, Kristen Schumacher, and Shaina Turner, thank you for helping readers find this book!

To ACFW and the many writers who've read my work and helped me hone my craft over the years—Tessa Afshar, Melanie Brasher, Edwina Cowgill, and Nicole Miller. A special thank-you to Sandra Ardoin for her valuable insight and encouragement during our weekly check-ins, and to Melissa Jagears for not only being a wonderful friend and mentor, but for squeezing me into her own busy schedule when I'm struggling with those stubborn plots and characters.

This book would never have come to be if not for Susan Brower taking the time to read the first draft and give me advice to make it stronger.

Thank you to David Lambert, chief genealogist at NEHGS in Boston, for sparking an idea that helped tie these two stories together.

I'm very grateful for my local librarians. Thank you to Carol Gafford, who explained some genealogical research to me, and to Kaija Gallucci for organizing our local writers' group.

Thank you to my church family at WDCC, and especially to John and Pam McPherson, who showed me how truly sufficient the grace of Jesus is.

Thank you to my parents, Scott and Donna Anuszczyk, who've taught me that real love is hard work, but it is *so* worth it. I love you guys. Mom, sometimes when I write words on paper, I hear you in them. I'm convinced your side of the family gave me this writing gene, and I'm happy to have inherited it. Thank you for teaching me to pursue my dreams.

Thank you to my sister, Krystal, for listening to me whine about all those rejections, and for being not only my sister, but one of my closest friends.

Thank you to my sons, James and Noah, for putting up with my computer, for jumping up and down with me at news of a contract, and for making every day both a joy and an adventure. Boys, I'm so proud to be your mom. I love you to the moon and back.

I am so incredibly grateful for my husband, Daniel, who not only encouraged me with words, but who worked many side jobs to help me afford travel to conferences. I could never write a fictitious hero without the inspiration of a real one right in my kitchen. Thank you, honey.

Last, but far from least, I am amazingly thankful to my God. He pursues me with a grace I don't deserve, then gives me my dreams on top of it. Jesus, you rock.

PROLOGUE
Anaya

Death's threshold overwhelmed me in a swell of instant silence and intense heat. The minute before the flash of white and loud *pop, pop, pop,* I'd been pushing the burning muscles of my legs forward in a last throttle of energy, my eyes on the blue finish line of the Boston Marathon. I'd heard my sister's cheers from behind the nearby barricades that separated the racers from the spectators. I knew my niece was with her, and I searched them out, spotted them. Lydia in a Red Sox cap, her daughter, Grace, bouncing with excitement beside her. An insatiable urge to hug them now, in this moment, overwhelmed me. Especially Grace, who trained with me the last four months but would have to wait a few more years to be eligible for the race. Grace, who I knew expected me at the finish line at least fifteen minutes earlier.

I ignored the burning in my lungs and lifted my arms

to reach over the barricade to hug my niece, her eyes bright and dancing.

I never touched her.

I was late. Too late.

Now the foggy quiet fell over me in a thick cloak. I lay on the road, marveling at the blue sky through the sulfur-scented haze. I opened my mouth to cry for help but could not hear my own screams. I lifted my head to see a blur of mangled limbs and blood and glass on the pavement of Boylston Street. The crush of hurting people transformed the celebratory race finish into a hot, smoky place of torture. The scent of burned flesh assaulted my nostrils. Sour bile pooled in the back of my throat. I didn't allow my eyes to roam my own body but let my head fall back on the street.

I would die. Here, alone.

I ordered my harried thoughts to grab an assurance, a sense of peace, about dying. None could be found. Truth was, I hadn't given the afterlife much thought until now.

My eyelids grew heavy, and I knew if I succumbed to their pull, I would be in eternity—whatever that held—in the next moment.

Only thoughts of my sister and niece made me fight. They'd come to support me. What if one of the distorted limbs or lumps of flesh I saw belonged to them? What if they lay somewhere . . . dying?

I cried for help again, my voice faint this time. Muffled sound—animalistic screaming—faded in and out, and then *he* was beside me.

In a place where I questioned whether I'd ever feel human touch again, his warm hand found mine and squeezed. I pressed back and clung with the dregs of my strength.

"You're going to be okay." The words sounded through the muted fog, but I latched on to them as if they were life.

He wrested his hand from mine and then his arms were under me, lifting me. My eyelids fluttered and I was only conscious of the feeling of security against the blue Red Sox sweatshirt, of pressing my nose into it and smelling something spicy and woodsy to replace the smog of sulfur and singed flesh clinging to my nostrils.

I must have blacked out, for when I woke, an EMT pushed a needle into one of the veins in the back of my hand. The tightness of the ambulance confines tugged a surge of rebellion through my belly. My rescuer would leave me.

"Don't go!" I didn't know what I was saying, and I did. I grabbed for the stranger's hands, and he pressed something cool into my palm, placed my fingers around it, and then laid my hand on my chest. His words faded in and out. Others needed help. Like Lydia. Like Grace. He'd find me.

He said he'd find me.

Some time later, I woke in a hospital bed to hazy thoughts. I tried to comprehend that I'd been in some sort of explosion, that I still didn't know the fate of my sister and niece. In my loosened palm lay the object the stranger had pressed into my bloodied fingers.

A gold signet ring. The flat oval bore an engraving of a shield. An anchor was set in gems at the bottom left of the shield, and at the top right, the symbol of a horn. I skimmed over the Latin inscription on the top and read the name *Smythe* written in dark-green jewels beneath. The weight of the ring and the worn edges whispered of stories of long ago, stories that had lain dormant for generations.

It felt like a holy relic of sorts, one that had whisked me away from terror and explosions and mangled limbs and broken people.

My arms burned with a sudden longing to hold Grace as the explosion hadn't allowed me to do. I curled the ring in my fist and pressed the call button for the nurse with my other, trembling hand.

In a moment I heard the slight shuffle of rubber shoes against linoleum, coming toward my room. I inhaled a tight breath, pushed aside the horrifying visions from the finish line, and prayed the nurse would have good news of my family.

CHAPTER 1
Anaya

I stared at the potted lily in my hand, its pure white petals fresh against the backdrop of my sister's stained wood door.

Maybe flowers were overkill. I wasn't looking for a date, after all. I was looking for . . .

What was I looking for? Why was I here?

The unexpected phone call with my mother the night before replayed in my head, along with the news she had shared.

"I talked to Lydia today. It looks like Roger's going to take a job in the UK."

1

The statement ripped through me. I hadn't seen Lydia or her family in over a year and a half, but this news broke on me with the sudden realization that I might never see them again.

So here I was, after nearly seven hundred days of silence. Trying to reconcile the fact that each day I could have picked up the phone, tried to mend the fragments of our relationship, but I hadn't.

I closed my eyes, concentrated on the familiar weight of the object attached to the chain at my neck. The ring, Red Sox Sweatshirt, my sister, and my crippled niece—they'd all jumbled together the last two years to create a fierce, writhing fairy-tale nightmare that wouldn't release me from its vicious hold.

I freed a quaking breath, clutched at the cool plastic of the flowerpot in my hand. *Qui fortis salutem tribuet.*

It was the Latin inscription on the ring belonging to the man who'd never bothered to find me after the day of the bombing.

I breathed around the preposterous feeling of abandonment, focused instead on the meaning of the words, tried to draw strength from them, from the ring itself. *Victory belongs to the one who is strong.*

Boston Strong.

I shook my head against the slogan that had rallied Boston to its feet just days after the crisis that rocked the city. I shouldn't think of it now. It only taunted me. Whether on T-shirts, hats, sports memorabilia, bumper stickers, billboards, or even the destination signs on buses, the two words tormented me, calling me to be something I wasn't.

Strong.

Why I thought I could suddenly draw hope from these etched words just because I stood at my sister's threshold, I hadn't a clue.

I turned around instead of knocking again, convinced I needed something more to face what was behind this door. But the hinges creaked behind me. I turned, and there she stood.

She'd gotten more beautiful the last two years, young womanhood making her blossom and mature. And I'd missed it all.

"Grace . . ." I could scarcely push her name past my lips, for the sudden emotion in my throat. She stood at eye level with me. I'd expected a wheelchair, a crutch, something. But a quick—what I hoped to be discreet—scan of her lower half revealed two legs clad in skinny jeans. She looked like a healthy, normal teenage girl, thanks to prosthetics.

I would not cry.

"Auntie Annie. Wow, you're here."

"I—um, maybe I should have called first, but—"

"No. No, this is great." She opened the door wider, threw her long, honey-colored ponytail over her shoulder. "I was just thinking about going for a run, but that can wait. Mom's out catching up on some errands, Dad's fiddling in the garage, Joel went to a friend's, so, like, it's just me." She closed the door behind us. "I hope that's . . . okay."

She was about to go for a run. A run. I thought she'd never walk—never mind run—again. I knew in my head people who lost limbs could still do many things others could do, but in my mind Grace was as I'd last seen her. Crippled, in a wheelchair. Bruised both inside and out.

I inhaled the scent of pine furniture polish, the house as tidy as my sister's room when we were kids. On counters and hutches were dried flowers of every type—hydrangeas, carnations, larkspur, peonies.

"Let me take that." Grace held out her arms for the lily and I released it, noticing the slightest of limps when she walked to the kitchen counter to set the pot down.

I found my voice. "You look great."

She smiled at me, revealing white, straight teeth. No braces anymore. "Thanks, so do you."

I knew she was being nice. While I'd been severely battered by the bombing, I'd also been fit and trim. Not so much anymore. I hadn't pulled on a pair of running sneakers since the morning of the marathon. I likely never would again. I could live with these fifteen extra pounds for the rest of my life if I had to. Kind of even liked them—a buffer zone of sorts.

"Do you want some coffee?"

I raised my eyebrows, shook my head, and sighed. "I can't get over how grown-up you are. Sorry, yes. I'd love some coffee."

She opened one of the perfectly distressed white cabinet doors and pulled down two mugs. I sat on a barstool and drew a greeting card from my purse. I slid the card along the counter.

"Happy belated. Sorry it's late."

It was an improvement from last year, anyway, when I sent nothing.

Her green eyes brightened. "Hey, thanks." She ripped open the card, moving aside the fifty-dollar bill as she read the greeting. Nothing fancy or personal. I didn't want her to think I was trying to flatter my way back into her life.

"Thanks, Auntie." She placed the card on the counter and came around the island to envelop me in a brief, awkward hug. I was relieved when she went back to the kitchen.

"How many sugars?" Grace opened one of the Pfaltzgraff containers and spooned a teaspoonful of sugar into one mug.

"Two please." I put a hand on my stomach. "Though I'm trying to work down to one and a half. It stays on so much easier these days."

Grace smiled and in it I saw she didn't harbor anything against me. I loved her all the more.

"So seventeen, huh? Driving yet?"

"Got my license a few months ago. We've been looking for a car. Mom's freaking."

I laughed. "I'll bet." I scurried for more meaningless small talk. "How's school? Any boyfriends?"

She shook her head. "No on the boyfriends. Good on school. Except for pre-calc. Struggling with that."

"I could help you sometime if you want. With calculus, I mean." I could have knocked my head against my sister's quartz countertop. Who did I think I was, waltzing into my niece's life after nearly destroying it, offering to help her with math?

But nothing seemed to faze Grace. She kept smiling at me, like she was actually glad I came, glad I sat in her kitchen. "I'd like that."

The coffee dribbled into the mug, releasing a French-roast scent into the kitchen.

"So how about you?" Grace switched out the mugs in the Keurig, grabbed cream from the fridge. "Like, what have you been up to? Any boyfriends?" She gave me a sly smile as she placed a cream-colored mug in front of me. I recognized it as one I gave Lydia on her thirtieth birthday. It said *Sisters* on it in large cursive writing. Around the word in a circular pattern was a collection of words about sisters. I didn't want to turn the cup and study it with Grace beside me, but I did glimpse one sentence. *As friends we have pulled together.*

I was surprised Lydia hadn't tossed the cup sometime over the last two years.

"Auntie?"

I shook my head. "Sorry. No—no boyfriends." Not serious ones, that is. "I relocated, actually. For work. Still with the bank. I'm renting an apartment above a garage in Lexington now. Not too far from here—on Belfry Terrace."

"No way."

"Yeah, I like it. Peaceful, you know?"

"Try going to high school. There's nothing peaceful about it."

"Thought you said school was good?" I let the heat of the mug seep through to my skin, then sipped the coffee. It slid down my throat, warm and comforting. This felt . . . normal. I hadn't expected such an easy transition.

Grace waved a hand through the air. "Oh, it's fine. Just the usual, I guess. Immature boys; gossiping, shallow girls. I don't fit in, you know?"

If someone had told me the day before that Grace would confide in me that she didn't fit in anywhere, I would have instantly blamed it on the terror attack, on her leg. But sitting here with her now, I knew that's not what she meant.

"The bombing made you grow up faster than them." I stated the sentence with confidence. It wasn't a question; I saw the evidence before my eyes, in the way Grace handled herself, in the way she received me with such poise and mercy after all these months of silence.

She shrugged, blinked fast. "I guess so."

I reached for her hand, the awkwardness from our previous physical contact now gone. I may have come for myself, but in this moment I could only think of comforting the young woman before me. "I'm so sorry I haven't called, Grace. I got your letter. It was just—I have no excuses. I'm so sorry."

"I'm not, like, holding any hard feelings—but maybe sometime we could talk about what happened. I mean, you were there through my surgeries, skin grafts, therapy sessions. Then not long after I moved to rehab, you just stopped coming."

Like I said, I had no excuses. Still, I opened my mouth to explain myself, but not before Grace squeezed my hand.

"Not today, Auntie, okay? Today let's just be happy together."

Tension eased from my body. Tears pricked my eyelids at the simple act of grace. "Thank you." I wiped my trembling lips with a napkin. I couldn't hold it together much longer in front of her. "Is it okay if I use your bathroom real quick?"

"Of course. I'll see if I can scrounge us up some comfort food."

I laughed around my tight emotions and started down the hall. Once in the bathroom, I opened the window and allowed the cool air to calm my nerves, as frayed as an overused toothbrush. I wiped the corners of my eyes with a tissue.

Let's just be happy together.

How simple and sweet. I could do this. I could be happy again, couldn't I?

If only Lydia would be content with the same.

I opened the bathroom door and a whoosh of air from the still-open window swept across the threshold and into the living room, across the hall. The pages of a book on top of an end table fluttered and a small card flapped to the ground, swirling like a feather near my feet.

I turned to close the window before picking up the business card. When I did, my stomach clenched.

It wasn't the name on the card. Or even the business, a construction company of some sort. It was the emblem on the card that made my skin grow hot, then cold with goose bumps. My lungs constricted around my thrashing heart.

I didn't need to fish the ring from beneath my sweater to know the same crest adorned the signet ring I'd been given almost two years earlier. The anchor, the horn symbol, even the Latin I'd memorized at the top.

I glanced at the name. *Bradford Kilroy.*

"Auntie?"

"Be right there," I called.

I lifted the cover of the Bible the card had fallen from and moved it toward the feather-light pages of the book of Psalms. Just before the sharp edges touched the binding, I drew it back. If I released the card to the clutches of the solid book, I might never see it again. It belonged to me. I knew it. And yet how could that be? Lydia knew I had looked for the man who'd helped me that day. Surely she would have said something in the weeks after the bombing.

I stared at the emblem, an exact replica of the engraving on the ring. Somehow this card was connected to Red Sox Sweatshirt; I was sure of it. Somehow my sister had played a part in keeping it from me.

I tucked the card in the back pocket of my jeans and stood in Lydia's dust-free living room, reluctant to go back into the kitchen so shaken up. I tugged on the chain at my neck, freeing the ring from beneath my sweater. I clutched it in my fist and wound the chain around my pinkie finger.

I'd read somewhere that ancient Egyptians would adorn themselves in jewelry—particularly gold—believing it imbued them with special powers. Like the Egyptians, I'd often looked for spiritual influence in the ring—a magical amulet of sorts left by my mysterious savior. And while a part of me felt silly for putting so much stock in an inanimate object, another part panicked at the thought of not having anything solid I could turn to. At least the ring offered me a tangible connection to the supernatural—something to believe in.

I opened my eyes and slipped the ring back beneath my sweater. I started toward the kitchen, vowing not to let the card's discovery tarnish my time with Grace. She stood at the counter, shaking popcorn out of a bag and into two bowls.

I sat at the bar, suddenly desperate for conversation. "So the UK, huh?"

Her face registered nothing, the bag of popcorn frozen in her hands.

I fumbled for words. "I talked to your grandmother. . . . She mentioned your dad taking a job. . . ."

Grace shook her head and placed the popcorn on the counter. "I—I hadn't heard. I thought—"

I reached for her hand again, a heaviness in my chest traveling downward. "I'm so sorry. You know your gram. She gets ahead of herself sometimes. She probably—"

The kitchen door opened. On the threshold stood Lydia, a brown Stop & Shop bag in her hand, her expression one of stone.

Her gaze took in my presence, saw my hand connected with Grace's. The bag dipped in her arms. She recovered quickly and placed it on the counter.

"Well, isn't this cozy." She shut the door, tossed her keys in the small basket on the counter.

I snatched my hand from Grace's and stood. "Hi, Lydia."

"Nice of you to drop by." She didn't sound like she thought it was nice. She sounded as if she'd rather have a visit from an angry skunk.

"I—um, I should have called."

Grace stood beside me. "No, Auntie. It's good you came. Right, Mom?"

If smoke could have poured from my sister's ears, the fire alarms would have been going off at the neighbor's house.

"No, Grace. Your aunt is right. It would have been better if she'd called."

CHAPTER 2
Liberty

Just when I thought the mercy of morning might never ascend, faint ribbons of pink light shone through the second-story window of the officers' house. With it, a burst of something familiar in the core of my being. 'Twas a feeling of long ago. An emotion I no longer deserved or expected.

I swiped the canopy curtains aside and slid from the warmth of my bed, musing why this foreign sensation of promise should come to me this day. Perhaps it was the longer days, or perhaps something more. A premonition of sorts? My heart thrummed beneath the thin covering of my shift.

Perhaps today would be the day I finally found James.

With soundless movements, I washed my face, then threw the water out the window into the gutter. I stood on the rag rug beside the bed and donned my petticoat and gown. I laced my boots with deft fingers, pinned my mobcap to my head, and attempted to blow away the cloud of gray fog that often took up residence in my spirit at day's dawn.

I hadn't a choice. Starve and freeze on the streets while I waited for my younger brother's ship to come in, or accept the position in the officers' house. Yes, many labeled me a traitor—many presumed I did more for the captain and the lieutenant than keep a tidy house, and yet what did they know of being seventeen years of age and alone? What did they know of being cold and hungry?

I left my room and walked first past the lieutenant's chambers and then the captain's. My footsteps fell soft on the stairs, and once in the keeping room, I lit the candles. They gave off a cheery light in their copper holders. I fetched fresh wood from the box and laid kindling down on the glowing embers from the night before. Soon small flames licked the wood, sending light to the bunches of dried herbs in the shadows of the rafters overhead. I stood and stretched.

First order, tea.

The thought of the "baneful weed," as the Liberty Boys called it, set my mind to spinning like a child's toy top. The so-called *Americans* in the town refused to drink the beverage. Indeed, a boy named Seider had died just days earlier as the result of a fracas in the North End over the matter of importation. I tried not to think much on the herb, to serve it without question. But my conscience forbade me to imbibe any myself.

Booted footfalls echoed down the stairs, and my traitorous heart quickened as Lieutenant Smythe appeared, his red wool coat and crimson sash over his arm, his hair tied neatly back in a queue. Unlike the captain, who slept until the sun shone brightly over the harbor, the lieutenant fancied his early starts.

I would not flatter myself by assuming he fancied my company as well.

The lieutenant nodded to me and hung his attire on one of the straight-backed cherry chairs. "How do you do, Miss Liberty?"

I placed a bowl of preserves and biscuits on the table, conscious of his gaze upon me. "Well, thank you."

He sat, but I did not miss his grimace, the way he held his hand to his cheek.

"Mayhap simply some tea this morning, sir?"

He removed his hand from his face. "Yes, that would do me well, thank you."

I did not wish to pry, and yet seeing a person in pain stirred up an irrepressible urge in me to heal. One of many ways I took after our grandmother, James had always said.

"I could journey to the apothecary today, sir. I am low on herbs, but I think a powder of cloves may help your tooth."

The corners of his mouth pulled into a smile, and I noted the indent on his left cheek, a charming addition to his well-formed face. "I did not mean to be so obvious."

I dipped my head. "I would like to think I am simply perceptive to one's pain."

He laughed, a soft sound in the still-quiet house. "That sounds agreeable to me."

I shaved the tea brick into the lieutenant's tin cup, the heat from the stove warming my back. I scooped a teaspoonful of sugar and covered the herbs with hot water from the pewter pot before bringing it to the table.

When I placed the cup before the lieutenant, he took it, and my fingers brushed against the warm metal of the signet ring he wore, its bonny brilliance of gold and bloodstone playing with the light of the candles.

I snatched my hand away, tried to censor my reaction to the subtle scent of cedar and soap that belonged to him. It reminded me of my first night in Boston, when I met the lieutenant. How he shielded me with his cape after those horrid boys had tried to take my innocence in a dark alley. How he had threatened to have them hanged on the Common. And how, when he learned I had no home or family to be found, he'd taken me to the officers' house, offered me my own bed. The next morning he rescinded his employment advertisement at the Royal Coffeehouse and offered me the position of housekeeper.

I was a foolish girl to allow myself to fall in love with one of the king's men. James would disown me if he ever found out.

He wouldn't, of course. I would see to that.

"Thank you." The lieutenant raised the cup to his lips, took a sip of his tea, then placed it upon the wood-plank table.

I turned to tend the fire.

He cleared his throat. "Miss Liberty, I was wondering if you enjoy poetry?"

"I—poetry, sir?"

"Yes. My little sister was quite taken with it back in England. . . ."

I attempted to push flustered words forth. None came. No matter how I tried to see this red-coated man as a monster, as my brother's letters claimed all Regular soldiers to be, I could not manage it here, beside the lieutenant, as he revealed fresh bits and pieces of himself to me with each new rising sun. Part of me wished to know nothing of him and his life back in England. Another, more rebellious part wished to know every nuance and detail of the man—far from a monster—before me.

"I have not had opportunity to read much poetry, sir." Did I imagine it, or did his face register disappointment? I wished nothing more than to fix it. "Yet I think I should like to."

His face brightened, and he stood, drawing a small book from the red coat behind him. "I thought of you when I saw this at Henry Knox's bookshop." He shook his head, seemed to fumble for words, then held the book out to me. "It is yours, if you'd like."

I took the book, my fingers hesitant. I had never received such a valuable gift. The cover read, *Miscellany Poems, on Several Occasions* by Anne Kingsmill Finch, Countess of Winchilsea.

"I hope it is not too presumptuous of me, but I noticed you've taken a liking to the *Chronicle*, and if it is not too bold of me to say, I saw your interest in *The Odyssey* on my nightstand as well."

I fought the blush creeping up my neck. I thought I'd been discreet when polishing the furniture in his room. "My father taught me to read when I was a girl." I whispered the words, the book of poems still held in midair.

The lieutenant pressed the book into my hands and then released it. "He must have thought much of you."

He had. I ached for my brother all over again at the thought of my doting father, dead beneath the smallpox flag more than a decade ago.

"It is my hope that you enjoy it. And if you wish, *The Odyssey* is yours to borrow as you please."

I gathered myself, hugged the book to my chest. "Thank you, Lieutenant. It is indeed a thoughtful gift."

He gave a slight nod before returning to his tea.

At the sound of the captain's boots on the stairs, I slipped the book into the pocket of my dress and continued shaving herbs from the block. The captain greeted the lieutenant, then pushed himself behind me to get to his seat. I felt the scratchy red wool of his coat against my sleeve.

"Good morning." He leaned over, his nose touching my mobcap, the cloying scent of pipe smoke nearly smothering my breath. And then, as quick as he'd pressed against me, he was gone.

More and more often, he'd made a habit of familiarity

with me. I hadn't much experience with the stronger sex and wondered if I perhaps thought too much of his seemingly friendly manner. Still, I fought the remnant of a chill pulsating through my body at his closeness.

When I turned, the lieutenant's jaw was clenched. I bade myself remember the cloves for his tooth as I went about my day.

After the two men broke their fast, they grabbed up their silver-laced tricorns and Brown Bess muskets, then left for their posts. I watched them from the keeping room window and saw the lieutenant call ahead to the captain, then turn back to the house. I busied myself with dishes at the sink when he reentered the house, opening the door to a town brewing heavy with rattling carts and horses clopping, people beginning their day.

When I didn't hear his boots on the stairs, I looked up. He stood, his gaze intense on me.

"Can I retrieve something for you, sir?"

He shook his head, fast. "Miss Liberty—I . . ."

My hands stilled in the warm water.

"I—I would not have the captain become too familiar with you."

I swallowed, my thoughts racing to piece meaning to his words. I was not some camp girl. After months of knowing me, did he think so little of me?

I dried my hands on my apron and turned to better face him. "I would not have it so, either."

He stepped forward. "What I mean is, I will not allow

him to be. I do not want you to feel unsafe in this house, ever. Please . . . will you come to me if—if the captain makes you feel so?"

My heart near leapt forth from my chest at the sight of the man before me, vowing to once again keep me safe, to be strong where I only felt weak.

"I will, sir. Thank you."

He left, and I again pondered the bursting hope in my chest, longing to be set free. I attempted to convince myself it was due to the impending arrival of spring and the prospect of seeing James, of both of us finding a way together at last. But deep in my heart, I knew it was more.

It was the book in my pocket. The lieutenant's promise of protection. The way he looked at me as if he wanted to care for me.

How long had it been since someone had taken care of *me*?

And yet there could be no way for us. I was a traitor to the Sons and Daughters of Liberty to even entertain such a notion, to be living in this house to begin with. The lieutenant belonged to the king, and I had vowed to stand by my brother and forever be counted a Patriot.

CHAPTER 3
Anaya

I STARED AT the television screen, the last warm puff of Anna's animated breath dissipating against the backdrop of white, her body turning to ice.

I'd started watching Disney's *Frozen* with Emilia, my landlord's eight-year-old daughter, yet her mom had called her in for bed before we'd finished the movie. The girl knew all the songs by heart, singing them without shame.

Now I watched alone as Elsa cried over Anna's icy body.

I glanced at the business card I'd found at Lydia's house earlier in the day. It lay on my coffee table beside an empty popcorn bowl, kernels congealed to the bottom in now-hardened butter.

I dug the ring from beneath my sweater, warm from sitting close to my skin. I compared the identical emblems once again. Where had Lydia gotten the card?

So many questions. So many walls to break down. And I'd likely created another one by spilling news of the move—something my sister hadn't yet mentioned to Grace.

I ran my thumb over the card. The crest was only a small portion of it. The other, larger image was of a wooden arbor.

Kilroy Construction
Carpentry, Design, Restoration
Helping your home tell its story.

The number on the bottom glared up at me. I remembered the weeks following the bombing, the promise of the man in the Red Sox sweatshirt to find me, the empty passing days where chances thinned that he would keep that promise.

I let the ring drop from my fingers to hang at my neck. I couldn't imagine broaching the subject with Lydia after our icy reunion that afternoon. If I wanted to find out whether this man belonged in my fairy-tale nightmare, whether the man on the card belonged to the ring, I would have to find out myself.

I scooped up my cell phone and, without dwelling too much on the consequences, punched in the numbers, my fingers trembling.

On the first ring, the possibility that he just didn't want to find me hung in my mind. On the second, I pondered whether the signet ring wasn't truly valuable at all and my mystery hero gave duplicates out to every woman in distress. On the third, I felt certain his wife would pick up.

The fourth ring was cut short. "Hello?" A male voice.

I swallowed, my bottom lip quivering. "Hi—um, I'm looking for Bradford?"

He laughed—a deep, pleasant sound. "You must have my business card. Don't know why I ever decided to put my full name on there. Yes, this is Brad."

I was able to draw a breath around my anxiety. "Hi . . . my name is Annie David. I—well, this might sound strange, but I was a victim in the marathon bombing a couple years ago and . . . I have this ring. Someone gave it to me that—"

"No way."

I held my breath. Was that . . . recognition? "Is it—is it yours?"

I listened to a whoosh of air releasing on the other end. "Wow. I mean, yes. Yes, it is. I thought I'd never find you again."

Find the ring. Of course he meant he thought he'd never find the ring, not me personally.

"You were the one that day, then? The man who saved me?"

He chuckled. "I don't know that I saved you. By the time I got to you, the blast had already done its work. But yeah, I helped you that day."

But he'd done so much more. He had to know. While everyone was running away from the explosions, he ran toward them. "I've wanted to thank you for so long. I—" Words escaped me. It felt foolish to gush to him over the phone when he seemed so nonchalant about the whole thing. "Your ring—I've wanted to return it since I woke up in the hospital."

I fisted the gold in my palm once again, tried to imagine parting with it. For goodness' sake, I'd treated the object like some sort of spiritual talisman these past two years. I'd feel naked without it.

But it didn't belong to me. I'd known that from the beginning.

"Great." He cleared his throat. "I'd love to meet you. Please, name a time and a place. I'll be there."

"Are you local, then? I live in Lexington."

"No kidding. My family's been there for years. Nice place. I live in Quincy, actually."

All this time, and he'd been no farther than the Red Line. Paul Revere on horseback could have gotten to him faster than I had.

I scrambled for a meeting place. As much as I hated to admit it, Boston made the most sense. "I have a meeting near Faneuil Hall tomorrow. Maybe we could grab some coffee around five?" Downtown Boston didn't bother me much. Up until a couple months ago, I'd worked there, breathed in Boston's historic district. It was the Back Bay and its taunting memories I tried to stay clear of.

"Absolutely. Union Oyster okay?"

"Perfect."

We said good-bye and hung up. I unclasped the chain from my neck and slid it from the ring.

I felt good. I had taken my fate into my own hands instead of waiting for it to be handed to me. This was a new feeling, a new achievement. Taking the initiative, creating my own possibilities, had never been my strong suit. I'd gone to college for finance because that's what Dad had suggested. I'd signed up for the Boston Marathon because Grace had urged me to. Heck, I barely ever made so much as an eye doctor's appointment without getting the reminder in the mail at least twice. But this—calling Brad Kilroy, finding my rescuer—this I had done. Without anyone else's help, particularly my sister's.

I looked down at the gold anchor, the Latin words I'd long ago memorized. How many times had I wondered over its story, imagined it entwined with my own? I hoped Brad could fill in some answers for me—about the ring, about that tragic day that still haunted me like a persistent ghost, about how my sister had come to be the keeper of his card.

I dug my hands in my pockets as I exited the bank and turned right. Snow piles huddled at the corners of buildings, the recent winter storms unrelenting, even into March. Across State Street and in the midst of the pedestrian bustle ruled by traffic signals lay Boston's Old State House. The brick building was the oldest still standing in the eastern part of the United States, the very same pictured in Paul Revere's engraving of the Boston Massacre.

Before the bombing, I used to frequent the sites of the Freedom Trail, eager to learn about the city's rich history. Why had I stopped? None of the sites would take me to the Back Bay, that part of Boston being nonexistent in colonial days. Yet somewhere along the way, I'd given up things I loved. Running, hiking, exploring Boston like an overeager tourist instead of the resident I'd been since college.

I braced myself against the wind, ignored the news vans, and walked north toward Union Oyster House. Passersby walked quickly and with purpose, dressed in skirts or suits. A family of four posed beside Samuel Adams's statue in front of Faneuil Hall.

I arrived at the restaurant early, but the hostess led me past the semicircular oyster bar and seated me, promising to point Brad in my direction.

I inhaled the scents of corn bread, melted butter, and lobster and looked at the painted reliefs on the wall beside me. The painted musket pointing in my direction did little to calm my nerves. The red-coated British gentleman on the other end of the firearm seemed to stare at me. Above him hung a plaque in fine cursive as if announcing a wedding rather than the historic death of Patriot men. *The Boston Massacre.* March 5, 1770. Exactly two hundred forty-five years ago this very day—the day after the bombing trial began.

Victory belongs to the one who is strong.

I reached into a small compartment of my purse and felt for the gold. When I found its round coldness, I drew it out and placed it on the table. I already missed its steady weight hanging at my neck. But meeting my rescuer would be worth it, wouldn't it?

My chest trembled against a long breath. This was it. I was finally going to meet my hero. The man behind the ring would no longer be a mystery.

"Annie?"

I looked up to see . . . Paul Bunyan? The big man in the flannel shirt couldn't be Red Sox Sweatshirt. He didn't look all that athletic. Or heroic. Or how I remembered. A pencil stuck out from his *Kilroy Construction* hat, the pink eraser pointing toward his neatly trimmed beard.

I gathered myself, chastised the inner girl in me longing for a Prince Charming. I stood and reached my hand to his own extended one. It felt warm and solid. "Brad, right? So nice to finally meet you."

He smiled, the gesture crinkling his sea-green eyes. "You, too." He sat, took off his hat, and placed the pencil in it. "I had all intentions of cleaning up before meeting you, but I got held up at work. One of my guys went a little too demo-happy, and we had a hole to close up before we left. Sorry."

"No need to apologize."

The waitress came over and placed a basket of corn bread on our table. Brad picked up his menu, pushed up his sleeves. I glimpsed a tattoo of a cross on the inside of his forearm. Whoa, definitely wasn't expecting a tattooed savior.

"Can I treat you to dinner instead of coffee?"

"Sure." Some food might help the sudden light-headedness

taking over my brain. It would also give me more time to solve the many mysteries surrounding the day that haunted me.

After the waitress took our orders, Brad's gaze caught the ring sitting on the table. His thick fingers reached to grab it, but just before the calloused skin touched the ring, he stopped. "May I?"

Crazy that he should ask, and yet it seemed fitting. I nudged the ring a couple inches toward him. "Of course. It's yours, after all."

He picked it up, stared at it beneath the dim lights of the restaurant, tried to push it on over a massive finger, and chuckled. "Guess I haven't lost any weight the past two years. Still doesn't fit." He placed it back on the table.

I smiled. "Thank you for leaving it with me that day. I'm not sure why you did—or even why you chose to help me—but thank you."

He shifted in his seat, seeming uncomfortable with the expression of gratitude. "They were able to save your foot?"

"Good as new." I stuck my foot out from under the table and wiggled it. I felt only a small pinch in the back of my leg. A shard of glass had lodged itself there on the day of the bombing. Though the X-rays showed all the glass had been removed during surgery, I could still feel the slight pain when I flexed my foot, but I had never complained to the doctor. In some twisted way, I liked it there. Such a small reminder of the pain others—like my niece—would have to endure for a lifetime. The pain I'd run away from. The pain I was now being shut out of.

I blinked, brought myself back to the present. Brad's arms rested on the table, his gaze intense on me. The woodsy scent I vaguely remembered from the day of the bombing plucked chords of emotion against my heart. I looked away, tried to conjure up the mental checklist I'd written. There were so many things I wanted to tell him, so many things I wanted to ask.

I wiped my hands on the legs of my pants. "This might sound silly, but I want you to know how you gave me hope that day, that week. Since then, whenever I felt the world was collapsing in on me with its evil, I'd look at that ring and remember what you did. I remembered that there was still good in it. Thank you."

He smiled and a slight quivering started in my chest. He really did have a nice-looking face. Who said Paul Bunyan couldn't be handsome?

"You know, that's not the first time that ring's given someone hope. I think that's why I thought to leave it with you."

"Oh?" I tried to draw him out with the one word.

"I kept the thing in my pocket all the time. Went right in with my wallet and phone every day. It's some sort of a family heirloom, but no one knows the entire story. It belonged to my great-great—like five-times-great—grandfather." He sipped his water. "When I was deployed in Iraq . . . I went through some tough times. My dad sent it over to me with a letter. He died the day after he mailed it."

"I'm so sorry," I whispered.

His eyes shone beneath the dim lighting of the wall

sconce. "I didn't want to leave you that day. I didn't, but I had to help. It's who I am. I thought the ring would keep us connected."

I felt suddenly warm. I wanted to take the glass of ice water before me and press it to my forehead. I blew an upward breath, pushing my bangs off my face instead. "That ring was the only tangible evidence I had that you'd been real. If I didn't have it, I would have convinced myself long ago I'd made you up."

The waitress brought my broiled scrod and Brad's lobster ravioli. I smoothed the cloth napkin over my lap.

Brad scooped up the ring, held it out. "You know, I think you should keep it a little longer."

"What? No. Absolutely not."

"I can tell it means a lot to you. I've been without it for almost two years now. I gave it to you that day. Keep it. Please."

"Don't be ridiculous." I refused to reach for the proffered ring. "I'm not taking your family heirloom. You gave it with a promise to find me. You have, so now we're even."

He placed the ring between our plates and split a ravioli in half with the end of his fork. Creamy pink sauce oozed around the edges of the lobster-stuffed pasta. "Only I didn't find you. You found me."

"That's neither here nor there." Only, was it? I wanted to know—needed to know what had happened. I squeezed a lemon wedge over my scrod.

"Truth is, I was expecting a call a lot sooner." He picked

up a piece of corn bread and began buttering it. "When a month went by, I thought that was it. You weren't going to call."

I dipped the tines of my fork through the bread crumbs coating the top of my scrod and into the flesh of the fish but couldn't find the strength or the appetite to lift it to my mouth. "I—I found your card at my sister's house the other day."

He chewed, seeming thoughtful. "Huh. She never gave it to you. I guess I shouldn't be surprised. She seemed really distracted that day at the hospital. Worried about you, probably."

"Her daughter—my niece—lost a leg in the bombing."

He nodded. "That explains it. I tried to stick around, but she really didn't seem to want me there. Not rude or anything. I think she just didn't want a stranger witnessing all the grief. Can't really blame her."

I could. "For weeks I talked about finding you. She never said a word." Not that I'd stuck around much longer to hear anything she had to say.

He shrugged. "Trauma can do a number on people. I'm just glad you found me now."

Yeah, two whole years later, and only because I'd been a snoop in my sister's house.

He must have sensed my bitter thoughts, for he briskly changed the subject by asking what I did for work. We chatted through the meal, getting to know the thin veneer that strangers first reveal to one another. When the waitress brought our bill and Brad insisted on paying, I fought off a dull pang of disappointment. I'd longed for this night for almost two years, and now it was over. I grasped at my mental checklist to keep the conversation going. There was still something I wanted to know.

I picked up the ring, still between us. "Do you know anything about the history of your family? I mean, what this crest stands for and all that? Like I said, it gave me hope. I've had two years to wonder what it all means, but I haven't come up with much more than the Latin translation."

He closed his wallet, put it on the table. "Victory belongs to the one who is strong."

We shared a smile. "Is that what helped you when you were in the Middle East?"

He shook his head. "Not so much the saying. I knew I wasn't strong enough to handle it all. It was the fact that my dad had given it to me in the first place. I knew he understood; I knew he was rooting for me. Praying for me."

I felt a strange sense of relief that the words hadn't magically transformed Brad into a pillar of strength either. "So you don't know anything about the emblem? The name?"

"Never really thought about it, I guess. My father never told me—likely he never knew." My expression must have showed my disappointment, for he rallied quickly. "But you know what, it could be interesting to find out. Maybe I could look into it."

"It's no big deal. I don't want to trouble—"

"Nah, no trouble. I want to. I'll make you a deal."

My heart thumped against my rib cage. "Okay."

"You hold on to the ring for me until I find something about it."

"That's kind of an open-ended deal." Was this his way of letting me have the ring in what he considered a gallant manner?

"That way, I'll work hard at uncovering the mystery."

"Because you want the ring back."

His mouth twitched and he put his hat back on, stuck the pencil up into the right side of it. "No. Because I want to have dinner with you again when I don't smell like sawdust."

CHAPTER 4
Liberty

I closed the door of the officers' house and burrowed farther into my go-to-market cloak, a basket clutched at my side. From across the street, the giggles of two girls reached my ears. They were about my age, and I smiled at them before realizing *I* was the target of their laughter. They whispered to each other, then turned away without bidding me a good day.

I tried not to take the snub to heart. I knew they believed I warmed the captain's and lieutenant's beds with more than warming pans of coals. In truth, most of the advertisements posted at the Royal Coffeehouse for housemaids stated rather boldly that virtue was not a requirement. I stared after the murmuring girls.

I envied them. Carefree, no doubt living beneath the roof of a loving parent. Not so very long ago I was in their place. 'Twas not my fault Providence had dealt me so difficult a hand. And yet, mightn't I have looked harder and longer for a respectable employ? Spent more than one night on the cold town streets? A stronger woman would have refused the help of the enemy.

On my way to the apothecary, I dodged the women bustling to market, chimney sweeps vying for jobs, piles of horse and donkey manure, and red-coated sentries.

Just ahead stood the brick Town House, the gold unicorn and lion of the royal crest standing proudly on top, a whipping post before it and the town pump not much farther. Toward the horizon and between brick buildings, I just glimpsed Long Wharf, packed with warehouses, counting houses, and the great naked masts of ships at port. I craned my neck for a sight of blue sea. With the hum of spring, the wharf would soon be filled with casks of wine from the island of Madeira and hogsheads of fruit and sugar from the West Indies and Canary Islands.

A crude word cut through the busyness of the streets. At the Customs House, across from the Town House, a red-coated sentry, not much older than me, stood guard. His musket was planted firmly over his shoulder, and he walked back and forth, turning smartly on his heel with each change of direction even as a nearby boy called obscene names at him. I thought to shoo the boy away but lost my courage at the prospect of a South End mob turning against me.

The apothecary shop was just beyond on Royal Exchange Lane. I would pick up the cloves and perhaps some catnip for the lieutenant's tooth as well as some camphor, linseed oil, headache powders, and beeswax, as my supplies were running low. On the way home I would visit the Customs House and see if news of James's ship, *Defiance*, had come in. While ships were not required to be registered upon their arrival, my best hope of finding news of James was here. Yet even as I held on to the hope I'd felt that morning, the scent of snow thickened the air, reminding me that ships traversing from the West Indies didn't often pull into port in early March.

A crumpled newspaper swirled at my feet. The rattling of a cart came from behind, and I stepped aside, turning to see a boy wheeling a load of firewood. He rushed past, and out of the corner of my eye I caught a figure leaving the print shop of Edes & Gill, publishers of the *Boston Gazette*. Something jumped in my belly. Even with the tricorn hat and cape, I'd know that form anywhere. I'd cleaned up his toddler hands caked with mud after playing in a summer rain. I'd watched his eyes light up at the sight of seedcakes, warm from the oven. I'd hid those same eyes from our parents' corpses, riddled with smallpox sores. At sixteen, he might no longer need me, but I desperately needed him.

James turned in the opposite direction, and I half skipped, half ran after him. When I drew closer, I called out, "James!"

The man didn't turn, and for a moment I doubted myself. But certainly I wasn't wrong—no one could walk with such a step as my brother, who'd had the lung fever at age ten and who still suffered his breaths when he walked, taking deep cleansing lungfuls that arched his back with each draw of air.

I quickened my pace, not entirely missing a manure pile. "James!"

He stopped, tilted his head, and turned. I couldn't deny my joy at his surprise, his jaw open and his eyebrows raised. "Liberty?"

I drew closer, ignoring the manure now, and flung myself into his arms. "I can't fathom it. You're here. You are truly here!" I pulled back, examining him. "You look wonderful. No doubt the sea air agrees with you, little brother." He'd filled out since I last saw him, no longer the scrawny boy whose clothes I'd pressed.

His hands stayed on my arms. "How did you come to be in Boston, dear sister?"

"An old farmer took pity on me on the King's Highway from New York. I gave him the last of my shillings."

James blinked. His nose twitched. "Why did you not stay at home? What of Grandmother Caldwell?"

"Mayhap we should exit the streets. . . ."

He nodded, his mouth firm, and offered me his arm, which I took gladly. Though I was the elder by more than a year, he was now the man in our pitiable family of two. I would have to put myself under his protection—and willingly I would. No longer would I be criticized for serving the redcoats, however charming one could be. I now had a family, a place to belong.

James led me several blocks away from the main

thoroughfare. The Common loomed before us, and he ushered me to the Old Granary graveyard, where a high stone wall hid us from view of the street. A lone woman stood at the grave of the Seider boy—perhaps his mother? The Liberty Boys had ensured a magnificent funeral for the twelve-year-old boy, shot by one of the king's customs officials in the middle of a violent row. Standing there, looking at the grieving woman, I could understand the vehement passion of those who called themselves Patriots. After all, what sort of suppression led to the needless death of a child? Why didn't they just let us alone to run our own land?

The woman brought a handkerchief to her nose, her mouth moving. I wondered how many of the five thousand funeral attendees would come to visit the boy's resting place over the coming days. Likely only a handful. The funeral was more a show of Whig loyalty, meant to incite the Patriots' fervor for their Cause. I swallowed a lump of empathy for the woman at the boy's grave. She was the one who would truly mourn.

James and I strolled the crude paths between mottled headstones.

"Grandmother fell to the throat distemper last autumn. We had little in those final days, littler still as we laid her in the ground. I could think of nothing but to find you."

My brother's stubbled face showed the distress the news brought him. "I—I'm sorry, Libby."

My bottom lip trembled at the sound of my childhood nickname. "There is naught to be sorry for. I miss her terribly, but she passed to the next life with her unwavering faith as her comfort. And we are together now, James; that is all that matters. Tell me, when did your ship finally arrive?"

"Finally? I have been here all winter, sending word to New York for news of you and Grandmother. Now I see why I have had no reply."

I stopped walking and stared at a chipped headstone. James had been in Boston the whole of winter? While I stooped to serve the enemy—while I near lost my heart to one—my brother had been within arm's reach? "W-when? I checked the Customs House registers every day. I saw no sign of the *Defiance*."

"I was not on the *Defiance*. At the last moment I switched to the *Hawk*. I was certain you'd have received my letter."

I wanted to crumple atop the graves and sob. What waste! What ridicule I could have escaped. What guilt I would have been able to spare myself. Yet I could not let on with my brother watching me so intently. I drew in a large breath and fixed my chin firm.

"We are together now," I reiterated. "That is what matters. Where do you stay, James?"

"In a back room of the *Gazette*. Captain Morton is a friend of Benjamin Edes. I am looking for a way to make a living on land." His face turned a faint shade of green. "The ocean did not agree with me as I would have liked. Delivering papers suits me better."

My hands began trembling, along with the rest of my body. I ordered them rigid. There would be no coming beneath James's protection. Would I make a home in the back of the *Gazette*? Hardly. Would my brother soon be able to support us delivering papers? Likely not.

James's warm hands grasped my own. "Don't be glum, Libby. I feel I am a part of something—something important—at the *Gazette*. I may only ride for them, but I'm helping the Cause of liberty. It is a worthy Cause, one you can be proud of."

"Cause . . . Oh, James, do be careful. Please don't put yourself in the midst of the Liberty Boys' troubles." Once again, I very much felt the older sister, my task at hand to set my wayward brother straight. While one might inwardly support the Patriots, it was another thing entirely to risk one's life for them. After all my loss, I could not bear to lose the last precious family member I called my own. "Have you seen the handbills posted in the streets of late?" They informed the "rebellious people in Boston" that the Crown's 14th and 29th Regiments of Foot were determined to join together against the rabble who opposed them.

James stared at a spot to the left of my shoulder, his lips pressed together, his eyes unblinking.

Though I didn't see him waver, I continued. "A boy died last week because of this Cause you speak of. The Sons, they stir up trouble for all of the town. Perhaps all of the colonies, even."

James dropped his hands from mine. "And why should we be content to be ruled by a king thousands of miles across the sea? Why should we be content to give him our money without a by-your-leave, without a say in the matter?" My brother's voice rose with fervor, his cheeks red. "He sends these bloodybacks over here to intimidate us. What do they know of this land that is ours?"

I put my face in my hands. "Oh, James, you talk treason. I fear for you, is all."

He sighed, put a hand on my shoulder. "I am well able to look after myself. Now that I know you are here, though, I must look after you as well. Tell me, Libby, where do you stay? How have you fared?"

"I—you will not be happy should I tell you."

"Have you become a camp woman, then?" He smiled, his joke attempting to lighten the mood. It failed miserably.

I straightened my posture, prepared myself for my brother's condemnation. "I am the housemaid in one of the officers' homes. I make their meals and keep their rooms in exchange for room and board. I am also paid a shilling a day."

James clenched his fists. He took a particularly deep breath and I heard the wheeze in his lungs. "For those lobsters? You stoop to serve them? You must stop this at once, Liberty."

"You shan't tell me what to do. I came here to find *you*. I am a single woman in a strange town—what else am I suited for?"

"You must find something else."

I released an unladylike snort, fury whirling in my chest. If James had found me earlier—if I had found him—we wouldn't be having this conversation. We would have discovered a way, together. Now . . .

"I am suited for nothing else."

"There must be something. I will ask around at the *Gazette*. I'm certain there are plenty of Patriots in need of housemaids. Or perhaps a midwifery assistant. . . . How did you come by the position for those lobsters anyhow?"

I continued walking, not willing to look at my brother as I told my story. "I was accosted my first night here. One of the officers I now work for came to my rescue."

James stopped my steady gait, grasped my arm a mite too hard. "Were you harmed?"

"No."

"And now you are expected to repay your debt to the king by living with those fools."

I snatched my arm from his grasp. "You've no right to speak in this manner, James. You do not know this man—and yes, he is a man, just like you. He fights for a cause, just as you do. If not for him, I would be left for dead on the streets."

As I defended the lieutenant, I gave little thought to the captain's too-close, rum-soaked breath, his overly familiar gaze, the way he took snuff and then sneezed into a white kerchief I would later have to launder. All I saw was the lieutenant, the folds of his cape and tall form protecting me the night I first met him. His strong fingers, adorned with a single signet ring, holding out a precious book of poetry to me. His bold words, vowing to protect me from the man from whom he took orders.

And I thought James was wrong.

All British officers were not fools.

CHAPTER 5
Anaya

I GROANED AT the knock on the door and pulled the ties of my terry cloth robe tighter. In the bathroom, the steam from the water filling the tub rose in swirling wafts. I really didn't want to see anyone. I wanted to escape to my hot bath and wash away the stresses of the day. A teller's drawer that hadn't balanced. A snooty assistant manager who seemed bent on disliking me. A man I couldn't keep from my dreams, either in fairy tale or nightmare.

Maybe . . . but no. Brad didn't have my address. If he was going to contact me—and after a week of silence, that was a big "if"—he would call. I shut off the water and went to the door. It was probably Emilia, inviting me to dinner.

I'd accepted a couple times, and while I felt a true affection toward the family of three that made up my landlords, I didn't want them to feel obligated to take care of me just because I lived on their property.

I turned on the porch light and opened the door. My sister stood, shifting from side to side, hands tucked into the pockets of her coat.

"Lydia. Hi."

She took in my attire, or rather, lack of. "Hey. I know I shouldn't just show up, but I was coming home from Stop and Shop, and Grace told me what street you lived on. I saw your car."

Her blabbering put me at ease. She was nervous, vulnerable. Good.

"Come on in."

She gave me a tight smile and crossed the threshold. "Cute place." Lydia closed the door behind her and stood a foot past the threshold with her coat still on, her arms in front of her chest. I noted the new lines around her eyes and mouth. How many were there because of me?

"It's small, but it's all I need." I mimicked her posture, suddenly feeling exposed in my robe. I thought of Brad's card. I wanted to ask, but I couldn't risk her closing up. My questions—my horrible need to place blame at Lydia's feet instead of mine—would have to wait. A forgotten business card could hardly compare to my crimes. After the bombing, I had gladly identified as a victim, but not in this situation. The victim was Lydia. Her family. And I was the perpetrator.

"Nice landlord?"

"Yeah, they really are." I held out a hand. "Can I take your coat?"

Lydia wavered in her stance, reached for a button of her coat, then let her hand fall. Whatever her doubts were—and there must have been many—they won out. "I really don't have much time. I have to get home and get supper going."

"Time for coffee?"

She shrugged, unbuttoned her coat, but kept it on. "Okay."

I filled the Keurig with water. "How's Joel?"

She turned to me from the middle of my living room where she stood, somewhat aimless. "He's good. Getting ready for baseball."

"Nice. When's his first game?"

She shook her head. "I'm not sure yet. Beginning of April, I think."

I placed two napkins at the table. "Roger still away a lot for work?"

"No. After—after everything he took a different job in the company. Less responsibility, less travel." A hint of a smile appeared at her lips. "I guess Mom told you that might be changing."

She didn't seem angry that I'd accidentally told Grace about the possibility of a move, but I still winced at the reminder. "Yeah, sorry I spilled the beans the other day. Mom made it sound like it was happening next month."

"We're only considering. We don't have to decide until the

summer, figured we didn't need to work up the kids over a possibility." She fiddled with the bottom button of her coat. "He took a pretty drastic pay cut the last two years. This move would give us a chance to get back on our feet."

Why did I feel like all that was my fault? Was it? In my head I could reason that none of that day was my fault—the bombing, Lydia's minor injuries, Grace's severe ones. But at the end of all the reasoning, one fact remained: they wouldn't have been at the Boylston Street finish line that day if it weren't for me. If I had gone faster that day, we all would have been gone from the scene when that first bomb went off. And if I'd been around to help them the months following, perhaps Roger could have kept his old job. Perhaps my sister and her family wouldn't be contemplating moving halfway across the world now.

I flexed my foot and felt the familiar pinch of pain in my calf. Memories of Lydia and me playing "tea" as girls with our stuffed bears and dolls pushed to the forefront of my mind. She was older by six years, so there was a lot of overlap time where we just didn't have much in common. But there were a few precious years, from the time I was about three to when I was six, when Lydia wasn't too mature, too busy with friends or school or boys to pull on galoshes, grab one of Mom's umbrellas, and sing beneath a gently falling summer drizzle.

High school and college found us separated more often than not, but we drew closer again as Lydia married and had children. I'd come frequently to help her with Grace and Joel and talk to her about my own struggles with school and work and life. We found each other then as something akin to friends. I didn't see how we would ever get back to that place.

I pushed aside my thoughts. If I was to survive this visit and move forward, I couldn't dwell in the past anymore. I scrambled for a question to keep the conversation going. "And work for you? Your patients treating you okay?"

She looked at me a long moment then. I couldn't keep eye contact, and focused on arranging the saucers beside the Keurig instead.

"I thought Mom would have told you."

"We don't talk that much, really. Kind of a freak thing that she mentioned you guys moving to me the other day."

Lydia stared at the tan linoleum of my kitchen floor. "I left nursing. Too much for us right now. The kids—they're not going to be home for much longer. I want to be there for them, as much as I'm able. Life can be too short."

I breathed around the tightness in my chest.

"I'm a teacher's aide now. At the high school. I get to see Grace every now and then, help struggling kids. It's not bad. If the nursing position at the school ever opens up, I'll apply for that."

Guilt wormed its way inside me again. I had been living my life worrying about no one but myself for the last twenty months. Meanwhile, my sister's life was entirely rearranged. I couldn't help but wonder if her job move was a healthy one. Had she taken the job for the sole purpose of watching over Grace? I mean, the girl was seventeen. She didn't need her mom hovering over her every minute.

"You loved nursing."

"And I'll go back to it. Someday." She readjusted her purse, glanced at her phone. "Yikes, didn't realize it was so late. I really do need to run home. Joel's got a friend coming for dinner."

She wanted out. Out of my apartment, out of my life, probably. I couldn't let her get away so easily. She had made the choice to come. There must be some part of her that wanted things right between us again. "But coffee . . . ?"

She closed her eyes, shook her head, dark hair swinging around her chin. When she opened her eyes, it was with an exasperated sigh. "I'm trying here, Annie. Really I am. But you don't get it, do you? You can't waltz back into our lives after all this time of silence and expect everything to be like it used to. I mean, listen to us. We don't know anything about one another anymore. We're—we're different people than we were two years ago."

"I—I know. But—"

"We *needed* you. Grace and I needed you. But you bailed. Now that the mess is over, now that we're not waiting on doctors every minute of our lives, now that I'm not lying with her in bed at night just to reassure her everything's okay when she wakes up and remembers she doesn't have a leg, when she wakes up screaming that her foot—the one she no longer has—is killing her with phantom pain—now you want in? Sorry, but I have a family to protect."

The comment made blood rush to my limbs. True, I already saw myself as the culprit. But to hear Lydia claim she had to guard her family from danger—from me—was just too much. "I know I made a mistake, and Lydia, you have no idea how very sorry I am. But believe me when I say I never meant to hurt you or Grace." I didn't know what words could make the situation better. For whether I'd intended to or not, I *had* hurt my sister and niece. I looked at the carefully arranged coffee, knew it would be entirely inappropriate to ask her if now was a good time to choose a flavor. Instead, I swallowed, made an effort to mollify my tone. "I know I don't deserve—"

"You deserve nothing." Lydia reached for the door handle. "I came here for Grace, but you know what? Maybe it's time I think about me. Because seeing you—knowing what you expect—"

"I don't expect anything!"

She froze at the threshold. "It's just too hard right now, Annie. For me. Please don't call or come by." Her gaze flicked to my feet and her voice softened. "Not yet, anyway. I just—I need more time."

Then she was gone, her footsteps echoing on the wooden stairs of my apartment.

I rubbed my eyes, waited for her car to pull out of the driveway before I shut off the outside light and flopped onto the couch. I'd known this wasn't going to be easy. But Lydia's visit grounded me thoroughly in that reality.

Before visiting Grace the other day, I thought Lydia and I could take some time, work out our problems, and eventually reconcile. Now I realized that if we ever came to the point of understanding, there would still be this ugly thing hanging between us. This harbor of resentment. Maybe it would ease with time. Perhaps the sting would settle to a dull annoyance—like the pain in my leg—but I couldn't imagine it ever going away.

On the coffee table, my cell phone vibrated. Christina Perri's voice sang out "A Thousand Years," and I scooped it up. Brad Kilroy's name flashed up at me and I tried to push the disappointing visit with my sister from my mind and focus on the call I'd been waiting for all week.

"Hey, Brad."

"Hey yourself. How's it going?"

"Okay." A trite lie to the guy who saved my life didn't bode well for my conscience, so I settled for the truth.

Maybe should've gone for the lie. I sounded like a definite downer.

"Rough day?"

"Kind of. . . . My sister just stopped by—you know, the one you gave your card to. It didn't go so well."

"Sheesh, I hope I didn't cause any problems between the two of you."

I laughed, a dull, humorless sound. "No, we're pretty good at causing problems on our own." I shook my head, as if he could see me. "Anyway, sorry. Didn't mean to vent. We're not at that stage yet."

I could've kicked myself for the overly familiar comment.

"I don't mind." He cleared his throat. "But I did want to talk to you about something I stumbled upon today."

My fingers found the ring at my neck. "About the ring?"

"I think so. I wanted to see what you thought."

I sat up, pushing my feet farther into my fuzzy slippers. "You have my attention, that's for sure."

"I found something in the newspaper today. Are you up for a ride and maybe some dinner? It might be better to see this in person."

CHAPTER 6
Liberty

"'My soul impels me! and in act I stand to draw the sword; but wisdom held my hand. A deed so rash had finished all our fate, No mortal forces from the lofty gate could roll the rock. In hopeless grief we lay, and sigh, expecting the return of day.'"

I listened to the lulling cadence of the lieutenant's voice as he read aloud to me the struggles of Odysseus in the Cyclops's cave. The fire crackled in the small sitting area, and I kept to the task of darning the captain's socks.

When the captain had left for Deblois's Concert Hall on

Queen Street a few hours earlier, the lieutenant had stayed behind. I couldn't help but feel a thrill of excitement when he came down from his room to sit in the chair beside me, then asked if I might like to hear him read *The Odyssey* aloud.

He paused now, raised his eyebrows. "'Tis too gruesome for you? Shall I continue?"

I smiled. "I helped my grandmother midwife all manner of complaints. I believe I can handle Pope's translation of the death of Odysseus's two men."

"Yes, but 'the pavement swims with brains' is perhaps too gruesome for even me, a soldier in the King's Army."

If only he hadn't reminded me. For a short, blissful time I had imagined there were no such vast differences between us.

"Is something troubling you, Miss Liberty? Besides Homer's poem?"

I allowed my darning to fall in my lap. "I have found my brother." Three days had passed since James and I had spoken in the burying grounds. He had not tried to contact me since.

"That is good, is it not?"

Instant regret tore through my being in bumpy waves. With five words I had been disloyal to my brother, to my family. Was it not horrid enough that I worked for the Crown? Must I also discuss the person I loved most dearly with an officer in the King's Army? Inexcusable.

"It is nothing, sir. Please disregard a rambling lass."

He put down the book and leaned forward in his chair.

His long legs almost touched my skirts, and my heart took up a traitorous beat.

"Do you wish to leave our employ, Miss Liberty? Does your brother plan to provide for you? If that is your intent, we would of course understand . . . though I fear I would grieve your absence."

I raised my eyes to his solemn gaze, saw only sincerity. Heat traveled over my body, and quite suddenly the fire felt too warm.

He swallowed, the movement of his throat speaking of a nervousness I couldn't quite comprehend. "Perhaps 'tis not proper, perhaps I should not even say it, but I have come to—to care for you . . . Liberty."

The wings of a butterfly beat against my chest. An invisible weight drew me toward the lieutenant, and at the same time, I pictured James's clenched fists and tight jaw at the news I had shared with him three days before. I couldn't fathom his disapproval over my forbidden feelings for a man of the Crown.

"Lieutenant—"

"Alexander, if it so pleases you."

Alexander. His name was Alexander.

"Lieutenant, while I have . . . fond feelings for you as well, I do not see what could ever become of them. I—"

He scooped up my hands within the secure embrace of his own. The gold signet ring he wore pressed warm against my fingers. The scent of cedar and mint washed over me. "Then you care for me also?"

I tried to wrest my hands from his—at least in my mind. My disobedient body, however, would not obey. "It seems you are a sentimentalist," I whispered. "Perhaps you have read too much poetry."

He leaned closer to me until his knees touched my skirts, until we were but a breath away from one another. I would only have to close my eyes, lean the slightest measure forward, to close the gap. My limbs began to tremble at the anticipation. My mind swam. I should not encourage him so.

He looked down at our joined hands, did not move away. When he spoke, his voice was soft. "How old are you, Miss Liberty?"

The question caught me unawares. I pulled back but kept my hands resting in his. "I am seventeen."

He bowed his head and sighed, pressed our entwined fingers to his forehead. "So very young."

I slipped my hands from his, feeling the insult in a storm of turbulent emotion. "And yet I am not a child, Alexander." Using his Christian name would surely assure him of this.

"We are far apart in years. And with your position in the house . . . I do not wish to compromise . . . Forgive me, Liberty; I should not have spoken in this manner. I will wait—"

The door burst open and the fire shuddered, the cold air disturbing the warmth of the house. The captain's booted footfalls sounded from behind me.

"This is quite the snug picture." His words slurred even as he attempted to pronounce each syllable with precision.

The lieutenant stood, took a step back from me. "Sir. You are home early. You are welcome to join us, of course."

The chill of the captain's coat brushed against my arm as he came in front of me, his back to the lieutenant. He towered over me in full uniform—silver gorget, red coat, sash and epaulets, silver-laced hat. Snow melted off his boots onto the Persian carpet. He leaned down, placed his hands on either side of my chair. The scents of rum and pipe smoke and snuff swirled in nauseating waves around me. The sock I darned fell from my lap as my entire body took to quaking. "Perhaps it is my turn to get cozy with the help, eh?"

"Step away from her, sir. Now. You have had too much rum. You will not talk to Miss Liberty in that manner."

At first the captain didn't move. His addled gaze pinned me to the chair, and at Lieutenant Smythe's words, a lazy grin spread across his face. "And I suppose you, *Lieutenant*, are just the one to set me to rights?"

The lieutenant cleared his throat. "If need be, sir, yes."

The captain stood, swayed in front of me. Sounds from outside—shouts and knocks—pushed their way through the paned windows. Without warning, the captain spun, clenched the lieutenant's shirt in his hand, and drew back a tight-knuckled fist.

More noise from outside. A rapid knock on the door, and then a voice echoing down the street. "Town-born, turn out!"

Fire bells begged our attention, and I sat up, straining my ears for the sounds outside. The captain lowered his hands from their offensive position. In the distance, another bell took up the same call as the first. In such crowded confines, one fire could signal the destruction of the entire town. More shouts and frantic knocks. The clink of metal on metal—a shovel or bucket to fight the fire?

The captain seemed to sober quickly. He straightened his uniform and searched the room. When he found his musket, he grabbed it up.

"I fear 'tis not a fire this night," the lieutenant said, gathering his own coat and musket.

I thought to ask him what he meant, but I knew. He spoke of the tension that had built for months between the colonists and the king's soldiers. The fracases in the street, the mobs, the sentries taking abuse from schoolboys. The Sons of Liberty gathering at The Salutation on Ship Street, talking treason and working their rhetoric into the minds of the colonists through publications such as the one my brother worked for. The death of Christopher Seider and the great funeral that had followed. Just a couple nights earlier there had been another incident at the ropewalk. What would it all come to?

"Parcel of blackguard rascals. Those blasted *Americans*." The captain strode to the window, pushed aside the curtain roughly, and looked at the sight on the street. "Do not leave the house," he said to me. And then they were gone.

I scurried from the chair, tripped over the sock I'd been mending on my way to the window. Dark forms milled about the street, a great crowd, swelling in one direction—Queen Street.

My breathing quickened as I thought of James at the print shop on Queen. Of James and his ardent fervor for this living, breathing, fiery rebellion sweeping through the streets of Boston. I went to the keeping room and thought how to busy myself. I took two tankards from the cupboard, prepared to have cider for the men when they arrived home. Outside, the swell of people passed the window, lanterns and pine knot torches lighting up sticks and clubs and shovels. The bells continued their persistent ring, rattling my nerves further.

Then I heard it. Musket fire? I thought I recognized it from the many times the British infantry had taken up their shooting practice upon floating targets in the harbor.

Was this it, then? Had the Regulars—or perhaps the Sons—finally started their war? Or had the shots come from the harbor? Were they nothing more than a common drill?

My only thought was to help if in fact the shots had come from the center of town. At the risk of the captain's wrath, I left the jug of cider and searched the linen closet for old sheets to strip into bandages. Thankful I'd gone to the apothecary the week before, I grabbed a tincture of honey and camphor I'd mixed that morning. Who knew if I could help; who knew if my help would be welcome? Lord willing, the shots were to disperse a mob or merely a shooting practice, and no one would need aid.

My mind's eye conjured up an image of the woman grieving over Christopher Seider's grave in Old Granary. In this blistering town of chaos, bloodshed was possible, even probable. And all in the blasted name of freedom.

My petticoats dragged through the frozen mud and snow as I ran up Queen Street. The sound of drums echoed in the night, calling the soldiers to arms. The few paned windows that didn't hold latched shutters revealed curious little faces, a mother's skirts within grasp, no doubt behind bolted doors.

A din of conch shells and whistles, drums, and pounding feet. Then the haunting echo of shots rang through the air again, and unlike the last time, they were followed by an eerie sense of quiet that rippled from the center of town. Just as quickly, the din began once again.

I passed the Edes & Gill print shop, where I hesitated, yet instinct told me James would not be safe and warm in the back room with such a fabulous fray outside the door.

The crowd took on a life of its own as I neared King Street. I was carried along with the throng, fearful of its sudden force, cognizant that I would be trampled if I didn't keep up with the swell and press of it. Men, lads, and women joined around me. I tightened the basket I held against the crook of my arm. Someone stepped on my petticoats, and I tripped but caught myself, my skirts dirtying in the mud. A line of soldiers from the 29th Regiment formed what looked like a defensive barrier, their bayonets aimed at the crowd. I glimpsed a captain—Captain Preston, I knew, for he had come to the officers' house for tea—behind the barrier of grenadiers with their bearskin hats, along with the sentry I had seen tormented by school-age boys on more than one occasion before the Custom House, and several other soldiers. The crowd appeared mad for their blood, pushing toward them with shovels and catsticks despite the threat of the bayonets. The faint scent of musket powder clung to the air, as horrid as rotten eggs and a thousand times more terrifying.

Above us, from the balcony of the Town House, came a loud voice. I recognized Lieutenant Governor Hutchinson, calling for the crowd to return to their homes.

A man in the midst of the mass called up to the governor. "Order your soldiers to go inside the guardhouse, then, before we depart. See the position they are in, ready to fire on us!"

Governor Hutchinson's thin face wrinkled. "Indeed." He ordered them inside the guardhouse.

The soldiers of the 29th shouldered their guns and began to march inside.

Hutchinson again beseeched the crowd to go home. "Residents of Boston, believe me when I say I will see justice is done. I ensure a full inquiry on the events of this night. The law shall have its course; I will live and die by the law."

Slowly, the crowd began to disperse from King Street, their anger still united and burning. I wondered who had been hurt, who had been shot, for I could see no one in the midst of the tumultuous bodies.

"Light the tar barrels on Beacon Hill!"

"Yes—our town needs aid. Others should know!"

The comments swirled around me. From out of the chaos I heard my name.

"Miss Liberty!"

The lieutenant didn't appear to be in line with the other soldiers. The captain stood beside him. I dipped my head, bracing myself for his censure. The lieutenant spoke first. "Thank the Lord you are here," he said. "There are injured. Perhaps—"

The captain grasped my arm roughly. "There is naught to be done. We are all going home." He started away from the crowd, my skin burning where he held it.

"Captain, the governor has ordered us to the guardhouse. Miss Caldwell has supplies and knowledge these men can use."

Behind my employers, I felt the mob brewing, nudging one another over our display.

"I don't answer to Hutchinson," the captain sneered. "I take my orders from Colonel Dalrymple. We will go home now." He pulled my arm.

The lieutenant stepped close to the captain, his posture firm and steady. I hadn't realized he was taller than the captain until that moment. He spoke down to his superior, his nose nearly touching the captain's. "Use wisdom, sir. You will certainly hang this very night if you do not remove your hand from the girl this minute."

His words rang true. Behind him even now a burly gentleman struck a catstick against his open palm. "You bloodybacks shoot us, then dare manhandle a girl before us? You best run and leave the lass alone if you know what's best for ya."

The captain snorted and shoved my arm away so that I stumbled a step. "*You* best be home within the hour, Miss Caldwell, or you will find yourself out of employment."

"Yes, sir," I mumbled after him as he began, not toward our residence as he claimed was his intent but toward the guardhouse with the rest of the soldiers.

The lieutenant looked after him. "Do be careful, Miss Liberty. What has begun this night cannot be undone." He followed after the captain, his chin high against the jeering of the crowd, his musket firm at his side.

I broke away from the lingering stares to a spot where a dark form lay. He was massive, a mulatto from the looks of it. "I have supplies," I called to a man who knelt near the body, "and some knowledge of their use. Might he be moved to some semblance of a dressing station?"

"This one already be taken to eternity, miss. That lad yonder may benefit."

I looked in the direction he pointed, about ten yards away. A man lay on his side, his back toward me, the wounds exposed to the night air. The snow bled red beneath him. I cringed at the muddied scraps of shirts with which the man attending him attempted to stanch the flow of blood.

"Please," I called. "I have fresh bandages. And medicine. Allow me."

I fell to my knees in the mud, grabbed the linens in my basket. The man took away his scraps, the blood having soaked them through. Nausea gripped me at the sight of bone and flesh and muscle. I pressed a linen to the wound, knowing my skill was not enough to help the gentleman. "He needs a doctor. Where can the nearest be found?"

The injured man groaned, and I patted his shoulder, making shushing sounds as I did when James was a boy, crying over the death of our parents.

"Doctor Warren and Doctor Church have been sent for. We best not move him or he will lose more blood."

"I agree, and yet his temperature is dropping. He needs to be out of the cold."

The wounded man drew in a rattling breath. Something about it made me pause. He croaked out a sound.

And I knew. This man was not a stranger.

Heavenly Father, no . . . please let it not be so.

My hands took up a furious trembling, so much so that the man beside me took the linen from me. My breathing came rapid, and I tripped on my skirts in an effort to see the face of the suffering man.

I vomited in the snow beside me, barely had time to swipe at my mouth ere black spots danced before my eyes.

I reached for my brother's face, his eyelids fluttering. "James—James, I am here. A doctor is coming."

Flashes of my brother's youth assaulted me. James, running toward me in a field, his breeches stained with grass, his mouth all smiles, blue from berry juice. James, climbing into my bed, cuddling warm at my side, asking me to read

Robinson Crusoe. James, speaking passionately as a near adult about freedom and the Cause he served.

"Put more pressure on those wounds," I ordered through tears. "James—James. . . ." My frantic tone rose at the fierce convulsing of my brother's body. A line of crimson blood bubbled up from a mouth that tried to form words. It ran down the side of his face. I leaned closer, knowing he did not have much longer.

"I am here, James. I am here."

His pale mouth whispered unintelligible sounds. I leaned farther down. My cheek touched the snowy, footprint-packed ground, the scent of sour bile emanating from my brother's mouth.

"I . . . am proud . . . to . . . die for . . . freedom. Love you . . . Liberty."

"I love you, James." Tears froze on my cheeks, and I clutched my brother tight, willing my warmth, my life, into him. A moment later his convulsing stopped, and my sobs came harder, my chest shuddering against his cloak.

"Miss." The man who had tried to help me put a hand at my elbow, my brother's blood on his fingers.

I shook my head against James's shoulder, denying the words that would come from the man's mouth.

"He is gone, miss."

I breathed a last quaking sob, looked at James's vacant death stare. I clasped a hand to my mouth to suppress the gag that rose within me. The gentleman closed my brother's eyes. "I am deeply sorry, miss. Were you courting?"

My lips cracked when I opened my mouth. "No. He—he's my little brother."

I stared at James's body. My little brother. We should have been together. He never should have sought life at sea. I never should have let him go. I should have searched harder, hunted the streets of Boston for my brother instead of relying on a customs official. Then we would have been together. James wouldn't have taken up with the *Gazette* or the Sons or any such ridiculous call for independence.

"I can see to his body, miss. 'Tis not suitable for a lady to be exposed to all this. Tell me your address, and I will call on you tomorrow and give you news of where he is."

"Where he is . . . ," I said dumbly.

"Miss, might you tell me your name? Your place of residence? I give you my word to call on you tomorrow."

I gazed at my brother's body again, suddenly aware that a soldier of the Crown had done this. I blew my nose in my apron. The Regulars were responsible for murdering my brother. How could I admit to being in their employ? How could I not be ashamed to serve them, to sleep in a bed they supplied, to fall in love with one of them?

Bile rose again in my belly, and I quelled it with a press of a hand to my middle. I was the most traitorous kind of sister to allow myself to fall in love with a redcoat. I'd live on the streets if I had to. I'd die on the streets rather than crawl back to the officers' house, accept their food and fire.

I straightened, feeling a tangible target for my grief and

anger. Over my brother's blood, still reddening the snow, I addressed the man who wished to give me aid.

"My name is Liberty Caldwell. And you may give any news to those in the office of the *Gazette*."

Never again would I dance over the line drawn between Patriot and Regular. Never again would I betray my brother.

Or his Cause.

CHAPTER 7
Anaya

WHEN THE DOORBELL let out its single cheery chime, I grabbed my purse and opened the door to see Brad in khakis and a polo shirt.

I glanced down at my jeans. "Hey. Am I underdressed?"

He smiled, revealing a row of straight teeth. "No—you're perfect. I just wanted to make a good impression after phoning it in at our last dinner."

I locked the door and we walked to the car. "You know, I kind of miss the pencil."

"Pencil?"

"In your hat." I gestured to the side of my head.

He laughed. "Next time I'll be sure to take you to a fast-food place instead of Boston's finest. I'll wear my hat and pencil. I'll even clear off the passenger's seat of my work van and take you in that. My sister exaggerates—it's not really as bad as an episode of *Hoarders*."

I swallowed down the nerves climbing my throat. My mind skidded over the fact that he wanted to take me out again and landed on where we were going. "B-Boston?"

"Yeah—that okay? We were just there last week, so I didn't think you were against it." He opened the door for me, but I didn't get in.

"Sure, that's fine. Where are we going?"

"There's something I want you—us—to see at the Museum of Fine Arts."

Back Bay. I dragged in a deep breath, braced my hand against the top of the open car door.

"Annie?"

I exhaled, slow and steady. "My full name's Anaya." Why he should care, why I chose that moment to divulge such information, I didn't know. But I wanted him to understand. And if anyone could, it was him, wasn't it? The man who had shared the terror of that day with me? "It means 'completely free.'" I laughed at the irony. "I haven't been back to that part of Boston since the bombing."

"Ah, gotcha."

I flung my hand in the air, sat in the passenger's seat of his Accord. "Go, please. I didn't mean to make a big deal out of nothing."

He didn't close my door. "We don't have to go to Boston tonight."

HEIDI CHIAVAROLI

I breathed deep. "I'm tired of being a baby about the past. Yes. I want to go." At least I *wanted* to want to go. Same thing, right?

He shut my door and walked around to the driver's side. The inside of the car smelled like pine and woodsy cologne. The scent triggered something about that long-ago day. Something more hopeful than horrible, more wondrous than wearing. I clung to it.

Traffic ran light, and we entered the city a short time later. As the buildings pressed in around us, I reminded myself I had nothing to fear. Couldn't this even be an important step in my healing? Returning to Back Bay with Red Sox Sweatshirt?

"Are you afraid of another attack?" He pressed the brakes as we met a red light off the highway.

A news van pulled alongside us, reminding me that the trial I avoided rained upon the city. I wanted to know what went on in that courtroom, and I didn't. I would stay up to watch the ten o'clock news, and then shut it off when highlights of the trial popped up on the screen.

"No. It's the memories. The suffering. The thought of my niece, Grace . . . the thought of a boy the same age as my nephew . . ." I couldn't finish the thought. The word *killed* didn't seem to do justice to what really had been done.

"They'll find him guilty."

I scrunched up my face. "I'm not convinced that will fix everything." I shrugged. "People think it will—hey, maybe I'm wrong and it will make me feel better."

But it wouldn't change things. The bombing had still happened. That boy's parents still needed to live with the fact that they'd never see their son graduate high school, grow up, maybe get married. They'd never see what type of man he'd become. It had all been taken away. Stolen.

Just like my life had been.

My thighs tensed as we made our way through Boston's Back Bay and pulled into a parking garage.

"The museum doesn't close until ten on Wednesdays. Figured we'd get dinner after."

I forgot about the past, about my grief, and clutched the ring at my neck until the metal grew warm in my palm. "There's something about this ring in the museum?"

"I think so. But I wanted to see what you thought before I got you all excited."

I turned toward him. "Okay, spill it. What's this all about?"

Brad put the car in park and shut off the engine. His grin shone in the dim lighting of the garage. "Last December, some construction workers at the State House uncovered a time capsule from 1795. It was buried by Sam Adams and Paul Revere."

Goose bumps broke out on my skin. "I remember hearing about that on the news. It was a bunch of coins and newspapers and stuff, right?"

"And something else. A poem."

I blinked. "Okay."

"I remembered them opening the capsule at the museum

back in January. But I forgot about it until I browsed my newsfeed last night." He reached for his phone in a cup holder of the center console, opened an app, and handed it to me.

An article from the news section of a Boston website. It stated that beginning today, March 11, the Museum of Fine Arts would display the artifacts found in the time capsule.

I lowered the phone. "Neat."

Brad took it back, scrolled farther down the page. "The poem's by a woman named Liberty Gregory. There were a few words that caught my eye." He enlarged the picture of the poem, crinkled and yellowed with age.

I scanned the stanzas, incomplete in the picture. But my gaze immediately latched on to one phrase. "No way." My head swam with excitement. This shouldn't mean so much to me. It was Brad's family, after all. His ring. His ancestors, his inheritance. But I couldn't deny how it called to me, this story untold. I had waded through the last two years with this ring by my side. I'd clung to it, slept with it, imbued it with powers it couldn't possibly possess. Of course I'd be enthusiastic about the words before me.

Victory belongs to the one who is strong.

Beside me, Brad grinned. "Keep reading."

I skimmed the words in a rush. It spoke of a stolen ring. "You're kidding me. Do you think . . . ?"

"That's why I wanted us to come and see it. To read the whole poem. I'd been searching for information on the ring for days. When I saw this I thought it was wishful thinking."

I handed him his phone. "That would be a mighty big coincidence."

Brad nodded. "Unless someone made a lot of rings with that saying back then."

"Possible. But we're here now. Let's go see what we find."

We exited the car, and as we walked toward the entrance of the museum, Brad reached out and squeezed my hand. Then, just as quickly, he released it.

Before tonight, I thought I'd never set foot in this section of Boston again. I thought I'd never come so close to my living nightmares. But here, with Brad, anticipating Liberty Gregory's poem inside the museum, I felt . . . alive.

My hand tingled where Brad had squeezed it, and I thought maybe, just maybe, Brad Kilroy was still my hero.

CHAPTER 8
Liberty

I did not return to the officers' house that night. Neither did the townspeople manage a signal fire on Beacon Hill before Governor Hutchinson stopped them. I left my brother's body to the man—whose name I learned was Mr. Gregory—to take care of, James's blood still fresh in the snow. I took to walking the bitterly cold streets, my fear-filled mind numbing my senses to the near-freezing temperatures, the sound of baying dogs, rattling carts, and drunken, angry men. A herd of pigs had broken loose from their pens, and they ran by me, poking their snouts into the dirty gutters.

I replayed the events of the night over and over again in

my head. The stench of musket fire, James's blood in the snow, his final bold proclamation of being proud to die for freedom. His proclamation of love for me. He had loved me. Even though he knew I was disloyal to the Cause for which he lived. For three days I had known he was in Boston, willing to help me find another employ, and for three days I did nothing to change my situation.

Whether it was the consequence of my overtired mind or pure hatred that gripped me like a hard, angry vise, a potent need for revenge curled its talons around my heart, possessing me whilst I stalked the town streets into daybreak. As the ugly thing festered inside me, news from Faneuil Hall swept through the town—news that the troops, along with the customs commissioners, would remove to Castle Island, beginning the very next day, for their own safety.

Victory played a bittersweet tune across my vengeful heart. This was James's triumph, not my own. Not even Hancock's or Adams's. It all belonged to my brother. He said he was proud to die for freedom. Perhaps he had died believing truth.

The captain and the lieutenant would leave. Good riddance to both of them. These red-coated beasts had stolen all too much from me. My honor, my heart, and now my brother.

A need for justice swelled within my chest. 'Twas so great it demanded to be served. That was when the idea came to me. A horrible idea that I could not fathom as my own, and yet it was. As I walked in the direction of the officers' house, I clung to this, my only consolation.

While the plan was not a thing so honorable as my brother's death, I felt it was also perfect in its own way. I would prove my loyalty to James and his Cause, even if I had to do it with his soul beyond the grave.

I slid the key I'd taken with me the night before into the lock of the officers' house and heard it click softly. They did not lock the door except at night or if they were out and about, but I suspected in the aftermath of yesterday's events they would do so even if they were awake and in the home.

To my relief, the officers didn't occupy the keeping room. I heard no voices upstairs. I bolted the door and crept up the stairs like a thief, the task before me calling.

Once in my chambers, I made haste in obtaining my valise from beneath the bed. I opened the drawer of my dressing table and retrieved my underclothes and brush, shoving them in the depths of the case. Then my mobcaps, my stockings, my spare petticoat, and two dresses. I picked up the book of poetry the lieutenant had given me and tried not to waver as I left it on top of the cherrywood surface of my set of drawers. He would be hurt to see that I had left it, but I could not in good conscience carry around a gift from the enemy.

I scurried about, gathering odds and ends. The creak of the door from downstairs screeched up to my room. Dizziness swept over me; panic marched hobnailed boots over my chest. I would not get away with my plan if found out.

Shoving the open valise beneath my bed, I contemplated whether I should hide or pretend indifference, as if I had finally decided to come back. I chose the former, shimmying under the bed beside my satchel.

The cold wood pressed through my clothes as I listened to the steady thud of boots upon the stairs.

"Liberty!" the captain called, opening the door of my chambers. It was the first time he had used my name without a preceding *Miss*. It sounded overly familiar, and I hated him for it. I held my breath, praying he would leave.

"Has she returned?" The lieutenant.

"No. It appears she has chosen to leave our employ." I recognized the slur of his words. Truly, had he been drinking his rum so early in the day?

The lieutenant walked on to his chambers. Was it my imagination, or were his steps slow, defeated?

I squeezed my eyes shut, waiting for the captain to leave. Instead, his boots came along the side of my bed.

"And without her personal effects, it seems." The captain's words were lower. He closed the door behind him and bolted it.

My insides came alive with fire.

He knew I was here.

And now he would take pleasure in making me squirm.

"If Miss Liberty were to take her personal effects, she would most certainly take the book of poetry Lieutenant Smythe had given her."

How did he know? Had the lieutenant revealed such

personal information? It made me doubt both the officers, and I suddenly felt thoroughly alone. I remembered the way the captain had leaned over me the night before, tall in his full uniform, his words dirty and insinuating.

I wanted to weep, to disappear into the floorboards, to forget my ridiculous plan of revenge. What could I enact on this man that would make him flinch?

He may not have fired the musket, but he'd killed my brother just the same—he and every other invading redcoat. I saw that now. They shouldn't be here, any of them.

James was right. They were fools, every one.

The room quieted, but then my arm was pulled so violently I thought for certain it would dislocate.

My stomach and thighs dragged along the floorboards, my skirts catching, the fabric tearing on the roughened wood. "And what have we here?" The captain hoisted me up, shook me in front of him, his perfectly groomed queue not moving with the gesture, a sneer upon his hardened face. He reeked of rum and snuff, and I near gagged as his hot breath poured over me.

I didn't think. I spat in his eye.

The action surprised him enough that he released me. "You little chit."

I scurried for the door, but before I could unlatch the bolt, he caught me and dragged me, the heels of my boots skidding across the floor.

"So you have some fight in you after all, do you?" He

pushed me onto the bed. "Don't fret. I enjoy a bout with my women as much as an acquiescence."

I kicked; I scratched. To my extreme horror, he seemed to feed on my reaction, pinning my arms above my head, holding me down with a hard knee.

A loud knock upon my chamber door. "Open up at once, sir. You're making a fracas. Enough of this."

The captain looked up. "This is none of your concern, *Lieutenant*. Leave us or I'll have you . . . court-martialed for disobeying orders." The slur of his words discredited the authority he attempted to put behind them.

"You will find yourself in the gallows along with Preston and his men before that happens. You are angry about the events of last night, but do not be foolhardy—Miss Liberty has naught to do with all that."

The captain growled. The rough red wool of his coat scraped against my skin. He pushed me deeper into the straw of the bed. "The blasted . . . dunderhead is right." He removed himself from on top of me.

Without thought or hesitation I scooped up the pewter candlestick holder and brought it for a blow across his head. I struck twice before he wrenched the holder from my hand and repaid me in kind.

A black curtain closed before my eyes and blinded me to everything but the hurt of being struck. Sticky blood trailed down my face. I lunged for the door again, but he caught me with little effort and once more bashed my head with the holder. Then, in the most gruesome act of violation, he lifted my skirts and took me with a force that tore through me, leaving me hollow and destitute inside, both body and soul.

From outside my chambers, the lieutenant chopped at the door with a hatchet, but by the time the door was splintered open, the captain had finished his indecency and stood as smug and well-put-together as if he were standing before Colonel Dalrymple himself.

I jumped when the lieutenant shouted a dreadfully foul word at the captain and landed a well-placed fist across his nose, leaving a gush of blood to splatter down the front of his tidy uniform. Without remorse, he threw another blast, and then another. I watched as warm tears mixed with the blood on my face.

When the captain could no longer stand, the lieutenant stopped the blows. "You will most certainly pay for your crimes," he said.

The captain straightened, stanched the flow of blood with a handkerchief from his pocket. "We'll see about that, now . . . won't we?" He did not look at me or the lieutenant again as he stumbled past us, down the stairs, and out the door.

"Liberty . . ." The lieutenant held a hand to me, but I ignored it.

"Go," I whispered from where I lay on the bed in a ball, humiliated not only by what was done to me, but that it was witnessed by another.

"I can summon a doctor. You need medical attention. I will go with you to Hutchinson. The captain will pay for this. I cannot leave you." Through my blinding pain, I saw his bottom lip tremble. He reached out tentative fingers to stroke my shoulder.

I recoiled as if his hands had burned me. "Leave me!" I yelled with as much force as I could through quivering lips.

After a moment he did leave. The door of the house echoed closed again. Blessed quiet enveloped the abode. And yet I couldn't believe the lieutenant had truly left me. More than likely, he had gone to fetch a doctor. I would have to move quickly.

I pressed the coverlet to my bloodied head, not caring that I damaged the fine linens. With rigid steps, I pulled the valise from beneath the bed, my insides cramped and wasted. In light of all the captain had taken from me, my plan seemed ridiculous, childish. Indeed, it could not hurt him, and it would not satiate my murderous thoughts. And yet it would anger him. And by the time he found out, I would be out of his reach and he would be on his way to Castle Island.

With the linen still pressed to my head, I entered the captain's chambers. I opened his drawers, emptied them onto his bed, searched for anything of value—a pocket watch, a small silver plate, anything. I found a silver whistle with the king's emblem and a gold watch chain. In the bottom drawer, I found an inconspicuous wooden shaving kit. I opened it, unmindful of the razors spilling from the box. I glimpsed a white envelope, the red sealing wax pressed firm upon it. I lifted it, heavy in my hands. My breath caught.

I counted out ten pounds of British sterling silver hidden

in the shaving kit and did not feel an ounce of remorse at taking every pound. I emptied my shiny booty into the worn valise and proceeded to the lieutenant's chambers.

His room was tidy and smelled of him—cedar and soap. I went through his things with more care, finding nothing of interest and no silver. Then my eyes landed on his bureau, upon the signet ring I'd so often seen adorning his finger. I presumed he took it off to sleep, as I had found it left behind in this same spot when cleaning his chambers on particularly hectic mornings.

My conscience bade me not to touch the ring. And yet the shining gold, the bloodstones that formed an outline of an anchor, called to me. I stared at the ring, knowing I should not take it. The lieutenant had been kind to me, hadn't he?

And yet he had one fault I could not ignore.

He was one of *them*.

The brutes who forced themselves on a town who didn't want them. The brutes who forced themselves on young women. The brutes who had killed my brother.

I swept the ring up and placed it in a side pocket of my valise, along with the sterling.

Tonight I would seek and pay for my own shelter, by my own means, ill-gotten though they might be.

And by the next day at this time, all I loathed would be far from me, banished to Castle Island, all thanks to my brother's life . . . and death.

CHAPTER 9
Anaya

I FOLLOWED BRAD into the museum. Excitement threaded through my veins, yet even as Brad paid for our tickets, I doubted the feelings. Emotions could be fleeting and temporary. Hope, joy, excitement. All could be snuffed out in an instant.

I hated the dark thoughts and stepped an inch closer to Brad, choosing to cling to the feelings of a moment earlier.

The woman behind the counter directed us to the exhibit in Gallery 133: "Inside the Box: Massachusetts State House Time Capsule Revealed." The pamphlet she gave us stated that the contents of the time capsule would be on display until the middle of April. Then they'd be reburied at the State House for a future generation to find.

Brad grasped my hand again as we walked through the museum, the insides of our forearms brushing against one another. This time he didn't let go.

As we entered Gallery 133, I glimpsed boxes atop a table, along with a collection of green, copper, and silver coins and several sets of newspapers. The empty, weather-worn time capsule box sat alongside an inscribed silver plaque, commemorating the New State House on July 4, 1795, the nineteenth anniversary of the country's declaration of independence.

And there, at the end of the table, in its own box, lay a single, neatly printed paper, the edges yellowed, but otherwise none the worse for wear. The title read *Freedom's Ring*. My gaze flew to the bottom, where the signature *Liberty Gregory* stood out in neat swirls.

"Wow," I whispered, the need to be reverent overwhelming in this place. A place where, for just a few moments, history joined with the present in a dance so fluid and graceful a person couldn't tell one from the other.

We stood in silence, reading Liberty's poem.

FREEDOM'S RING

Across the swell of seas,
in the midst of church bells' ring,
you came to me.
Despised for the scarlet coat,
shadow of enemies at your throat,

you came to me.
Bitterness and betrayal won,
on that fifth of March the fight begun.
Sorrow and secrets I bore alone,
for guilt and remorse left unatoned.
The ring not mine but yours, I know;
untold grief was mine to sow.
My sins you chose to forget
in a final act of selflessness.
Come April on the Green,
you shed your blood . . . still scarlet.
I despise the color through and true.
I shall recall the symbol of love and strife
as long as God above may grant me life.
Forgive me for my blinded eyes,
freedom's ring and colors lie.
You were not the enemy after all.
And when at heaven's gates I call,
I remember. . . .

"Victory belongs to the one who is strong."
I will cling to Him all the dark night long.
A burst of freedom within my heart,
the ring I stole . . . my guilt departs.
As church bells ring and freedom chimes,
I remember.

Liberty Gregory, 1795

I stood over the ancient words, read them again. There was no denying the poem spoke of a ring—a symbol of love, likely bearing the same inscription as the ring around my neck. Brad's ring.

I slid a pointer finger through the generous circle at my neck, tried to contain my hope over the find. What were the chances this Liberty Gregory had actually owned *Brad's* ring? What were the chances she was truly Brad's ancestor?

Beside me, Brad shifted from one foot to the other. "Neat, right?"

No way I could deny that. "Crazy neat."

"And she's definitely talking about a ring with a quote that matches our ring."

I nodded, trying not to get hung up on the fact that he called it *our* ring. "A definite story."

He raised an eyebrow. "Up to figuring it out?"

Even if I wanted to, I couldn't have said no to that face, his stubble more of an eleven-o'clock than a five-o'clock shadow, the irises of his eyes speckled with the gold of hope, his ears almost wiggling with possibility. I wanted to spend more time with him, to delve into this mystery we shared. If I ended our journey now—if I gave him back the ring—I would be alone. Again.

I smiled, took out my iPhone. "I can take a picture, right?"

"Sure can." Brad slipped his own phone from his pocket. "I'm going to copy down the words as a backup, too."

As he finished, I looked out of the corner of my eye at Brad's scrunched-up face. His stomach rumbled. I poked his arm with my finger. "We don't have to stay here, you know. I—"

He grabbed my hand and pulled me in the direction of the exit. "Not that I don't appreciate history and fine art and all, but I appreciate fine food a heck of a lot more."

We hopped into the Accord and eased into downtown Boston. My breathing turned quieter when we headed away from Back Bay and into Boston's Seaport District.

"Like Del Frisco's?"

I hid a smile. "Fitting you should bring me to Liberty Wharf. And yes, seafood here's the best."

"I'm feeling like steak tonight, but they have the best of both worlds."

A smattering of people occupied the high-end restaurant—no more than I'd expect for a Wednesday night in March. Moonlight glittered off the frozen harbor as the hostess sat us at a table set apart from the circular bar. The soft lighting twinkled off empty wineglasses. Definitely romantic, though I couldn't be certain that's what Brad intended.

We unfolded our menus, and I searched for something under twenty bucks in case Brad insisted on paying, as he'd done a week earlier.

"No skimping. The scallops look good."

I closed my menu in defeat and sighed. "You read my mind."

He shut his menu. His foot brushed against mine, then retreated quick enough that the gesture must have been an accident. He dug his phone from his pocket, opened the note he had copied at the museum, and put the device on the table. "Up to some work, my dear Watson?"

I tapped the cover of the phone. "Don't you think we should have our dinner first?"

"An old-fashioned girl, right? No electronics on dates. I get it."

"So this is a date?" I cringed at the words that flew off my lips. *Monitor. Mouth.* I could almost hear the scolding Mom would be giving me.

He shrugged. "Do you want it to be?"

Trapped. I looked around the elegant restaurant, inhaled the scent of seafood and lemon and steak. He could have taken me to Burger King if all he wanted was some beef and to mull over the words of the poem. I decided to play it safe. "Do you?"

The waiter came to take our orders.

When he left, I sat back in my chair. "Saved by the bell."

He raised his Coke and took a sip. "Great show. Favorite episode?"

"You are unbelievable."

He grinned. "Why, thank you. So . . . favorite episode?"

I sighed, accepting his way of not dealing with the date question. "The prom one. When Kelly bails on Zack because her dad loses his job. Then Zack puts on a private prom outside the school for her."

He pressed his lips together, pretended serious contemplation. "Good one, good one. But I have to say the all-time best episode was the Save the Max telethon."

We shared a laugh. When the chuckles subsided, Brad grew serious. "Back to your question. Yeah, I'd like it if this were a date."

My skin heated. Did I want that? Was it emotionally healthy to get involved with a man I'd met *that* day?

He continued. "No pressure, though, you know? I mean, you've worn that ring all this time. You might even be attached to the guy who gave it to you . . . only you knew me for a minute in a moment of terror. I'll bet you conjured up someone spectacular in two years' time. Guess I probably don't measure up very well, huh?"

"I definitely didn't picture a tattooed contractor with a van from an episode of *Hoarders*," I admitted.

He nodded, his mouth pulled into a sad smile. I hated the regret it spoke of, but he was right. I'd clung to him for some sort of illusory hope the last two years. The hazy image, the feel of his arms carrying me away from horror. And yet his words frightened me. Somehow I would have to reconcile dreamy Red Sox Sweatshirt with real Brad. Would I come up disappointed?

"I bet you've had a few ideas about the heroine in distress you rescued too. Bet I don't fit the bill either."

"No, you don't. You're better than I imagined. You're real."

My body tingled at the affirmation. I only wished I could reciprocate the compliment. But while I did love knowing who my rescuer was, a part of me still had to come to grips with my fairy-tale nightmares, my countless daydreams in which Brad was the perfect hero of my world.

I had to come to grips with the fact that this was real life; there were no perfect heroes.

After the waiter cleared our empty plates, leaving nothing but two cups of coffee between us, we each took out our phones and studied the words to the poem.

"What do you think?" Brad sipped his dark coffee.

"I think I'm not an English major. But I still find this stuff fascinating."

"It is pretty cool. History revealed. And it feels . . . personal."

"It *is* personal. Brad, this woman could be your great-grandmother's great-grandmother." I scrolled the screen up and down on my phone, my pinkie finger tapping the table. "We need to find out more about Liberty." My sentence—my excited tone—hung in the air, and I realized how crazy I sounded. "Sorry. I'm not weirding you out, am I? I do realize it's *your* family history."

He shrugged. "Honestly, it's a little strange. Not in a creepy way. But I'm not sure I totally understand why you have such a strong stake in my family's ring."

That made two of us. I tried to mentally peel back the complicated attachment I had with the ring. From the moment I'd woken in the hospital with it clutched in my blood-crusted fingernails, I'd allowed it entrance to my soul. I sought the band at my neck, ran a finger along the thin chain securing it above my heart.

I shifted in my seat. "I'm going to be honest here and hope it doesn't scare you."

He nodded encouragement.

"You didn't just save me once. You saved me hundreds of times. Maybe thousands." I stared into my untouched coffee cup. "Every time I find myself reliving that terror, the worst moments of my life. Maybe my dwelling on it is unhealthy. But you and the ring—you're the happy ending of that nightmare. When I didn't want to set foot out my door for fear of what could happen anytime or anywhere, I'd remind myself that for every crazy person out there ready to hurt innocent people, there was a person like you. And your ring was a tangible reminder of that. You and the ring were the two sides of the hinge that held me together." I blew out a long breath. "No pressure, of course."

He chuckled, but it was stilted, and I felt the gravity behind it. When he spoke, his words were slow, measured, as if he feared breaking me with them. "I'm glad I helped you that day . . . and I'm glad the ring reminds you of the good in the world. But . . ."

"What? Say it."

"I'm not sure I can be a happy ending." He rubbed the back of his neck. I glimpsed the cross tattoo on the inside of his forearm. "I'm just a regular guy."

"You're right. I've made that day into some kind of fairy tale with a magic talisman and a knight in shining Red Sox sweatshirt, and that's not right."

"I didn't say it's wrong. How can I know, really, what you

went through?" He swiped a hand over his face. "Did you read *To Kill a Mockingbird* in high school?"

I nodded.

"There's a scene where Atticus tells Scout that you never really know a person until you climb into their skin and walk around in it. That's what I'm trying to do here, Annie. Understand you. Get to know more about you." He traced the handle of his coffee cup with a finger, then looked directly at me with new resolve. "It's my turn to be honest. . . . You fascinate me. Maybe it's the brief traumatic history we share, maybe it's your attachment to my family's ring, maybe it's more—I don't know. But I'm not some fantasy hero that pulled you to safety that day, and I don't want you to be disappointed."

I inched my fingers across to his. A squeeze would have seemed too forward, but the moment called for some sort of physical reassurance. I brushed the calloused skin of his hands with my own. I wanted to reassure him that neither he nor the ring could disappoint me, that they'd both already pulled me through the worst life had to offer, but I wasn't entirely certain of the truth of such words, so I stayed silent.

After another tense moment of quiet, I pulled my hand away. "Maybe we should look into your family genealogy. They have tons of stuff online now. There has to be a way to figure out if you were actually related."

"And what her story is."

I swiped my finger over my phone, examined the rest of the poem. "It seems she's writing about a British soldier. This soldier—she knew him somehow. Maybe even loved him? The fifth of March . . ." I thought back to the painting in the Union Oyster House, the burst of gunfire from the man in the scarlet coat, the date in fine script above. "That was the date of the Boston Massacre. It sounds like maybe he died that night."

Brad shook his head. "No Regulars died that night. Only colonists."

I looked at the next stanza. "Maybe in April, then? A month after the Boston Massacre?" I grimaced. "Or it could be any April up until the year she wrote it. But it sure does sound like he died."

"'April on the Green.' Reminds me of the Battle at Lexington."

"And what about the ring? How did she wind up with a ring from a British soldier?" The waiter brought us the bill. I reached for my purse, but Brad snatched up the bill and shooed me away.

"No denying the ring's there. Though it seems twofold— like she's playing around with words. You know, the real ring, and the victory of freedom."

I held up the gold circle at my neck. "Cool to think this could be the very ring she's talking about, but it's killing me that we might never know for certain." I slumped against my chair.

He lightly kicked my foot with his. "Don't tell me you're not up for a challenge. Come on, you're a marathon runner. You can't give up that easy."

I didn't correct him, though I knew otherwise. I used to run with that kind of purpose. But for two years I'd been running and hiding from my challenges, imposing silence on Lydia and her family.

I ran my finger over the indented crest of the ring. I didn't know if I was strong enough to change things, but I was tired of letting fear be in charge. I wanted to cling to something extraordinary. I wanted to know the ring's story, and I wanted to discover it with Brad.

He looked at me, probed gently with those green eyes that were becoming familiar and comfortable. I was thankful he had accepted my earlier honesty without judgment. I was thankful he was willing to continue exploring with me. I sucked in a breath and pushed aside my doubts.

"I'm in."

CHAPTER 10
Liberty

MARCH 7, 1770

The parade of redcoats boarding British convoys off of Long Wharf made my heart burst with a tune akin to freedom. And yet it had come at a heavy price. Within moments, the tune mellowed to a melancholy, mournful rhythm. True, the redcoats were gone. But what they'd stolen, I would never be able to retrieve. How could I go on choosing life beneath this heavy cloak of darkness? Only the memory of my brother prodded me to leave the warmth of my bed, to pull on petticoats and skirts.

For today, James would be my purpose. When I felt defeat this day, I would tamp it down with the memory of my brother's honor.

I waited until the ship had pulled away to Castle Island, each member of the 29th Regiment on board, before emerging from my room at the Golden Ball tavern. I'd requested a window facing the sea, the heavy sterling in my valise ensuring I would obtain the room I wanted or look elsewhere.

I pulled my cape tight around my shoulders and affixed my cap, careful to hide the ugly bruise forming from the blows the captain had given me. I felt for the heaviness of the captain's silver and whistle and the bold outline of the lieutenant's ring beneath the secret pocket I'd sewn into my dress the day before. Only when I'd placed the signet ring in with the nine sterling and closed it up did I feel a twinge of remorse that I had stolen from the lieutenant.

I brushed away the compunction with an image of James's body convulsing on the snowy ground in front of the Town House. I brushed it away at the remembrance of the captain possessing my body. As if he owned me. As if I were nothing.

In stealing, I had done what I needed to survive. I had played a small part in the Cause James had died for, fighting against the king and his soldiers.

The somber mood of the town fell around me as I hastened to the *Gazette*. I pushed open the doors. The smell of fresh ink, tobacco, and sweat wafted over me. A small group of men—some standing, some sitting—milled about the place. I recognized the stout build of Mr. John Adams and his cousin Samuel. Sitting at one of the desks was Mr. Revere, the silversmith. It appeared I'd walked into a gathering of the

Sons. With the regiments gone, they were brazen enough to meet in broad daylight.

"Can I help you, miss?" A gaunt young man came toward me. "Josiah Quincy."

I breathed deeply, the weight in my pocket and the worthy death of my brother giving me confidence in the task before me. "Yes, sir. I'm here to claim my brother's body. I was told he would be here."

"Your brother's body . . ."

"I am the sister of James Caldwell, sir."

Recognition dawned on his lean, handsome face. "Please then, Miss Caldwell, accept my deepest sympathies regarding your brother's death."

Samuel Adams came forward, extending a palsied hand. "We all offer our condolences, Miss Caldwell, for your brother's most worthy sacrifice."

Now, standing here with these men who had stirred up my brother's patriotic fervor, I wondered whether his sacrifice would mean anything a month from now. Yet I bit my lip to keep from arguing with the man. Didn't I, too, try to convince myself that James's death had not been in vain?

Mr. Adams continued, "I can assure you we are at this very moment planning a most honorable funeral for the four who bravely died Monday night."

I glanced at the surface of the desk the men surrounded. Beside Mr. Revere's ink-stained hand lay an engraving of some sort. I glimpsed only the Town House, redcoats, and smoke.

I ground my teeth. "That appears to be the most peculiar plan for a funeral I have ever laid eyes on."

Mr. Revere's face reddened. Mr. Samuel Adams laughed. "You are a sharp one, Miss Caldwell. And yet it is our job to ensure your brother's death is not wasted, wouldn't you agree?"

Though I did not have complete understanding of their plan, I could do naught but agree with the statement. "I understand, Mr. Adams. And yet I cannot help but fear my brother's funeral will be a show of politics rather than a memorial of his life, if left to you."

Mr. Adams clenched his deformed hands behind him and stared at the floor. When he spoke, his tone was soft. "I dare hope it can be both, Miss Caldwell. I dare hope that is what James would have wanted."

Blast him, I knew it was. I sighed. "Indeed."

Mr. Quincy's mouth tightened. "Unfortunately, Miss Caldwell, your brother's body is not here."

I clenched my jaw, inwardly ridiculing myself for leaving James with a stranger. "I—I see. I had spoken with a man—"

"Mr. Gregory."

"Yes."

"He did come here with your brother; rest easy, miss. But it was decided his body would be prepared for burial at the home of Captain Morton."

"Captain Morton? I'm sorry, sir. James was lost to me for months. I have little knowledge of his life at sea, nor here in Boston."

"He served on Captain Morton's vessel," Mr. Quincy said.

"The captain came yesterday to request that they prepare your brother's body. Apparently your brother was close to the Mortons."

I tried to hide my emotion at this unexpected news. There was so much I didn't know about James's new life. So much he had chosen not to share with me during our brief time together the week before.

"Might you tell me where Captain Morton resides? I should like to pay a visit."

Mr. Quincy directed me to Ship Street in the North End. I thanked him and turned to leave.

"Miss Caldwell?"

I spun, caught the attention of Mr. Adams. "Our purpose for tomorrow's funeral is to honor your brother and the other three who died beneath this tyranny. And I vow to do everything to ensure James's death was not in vain. I pray you see it as such."

Because James would have wanted me to, I gave a gracious nod to Mr. Adams and to the rest of the Sons in the room. "Thank you, sirs. Thank you for your efforts."

Mr. Adams gave a slight bow in my direction. "Miss Caldwell, if there is anything I can ever do for you, please do not hesitate to call on me again."

Although the next day was market day, shop signs read *Closed*, and the latched shutters indicated a manner more solemn than any Sabbath. No rush and rattle of carts and horses, no noisy bartering with vendors, no thump of hand looms echoing from the fabric store. Even the streets had been cleared of manure and washed. Captain Morton's nigra driver pulled James's coffin in a one-horse shay. I walked behind James's body in my go-to-meeting dress, Captain and Mrs. Morton behind me.

James's procession converged with the three others on King Street, where my brother's lifeblood had seeped into the snow just days earlier. I marveled at the immense press of people walking six abreast through the narrow streets. Behind us followed a train of carriages carrying the Boston privileged. I had not realized so many people existed in the colony, never mind the town. Certainly more people were gathered this day than were ever together on this continent on any previous occasion.

And all for James, and his Cause.

The bells of Old South cried out, then those of King's Chapel, followed by Christ Church, until all the church bells in Boston rang out a cry of mourning for their dead. Beyond the harbor, bells from the outlying towns echoed back in a solemn splendor that I felt did indeed honor my brother's sacrifice.

James was laid beside Christopher Seider in Old Granary, and after the crowd dispersed, I stood alone before my brother's coffin. I wished I had thought to bring a special offering to throw into the dirt above the wood of his final resting place—the petal of a flower, a note or poem of meaning, a trinket of Grandmother's. But I had nothing.

I felt the heavy contents of my pocket and my stomach lurched with possibilities. I did have something to offer my brother. I looked around. A few still stood paces away in the graveyard, but no one seemed to pay much attention to a lone grieving sister. I crouched to the ground, searched beneath my petticoats until I felt the pocket I'd sewn. I found a corner and pulled at the stitches, grateful my handiwork wasn't as tight and skilled as Grandmother's.

I shook the contents into my hands, putting the sterling into the pocket of my cape.

In my hand lay the lieutenant's signet ring and the captain's whistle. I vacillated, wondering which the more worthy to accompany my brother to eternity.

Truthfully, I would have liked to cast the lieutenant's ring into the pit. I felt guilt when I looked at its radiant beauty, the bloodstones in the shape of an anchor and horn above his surname, the Latin that boldly proclaimed that victory belonged to those with strength.

But this could not be about me.

I pocketed the ring. The whistle, symbolic of the men who had taken James's life, would be better suited beneath the ground for all ages.

I imagined the captain's ghastly lips on the silver, an image that recalled all he'd taken from me. I ran my fingernail over the engraving pressed into the metal—the king's emblem: the lion and the unicorn flanking the crest, proclaiming in Old French, *Honi soit qui mal y pense.*

Shame upon him who thinks evil of it.

Evil of the king, evil of the soldiers who had pressed their mighty hands down upon the throat of our town. Had my brother thought evil of them? Likely. I certainly had, along with many in Boston.

Shame upon him who thinks evil of it.

The words tormented me as I thought of those who would stamp my brother a traitor, to be shamed forever. I would not think on the notion. Instead, I let the whistle fall from my hands. It rolled down the dirt to the bottom of the grave, where it landed with a clink against the foot of the coffin.

There, my brother's feet would trample the monarchy for all eternity.

CHAPTER 11
Anaya

WHEN WE WERE LITTLE, Lydia and I used to play hide-and-seek on my grandparents' farm. Sunsets painted the sky pinks and purples, and chickens were given free range on the sprawling homestead where Gram and Pop lived. Best of all was the massive barn filled with Pop's many collectibles. The sagging, tired building was a maze of obscure spots in which to conceal myself, and I would inevitably go there to hide from my sister.

One day, as Lydia leaned against a porch column of our grandparents' farmhouse, counting steadily, eyes burrowed in the crook of her arm, I ran as fast as my six-year-old legs could carry me to the barn in the backyard. Long, dry grass brushed my bare skin, and the sweet scent of honeysuckle filled the air. Once I reached the barn, I waded through transistor radios, old furniture, movie posters featuring Audrey Hepburn and James Dean, a couple tackle boxes of fishing lures, and oil bottles, until finally I spotted the perfect hiding spot—a sturdy wooden trunk. Its hinges were tarnished, and iron bands studded with large brass buttons ran along its side. It was beautiful. And best of all, neither Lydia nor I had ever hidden there before. She'd never find me.

As my scrawny arms lifted the heavy top, I heard Lydia call out, "Ready or not, here I come!"

I waited a second for my eyes to adjust to the dark so I could be certain there were no unwanted guests in my hiding place; then, when I was sure of its vacancy, I hopped in, allowing the lid to fall shut behind me.

I muffled my excited giggles into my hands, my knees drawn up to my chest. I couldn't best my twelve-year-old sister at much, but this time I would certainly win. The thought made me giggle all the more.

I heard Lydia come into the barn, the sounds of her footsteps muffled. Something creaked, and then the sound of metal on metal as Lydia searched for me. "I know you're in here, Annie." She schooled her voice to make it go up and down in an eerie tone that caused me to curl more tightly into a ball.

She'd give up soon. I hoped so, anyway. The trunk's interior was becoming stuffy. The backs of my knees and my neck were sticky.

I didn't hear her anymore. I breathed in a last musty breath of trunk air and pushed on the lid, careful not to be loud in case she still occupied the barn.

It didn't budge.

In one moment, a game turned into a nightmare. Fear swallowed up my tiny body, and my breaths came in short, rapid spurts. I knocked on the lid. Again. And again.

"Lydia! Lydia, help!"

I banged and banged and banged. I'd never felt so alone. I was certain no one would ever find me, that I would die within the depths of the trunk and one day, years from now, someone would open it up and find nothing but my bones to prove my existence.

I'm not sure how long I was in there. Probably only minutes, but they stretched longer than a wad of Silly Putty.

I started to cry, and then I screamed, sure the trunk kept the sound of my voice to itself. A dizzy sensation swept through me and my stomach clenched. I swallowed the sour taste of my lunch—hot dogs and macaroni and cheese.

Then, miraculously, the lid opened and fresh air rushed in to revive me. Like an angelic being, Lydia stood over the trunk, pure natural light around her.

She reached for me. "Annie—oh my goodness, are you okay?" She hugged me to her in a rare show of affection, and I sobbed into her faded New Kids on the Block T-shirt.

Throughout our childhood, we'd had our ups and downs, but after that incident I knew one thing—Lydia would never let me down. She'd always be there for me, no matter how hard I was to find.

Or so I thought.

I sighed, stared at the many tabs lined up along my laptop's browser. The New England Historic Genealogical Society, the Massachusetts Archives, a search on Liberty Gregory, and another search on flight times from Boston to the UK. Just in case.

Beside me, my phone vibrated on the table, and I scooped it up, welcoming the distraction.

Lydia.

My heart scuffled out a few extra beats, and I grew warm at the thought of speaking to my sister, at the intimate memories of our childhood I'd just been pondering. I untied my robe and allowed the cooler air to flow through a thin T-shirt I'd earned by running a 10K several years back.

"Hello?"

"Hey, Auntie Annie."

"Grace! Hi." The wheels of my mind stopped and backtracked, like the wheels of a train moving in reverse. "How are you, kiddo?"

Bad. Shouldn't have used the nickname. We weren't at that stage yet. And Grace wasn't a kid anymore.

Lydia was right. I was expecting to step back into their life and presume everything could be the same.

"I'm good. I wanted to ask you something."

"Of course. Anything." Yes, desperate aunt was much better than overly familiar aunt.

I stood from the table and went to the window, where rivulets of rain streaked tears down the glass. I flexed my foot, allowed the pinch in the back of my calf to ground me.

"Well, my school is doing this run—a 5K. It's, you know, a fund-raiser." A shaky breath echoed over the line. "It's on Patriots' Day, and the idea is for a student to team with an adult to raise money for people who need prosthetics."

I groped the nearby kitchen counter, dizzy from the information—information I didn't want to dwell on.

Running.

Race.

Patriots' Day.

People who need prosthetics.

Grace must have sensed my hesitation. "It's an annual thing. They started it last year . . . to raise money for me to get my running prosthesis. Only this year I'll be able to run it, and the money will, like, go to another teenager, someone who loves to run just as much as I do."

I knew she didn't mean to remind me of all that I had missed, but that's just what her words did.

"Well, I was wondering if you'd partner with me . . . if we could, like, run together."

I scrambled for words, for an excuse. I was bailing again. I didn't want in on the reminders, the pain. And I didn't want to run—maybe not even for Grace.

I massaged my forehead as the truth of this hit home. I was being presented with another choice—run, or run away. I'd told Lydia I was sorry for avoiding them in their time of need, but if I said no to Grace's request, how was I proving my apology sincere? How was I changing the pattern of what I'd done every day for the past two years?

"Does your mom know you're asking me?" Better to blame my inability to participate on Lydia. I wrapped my fingers around the sharp edges of the counter. A particularly hard edge of laminate poked into my hand. I clutched tighter. I was a rat. Worse than a rat. A flea on a rat.

"I did run it by her. She didn't think you'd say yes, though."

Trapped. And Lydia had flipped the spring.

All I really wanted to do was dig a private hole and hide. But wasn't this why I had gotten back in touch? Lydia had cut me out, but now she was also giving me a way back in.

"Of course I will." I said the words because I couldn't disappoint my niece. I said the words to prove my sister wrong. I said them, knowing I'd regret them the second they left my mouth, yet knowing once they did leave there would be no turning back.

"Really? You'll do it?"

"Sure I will. I'm a bit out of practice, but—"

"We could train together. If you wanted."

If I wanted. Could I run by her side again? Move forward? Stuff the memories of the bombing deep in a place where they wouldn't bury me alive when I tried to run again?

"Um, yeah. I think that would be okay once in a while."

"Great."

"Great."

She rambled on for the next few minutes about sponsors and forms and websites and goals.

"Do you want to go for a run tomorrow afternoon? It's three-quarters of a mile around my block. We can walk once, run once, you know, see how it goes." Hope drenched her words. She amazed me, this girl I'd abandoned. I didn't deserve this. I didn't deserve her time. I didn't deserve her desire to be with me.

I cleared my throat to hide my emotion. "Are you sure it's okay with your mom? I don't want to . . ." Step on her toes. Barge in where I didn't belong. It all sounded too harsh. I didn't want to pit Grace against her mother.

"Yeah, absolutely. See you at three?"

"Looking forward to it."

I hung up, wondering if my last words were a lie. I did look forward to being with Grace again. In the context of running a race for prosthetics? Not so sure.

I rubbed my hands over my arms and trudged past my laptop to the couch, conscious of my heavy limbs, and sat down with a thump as I exhaled a loud breath and tossed my phone on the cushion beside me. I eased out of my slippers and perched my socked feet on the coffee table, leaned back and rubbed my forehead.

I tapped my head with one hand. I could do this. I could pump myself up. Just a little run around the block. No biggie.

But what if I couldn't? What if I panicked tomorrow?

Again my phone vibrated beside me. I thought it might

be Grace, calling to tell me a piece of information she'd forgotten. But at the sight of Brad's name, my stomach gave a little leap.

"Hey."

"Hey yourself. What's going on?"

"Oh, just sitting here trying to give myself a pep talk."

"Is it working?"

I flopped my free hand onto my lap. "No."

"Need someone to talk to?"

I scrunched up my face, shook my head. "How am I always the one spilling my guts to you?"

"It's okay. I don't mind. I'm on a break."

Like I needed to bother him with my problems when he was at work. "It's nothing. Grace—you know, my niece who was injured in the bombing—just called. She wants to run a 5K with me on Patriots' Day."

He let out a low whistle. "And you're not good with that."

"Not really. I haven't run since the morning of the bombing, and with Grace . . ."

"I'm sorry." His breaths traveled through the phone. "About the bombing. I—I know it doesn't change anything, but I wish it hadn't happened to you, or your family."

I shrugged, though I knew he couldn't see the gesture. "It's not your fault I'm so screwed up I can't bring myself to run anymore."

"It's a posttraumatic thing. Nothing's wrong with you."

I laughed. "You minor in psychology at Lincoln Tech?" I

closed my eyes. Why did I do this—push people away when they started getting too close? "Sorry, that was rude."

"Yeah, it was. Can't blame that on trauma."

"Brad, wait. I'm sorry. Really, I wish I hadn't said that."

He sighed. "I get that you're hurting, Annie. But you're not alone. And maybe I'm not a psychologist, but you're forgetting I was in a war. I know a thing or two about PTSD, and it comes in a lot of different forms."

Silence ate up the next ten seconds.

"So what do you think I should do?"

"Go for a run."

I almost choked on my next words. "What—now?"

"Don't think. Just do it."

"It's raining."

"Drizzling. You won't melt."

"I don't even know if I could find my sneak—"

"You can do this, Annie. Just a short one. Hey—you're right near the Old Belfry on the Green, right? Just make it to the top of that."

"Sure, then I'll raise my hands up and jump around like Rocky in front of that big building in Philadelphia."

He chuckled. "Now you're talking. Man, I love those movies."

I smiled. "I used to watch them with my dad to get me pumped up for track meets."

An air compressor went off in the background. "Hey, I gotta go. Meet you at one, right?"

"Yeah, looking forward to it."

"And Anaya?" I didn't miss the use of my full name.

"Yeah?"

"Today's a new day. I want to hear about your run."

I groaned after I hung up the phone. This guy sure had a way of getting to me. Yet I couldn't imagine disappointing him. And I knew he was right. Like it or not, I was running with Grace tomorrow. Things would go smoother if I could prove to myself today what I had to do tomorrow.

I dug my sneakers from my closet, grabbed a sweatshirt and yoga pants. On top of my bureau, Brad's ring lay beside my jewelry box. I picked it up, ran a thumbnail over the engraving, allowing it to catch on the tiny jewels that made up the anchor. I thought to hold it tight, to imagine some power hidden within its depths to strengthen me. But really, that had never worked before. Why would it now?

God, help me be strong.

I wasn't sure where the thought of praying came from, but in that moment it appeared more naturally than ever. I repeated the plea as I laced up my neglected sneakers and walked quickly down the drive until I reached the road. The scent of wet pavement clung to the air. I pushed my legs forward, faster. They dragged heavy from lack of use.

Brad recognized my problems—posttraumatic. The shrink had told me as much. But I hadn't been able to move past it, even with the help of a psychologist. I wondered what had happened to Brad in the war. I wondered if he still struggled with his past too.

I sucked in a breath and tried out a light jog—more like

a bounce-skip. I felt places jiggling I hadn't known were there. Yuck. That sure hadn't happened when I trained for the marathon. I sped up, wishing I'd changed into a sports bra before heading out.

I lengthened my stride, forced my shoulders down, arms pumping. Memories of the last time I ran came pouring forth. I hadn't felt great during the marathon. Cramps and nausea and an unplanned, but very needed, bathroom stop.

My goal had been three hours and twenty-five minutes, and I'd promised myself I'd make it—for Grace. Poor kid couldn't wait to be old enough to run. With her training and encouragement, I'd surprised myself by qualifying the fall before. The girl was fast and she made me, a moderately good runner, faster when she was by my side. During the final four months, we'd run the longer workouts on Sunday afternoons together.

If I had pushed myself harder on race day, if for no other reason than to show Grace her training efforts weren't for naught, I would have been across the finish line well before that first bomb went off. Grace and Lydia and I would have been on our way to a celebratory lunch instead of wading through broken glass and blood and terror.

The wind and rain whipped my face, melding with the tears on my cheeks. I held my breath tight to stifle the sob, but it came out anyway. I stopped running and walked, gasping for breaths between my emotions.

These last two silent years were lonely. Like I'd been stuck in that abandoned trunk in Pop's barn for all that time, but instead of calling for help I'd allowed the loneliness—the desperation—to eat me alive. What kind of person was I to shut everyone out, to seek excessive solitude, to abandon those I loved?

I turned left at the wooden sign that read *Old Belfry* and started up the steep staircase at a jog. It was a short trip up, but my thighs burned at the abnormal strain I demanded of them. The pain in my calf pulsated with a dull throb. I tried not to think much beyond one jagged stone step at a time.

By the time I reached the top, my lungs were tight as a jar of unopened pickles, my legs the consistency of custard. A brown belfry stood proudly at the top, seemingly alone on this cold March morning.

Drawing in deep breaths, I placed my hands on my hips and walked toward the belfry, a small wave of triumph washing over me.

I'd done it. I might not raise my hands toward the heavens like Rocky, but my soul did. I couldn't wait to tell Brad.

While I recovered, I read the sign posted on the side of the belfry.

This belfry was erected on this hill in 1761 and removed to the Common in 1768. In it was hung the bell which rung out the alarm on the 19th of April 1775.

Patriots' Day.
A day when the Lexington minutemen had been pitifully

defeated on the green just below me. And yet it had been the beginning of a glorious fight for our country's freedom.

I gulped down another breath. Would Patriots' Day forever haunt me with its taunting reminders of my weakness, of the world's potential for evil? I kicked at the slab of rock I stood on and admired the view of the Common. In another month or so it would be hard to see past the leaves.

Today's a new day.

I let Brad's words roll around in my head. Perhaps I could choose to cling to hope, to not allow that tragic day to steal more from me than it had already taken. I *had* gone running again. I didn't have to be defeated by reminders of a history that couldn't be changed. Instead, I could choose to find hope in that history.

Patriots' Day, after all, wasn't meant to be a reminder of devastation; it was meant to be a celebration of freedom.

CHAPTER 12
Liberty

MAY 1770

At the Mortons' supper table, I shifted slightly to the right, toward Mr. Dean, to allow for the nigra maid to pour water into my glass. On my other side, Mrs. Morton, in a teal silk taffeta dress fresh from the mantua maker, whispered to me, "Do you care for our seating arrangements this evening, dear?"

A breeze from the window at my back carried the scent of the sea, and I sucked it in, willing the simmering nausea I knew all too well of late to settle within my body. I forced a smile from my lips, though I couldn't ponder being smitten with anyone, let alone a man whose closest friend, Mr. John Adams, would help defend the soldiers who had shot my brother, claiming all deserved a fair trial.

I settled for a safe reply. "I am most grateful for your invitation, Mrs. Morton."

Since my brother's passing two months earlier, Captain and Mrs. Morton made it a habit to invite me to dine at least once a fortnight. To my pleasure, I found that James had shared much about me with the Morton family. We enjoyed small conversations over dinner, and while they were perhaps the closest people to me in this rebellious town, they knew me little. They didn't know of my recent employ, of course. Nor of how I had let my foolish heart fall for a soldier of the Crown. They were unaware of Captain Philips's atrocities against me, of my act of thievery . . . of the tiny life growing within my womb.

More than once I contemplated leaving Boston. Fearful the captain and lieutenant would attempt to find me for my last brazen act, I watched my surroundings with care, turned an attentive ear to the talk of politics in the street. Yet no sign of British troops disrupted the peace of the town. No sign of the two men with whom I had lived. I fancied the lieutenant would not wish to press charges, and perhaps the captain feared to, given all that I could report of him. Never mind the fact that after the night of March fifth, none in Boston would heed a British officer's complaint. The wounds were still too fresh, the hatred toward the Crown palpable, fed by the Sons and their propaganda, which included newspapers, pamphlets, and engravings such as Mr. Revere's "The Bloody Massacre in King Street."

For reasons I couldn't completely comprehend, I did not

wish to leave the heady clutch of Boston just yet. Never mind its unsettling memories and crowded confines, the thick air stinking of kitchen fires set too near one another, I could not bid farewell to it. The town gripped me with its bittersweet draw, with its promise to hold my brother in its depths forever.

And yet I knew, in time, I would have to leave. I would have to make a new beginning elsewhere. A new beginning couched in half-truths. A new beginning free of the heavy iron ball of my disgraceful past chained to my leg.

"And do you plan to attend the trial when it finally proceeds, Miss Caldwell?" Mr. Dean asked. His pleasant features hid shining eyes that bathed me in admiration. Mrs. Morton seemed to think us a perfect match, but then again, Mrs. Morton did not know my secrets.

"Yes, I think I shall." Though I feared I might encounter the captain or the lieutenant at such an event, my fears would submit to my longing to see justice served. Two weeks after the bloody fray that the Sons had dubbed "the Massacre," Mr. John Adams had requested that I call upon him, asking of the events of that night, of my brother's patriotic fervor. Mr. Adams had listened to my testimony that day with rapt attention. I'd been relieved when I found Mr. Adams did not plan for me to testify. I did not think I could bear witness before a crowd of Americans while the offspring of an English officer grew within my womb.

"I should think it would be good for you to be present." Mr. Dean said this so that only I could hear, and the conversation around us moved on to the indecency of the Townshend Acts. I wondered if any of the Liberty Boys had urged him to persuade me in this manner.

"Thank you, Mr. Dean. But I wonder, do you mean good for me, or good for the Cause?" I took a dainty sip of my oyster soup, concentrated my gaze on the elaborate wainscoting about the Mortons' dining room walls. The trial had been pushed back, perhaps until the fall. By then I would not be able to hide my condition any longer.

I imagined returning to New York with a story of a quick marriage and a husband's death. I placed my hand over my midsection, my womb hard beneath my fingers. More than once I had sat down to write a poem—even a thought—on my feelings toward the child within, but I could never make it past the first ink stroke. I could not bring myself to think much on it, on the seed of the man who had planted it there. And when I did dwell on the life within, I felt nothing. Indeed, I was a cursed woman.

I knew there were ways to rid myself of the unwanted child, and though the sin was like to be the greatest of all my sins, I could nearly justify it in my head when I relived that last day at the officers' house, the captain's brute force against my body. Surely nothing good—even a newborn babe—could come from such an evil act.

"It is Mr. Adams's job to defend the soldiers, Miss Caldwell. While I believe in the Cause, I believe in the law and justice even more. We both know Preston's soldiers were provoked relentlessly."

The table grew silent and I felt all eyes upon me to study my response. I opened my mouth but my bottom lip quivered.

Mr. Dean wiped his mouth with his napkin. "Forgive me, Miss Caldwell. Captain and Mrs. Morton. I did not mean to imply that Mr. Caldwell had done any provoking."

I studied the goose on my plate, alongside a portion of meat jelly. "Mr. Dean, I would not be surprised in the least if James had indeed provoked the Regulars. He was looking for a fight those last days, eager to begin what we have all felt coming for some time now. Nevertheless, I believe the soldiers were in the wrong. They *were* the first to fire, and I trust they will be punished under the banner of justice."

When I told the owner of the apothecary shop I was in need of a midwife for some womanly troubles, he urged me to first seek a doctor. After I pressed him a bit further, he gave me the name of Midwife Louisa, but warned me the woman was a bit eccentric and not all considered her reputable.

I did not need her to be reputable for my purposes.

Now I knocked on the wooden door of the address he'd given me on Union Street. It opened and a short, frail woman with pure-white hair stood before me, her face cratered with pockmarks. I thought to make my business quickly known, to forgo the telling of my name, to see if this woman would help me or deny my request.

"Good day, Midwife Louisa. A friend sent me. I hear you are a skilled midwife and I have a need . . ."

The woman gestured inside. "Won't you come in?"

I nodded and stepped through the doorway. The scents of comfrey and yarrow and mint and sage wound around me, placing me in Grandmother's cellar back in New York. With it came a homesick feeling—not for the place, but for the people I would never again see this side of eternity. Grandmother and James. Mother and Father. My family.

She ushered me past a long counter where it appeared she sold tinctures, ointments, herbs, and gargles, and on into the sitting room, bright and airy. "Tell me how I can help you."

"I—I have worked with my grandmother in the art of healing, yet there is one thing she never taught me." I swallowed. "I wish . . . I wish to cleanse my womb."

"Are you unable to conceive, child?" She tightened a knitted shawl around her shoulders.

"I—I fear the opposite is true. I have conceived a child outside the bounds of marriage." The words shamed me, and I scrambled to make her understand. "I was assaulted, Midwife Louisa." She needn't know the details.

"My dear child . . ."

I shook my head, throwing off her pity as one would throw out the contents of a chamber pot. I did not need her sympathy—it would only stoke the emotions I buried deep within. "I can pay you whatever you wish. Please, can you help me?"

She breathed in, her generous chest rising with the inhalation. "I cannot help you in the way you wish."

I allowed defeat to have its way with me for only a moment. Resigned, I stood. "Then my business here is through. I shall search elsewhere."

The woman followed me to the door. "Perhaps you may come tomorrow?"

"To what end, ma'am?"

"For employment."

"Employment?"

"I am getting on in years. I am weary making my calls. Even digging and pounding the roots and planting the herbs is tiring on this old body. I have no daughter or granddaughter to whom I may pass the knowledge and skills of midwifery. True, many now prefer doctors, especially in Boston, but there is still a need for midwives. Would you be interested in such a venture?"

I bit my lip, reeling from the turn in conversation. "I— I'm afraid you caught me unawares."

"Will you consider?"

"You don't know me. I—"

"Won't you think on the proposition and return to me?"

I could not ignore the sudden excitement growing in my chest. I had walked right into an opportunity to help and heal people—an opportunity I was skilled for. If only such a thing had happened last autumn.

If only, if only, if only!

I must stop such aimless thinking. What was done was

done. I could only move forward, making one choice at a time. Perhaps this endeavor would give me a new future—not one I had planned but one in which I could learn to survive. Though I had seven pounds and five shillings for the time being, even this would someday soon run out. I needed a life. I needed purpose.

"I think I do not need to consider your offer another moment, Midwife Louisa. It would be my pleasure to work with you."

Midwife Louisa nodded, as if she were not the least bit surprised at my decision. "I have a separate bedroom upstairs. Plenty of room for you and the child."

I shook my head. "I think we misunderstand one another, ma'am. This does not change my plans to—to . . ." The knot in my throat felt as big as a block of ice. I could not make myself say the words.

"But was not part of your reason for disposing of the child your need to find a husband to support you? If you stay here, you can support yourself."

"No, you don't understand."

"Tell me, child. 'Twould not hurt to talk this through. 'Tis a big decision that rests on your shoulders. Once the act is done, it cannot be taken back. You forfeit not only your child, but mayhap hope for future children."

I had not realized that. And yet what future lay before me? I would be labeled a whore, my child a bastard. "The child's father was a Regular. I—I cannot imagine loving it as a mother should."

She slipped her thin hand into mine, the loose skin warm. "All mothers love their children. I am willing to help you make the right decision in this matter, child. Have the babe. I will help you hide yourself, help you bear the child. If you do not love it as you fear, I will find a couple willing to take the babe. I know of many in Boston who are unable to conceive. I would present them the child—no one would have to know of your identity. It is not so uncommon a practice."

My mind swam. A way to carry the child to term and not live with its redcoat blood the rest of my days. It would be given a good home—one better than I could provide. A home with a mother and a father. It would live in ignorance of its sire's character, and I would be spared the stain of blood upon my hands.

The bell above the door rang out and a sturdy gentleman entered. Midwife Louisa walked around the counter to greet him. "Ah, Mr. Gregory! And how is your sister's fever this day?"

I recognized the man who had helped me the night of my brother's passing. He glanced quick in my direction, his cloak swinging at the second glance.

He nodded. "Miss—Miss—"

"Caldwell." I stepped forward. "Mr. Gregory. I fear I am long overdue in thanking you."

"It was my pleasure, miss, though I must express my sincere condolences for the loss of your brother."

Midwife Louisa slid a packet of mixed herbs across the

counter. Mr. Gregory handed her a few coins. I decided to take my opportunity.

"I will call on you tomorrow, Midwife Louisa. Does that suit you?"

The woman nodded. "Yes, child. I look forward to it." Her words spoke so much more than an outsider's ear would hear. Her tone, the inflection of syllables—it all spoke of anticipation . . . and understanding. She knew she'd given me much to think on. She also knew I was anxious to get away with my thoughts.

"Allow me to escort you home, Miss Caldwell." Mr. Gregory opened the door. The bright spring sunshine warmed the dung on the street, its odor rising to meet my nostrils.

"Certainly, thank you." He led the way toward the center of town, the sea breeze caressing the stray hairs on my neck. "I do not know many men who seek a midwife for medical advice, what with so many doctors in town."

He tucked the herbs in the pocket of his cloak, his thick fingers taking care with the delicate package. "My sister suffers a fever often. She claims Midwife Louisa's tea is the only thing that soothes it."

We walked in silence for a few blocks, the rattle of carts and clop of horses filling in where our words lacked.

"And how do you fare after the loss of your brother?"

When I did not answer, he continued. "I know 'tis a personal question, and yet I have wondered about you often. I wish there were more I could have done that night."

His compassion stoked to life something within me, something that I knew must be stomped out before it stirred to flame. "There was nothing more to be done, Mr. Gregory. Transporting James's body was the most decent service to me at the time."

"Mr. Edes told me your brother had no family save for you and a grandmother. Do you live with her?"

I squirmed within my boots, felt for the slight bulge of the ring in my pocket. Truly, why had I not tossed it into the harbor yet? "My grandmother passed whilst I was in New York. I am staying at the Golden Ball for the time being."

"Alone? At a tavern?"

I lifted my chin. "It is not unheard of, Mr. Gregory."

"But a young single woman in a place like—"

I stopped, turned to the man. My gaze avoided his, met his strong chin instead. "With all due respect, sir. You don't know me. I may be just such a woman to frequent taverns. Now, if you'll excuse me, I will take my leave. Thank you, Mr. Gregory."

I did not look to see if his eyes followed me, though I felt them. I wasn't sure what had come over me, but I hardly cared. I was tired of pretending I was innocent—in front of the Morton family, in front of Mr. Adams and Mr. Dean, in front of anyone I passed.

I should not have accepted the captain's employ to save myself from the cold of the streets. When I first felt uncomfortable with his lecherous advances, I should have run. I should not have softened my heart to the lieutenant—to a soldier of the Crown. I should have left the officers' house the moment I'd found my brother, perhaps even before. And now, wretch that I was, I pondered taking the life of a blameless child.

No, perhaps I was not so very innocent. And now, at least, one other citizen of Boston knew that very fact.

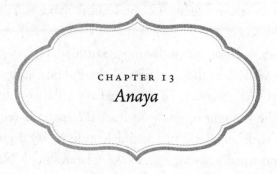

I CLIMBED THE STAIRS to exit Park Street Station, squinting against the daylight. I veered left, searching the Common for Brad. The scent of hot dogs from a nearby vendor mixed with that of cigarette smoke from a passerby. In the distance, someone jingled a jar of change, looking for handouts.

"Annie!"

I turned to see him walking toward me. In carpenter jeans, maroon *Kilroy Construction* sweatshirt, and matching hat—with pencil, of course—Brad smiled and waved. When he reached me, a split-second moment of awkwardness overtook us, as if we couldn't decide what sort of greeting to give each other. A handshake seemed too impersonal. A swift kiss on the cheek too intimate. A hug too . . . something.

In the end, I reached out and squeezed his forearm. "Good to see you again. I hope I didn't make you skip out on work too early."

"Nah, I cut out at twelve most Saturdays."

We walked in the direction of the Public Garden. After my run this morning, I'd promised myself I wouldn't seize up at the thought of going to Back Bay again. I refused to whine to Brad. Besides, I could handle it. We'd go down Commonwealth Avenue and take Clarendon to Newbury Street, where the genealogical society was located. We'd come back the same way. Boylston Street was another block farther. We wouldn't touch it. I would not be a baby about this anymore.

"So?"

I cast my thoughts aside to find Brad looking at me. "Oh, right. The run. I did it."

He nudged me with his shoulder. "All right. Knew you had it in you."

"Thanks. You helped me. A lot."

"And how'd it feel?"

We crossed over the bridge of the Public Garden. The naked, lazy boughs of willow trees hung over the lake.

"Good. Really good."

"So did you do the Rocky victory stance at the top?"

I laughed. "I refrained from that—but inside I definitely felt victory."

We waited for the traffic signal to change, and when it turned to a lit-up man, we crossed onto Commonwealth Avenue. Nearby a car backfired. Brad grabbed my arm and pushed me—kind of hard—toward the sidewalk. He recovered quickly, straightened from his bent posture, and brushed off the gesture with a casual "Sorry."

This time it was my turn to stare at his profile. His mouth was set in a thin line. His pencil drooped dangerously low from his hat. I resisted the urge to tuck it back up where it belonged.

"You react quick. From your time in Iraq, right? That's why you were able to get to me so fast that day."

He shrugged. "I guess."

"You know, if you ever want to talk about anything, I wouldn't mind listening. You've helped me. It's the least I could do."

He flashed me a fleeting, noncommittal smile. "Thanks."

Okeydokey, then. Best leave that alone.

I stuffed my hands in my pockets, put a little pep in my step. "So what's our game plan? I mean, where do you think we should start?"

The tension between us lifted. "I read as much as I could and watched a few webinars on genealogy. The first step is to figure out what we know so far and talk to living relatives."

"Right." I'd found out the same the past couple days, though I felt helpless to do any of that. This was Brad's family, Brad's ring. I almost felt I didn't have a right to want to know about it as much as I did.

"So I know the ring comes from my dad's side. I paid ol' Granddad a visit last night."

We turned on Clarendon Street, and against my will I sought out Boylston, just a couple blocks ahead. My breathing quickened, and the world suddenly felt a thousand times smaller. The streets pressed in around me. I ordered myself not to have a panic attack right there on the crowded streets of Boston. I made a sound of acknowledgment that I had been listening to Brad.

He slipped his hand into mine and squeezed. He began a loud hum of "Gonna Fly Now."

It worked. I couldn't contain a small laugh, and with it, the world righted itself, grew back to its normal proportion. "That song never fails." We turned left on Newbury Street. Boylston disappeared from view. Ahead, a brown-and-white *American Ancestors* flag hung from the society. "I'm sorry. How is your grandfather?"

"As ornery and stubborn as ever. Doesn't like to take his pills and still insists on splitting his own wood. But he's good. And lucky for us—" he tapped his hat—"sharp as a tack."

"You found out something about the ring?"

We stopped before the door of the society. Brad dug in his back pocket and took out a folded index card. He gave me a sheepish grin. "Sorry, this is about as organized as I get. I figured you might be willing to be our file keeper." He handed the paper to me, and I looked at the names on it as he spoke. "He remembered the ring, for sure. Said his dad gave it to him when my dad was born. It was given to the firstborn child down the line. But again, he didn't know any story to go with it. He made me promise to let him know when we found something. He was almost . . . excited."

I blew the bangs from my face. "I sure hope we don't disappoint him. I hope there's something to find."

Brad pointed at the index card. "I was able to trace back five generations just by talking to Granddad. That brings us to the mid-1800s—at least that was his best guess. I'm hoping we can find out more in here."

"Great work, Sherlock." I didn't bother to rein in the urge to nudge his pencil back up into his hat this time.

"I enjoyed it, really. Funny, but all this information would have died with Granddad if I hadn't asked him. Strange how we don't often look where we've come from."

I nodded. He was right. What did I know of my grandparents? Of their parents? Of the heritage my sister and I shared? Next to nothing.

Brad held the door for me, and after checking in and paying the visitor day fee, we headed to the seventh floor, where we were told someone might be able to help us get started. We placed our jackets and my bag on one of the chairs that surrounded a large table near the window, looked at the numerous books lining the walls, and swallowed down the feeling that our task was insurmountable.

Brad rolled up the sleeves of his shirt and approached the woman in one of two seats behind a large desk.

She looked up from her computer screen. "Hi there. How can I help you?"

Brad cleared his throat. "We're kind of new at this, but I'm looking for information about my ancestors."

She smiled. "You're certainly in the right place."

"We're trying to find out if a family heirloom—a ring I have—belonged to a certain person. We have a name, but we're kind of clueless where to start."

The woman nodded. "So you have a couple of puzzle pieces and you're trying to fill in the rest."

"Basically. But we're not even sure they're from the same puzzle."

She stood, propped a pair of pink glasses on her nose, and guided us to the computer near our things. "We have several websites, including our own library catalog, that can assist you in your search. How far back can you trace your family?"

"We're guessing around the Civil War."

"Great. I would start with Fold3—it's a website that specializes in the American military. If you know what town they were from, add that into the search. We also have many published genealogies here. Search your family's name in our catalog and see what comes up." She looked at two people standing by her desk. "Let me know if I can help. Good luck."

We thanked her and pulled two chairs up to the computer. Brad dug out a thumb drive and jabbed it in the USB. "Let's get searching. From what Granddad told me, the first-born of the last five generations were all males. Though if Liberty Gregory owned the ring, maybe it was passed down to daughters as well. Cross your fingers."

Brad clicked on the Civil War icon and typed in *Kilroy, Lexington*. Several results popped up, but nothing that clearly stated a name on our index card, or even the Civil War. Mostly city directories and federal censuses. A couple of women with the last name Kilroy, but no match. We finally clicked on an 1876 Boston city directory that listed about twenty Kilroys, their first names, occupations, and addresses.

None of them matched the names on our list.

All hope that this was going to be easy evaporated.

As the sun made its arc over the building, the room grew darker. We typed in different searches, different first and last names. We even found Brad's granddad's WWII registration card. Several times we'd find a name that matched Brad's list, but it wouldn't line up with the correct time period or location. I wondered how sharp the tack was that Brad compared his grandfather to, but I'd sooner look through five hundred more results than voice the question aloud.

Brad stretched his fingers, which had rested on the mouse for the last few hours. He navigated to a different website on the society's home page and clicked on an 1860 census, entering the name of his granddad's great-grandfather, the last name on our list, Allen Kilroy. He scrolled down the page.

We saw it at the same time. The 1855 Massachusetts State Census listed an Allen Kilroy of Lexington.

"That must be him, right?" Brad clicked on it.

The census stated that Allen's birth year was 1835. We clicked on the picture, and a black-and-white handwritten census list came up before us. Brad zoomed in on Allen Kilroy's family, three members including Allen—age twenty, occupation clerk; wife, Madelyn—age twenty; and son, Jonathan—age one.

Brad pointed to Jonathan's name. "Granddad's grand-father." We shared a smile at the small breakthrough. "Too bad it's not new information."

"But it is. Now we know Allen's exact birth year, and we can look for an older census—one where he's listed as a child with an age that matches his birth year—to find out who his father was."

He gave me a wink and downloaded the picture of the census. "I knew I brought you along for a reason."

I rolled my eyes and took out a notebook to sketch a continuation of Brad's family tree. "Maybe try an 1840 census. Allen should have been about five."

Brad arrowed back and clicked on the 1840 census. Though the federal census seemed to be set up a bit different from the state census, we did find an entry for a Thomas Kilroy of Concord.

"No Lexington entries," I said.

We clicked on the census that contained Thomas's name. It stated that the household of Thomas Kilroy contained one free white male between the ages of twenty-six and forty-five, one free white female between the ages of sixteen and twenty-six, one free white male under the age of ten, and two free white females under the age of ten.

"No names. Bummer." Brad clicked the download button.

"But the son who's under ten does match the age range for Allen." I wrote down the information on the tree with a question mark next to it.

"And now we're past what we know about the ring. Did it come from Thomas's family—if he is Allen's father—or did it come from his wife's side?"

I tapped my pencil on the notebook page. "We need to search for her name. Her maiden name. That might tell us which way to go."

We searched the society's library catalog. The published genealogies of several different families appeared, but none with the heading of Kilroy. "Let's just take a look at the first couple." Brad wrote down the call numbers, and we went off to search for the books in the many rows of the seventh floor.

We did find a handful of Kilroys in each book, but none that we could tell matched with Brad's family of Lexington. After a half hour of searching, Brad rubbed the back of his neck and pressed a button on his phone. "We should go. They close in ten minutes."

I fanned through one of the genealogies. Black-and-white pictures and the histories of individuals filled the pages. My eye caught the name Kilroy, and I looked, not expecting to find much. "Hey, wait."

I pointed to an *Allen Kilroy*. He was off to the left of the family tree, and the genealogy didn't show a wife or children.

Instead, it focused on his sister, Ava, and her children. Brad scooted his chair closer to me and ran his finger up to the parents of Ava and Allen. Father was listed as Thomas Kilroy, born in 1809, and his wife, Amelia Gregory, born in 1815.

I nearly bounced up and down in my seat. "That's it! That's him. And look at her last name."

"I—I can't believe it. But is this the actual Thomas and Allen we're looking for? They were fairly common names . . . maybe even Kilroy is a common surname. Look how many we found in all these books."

My hopes deflated when I looked at Allen's birth year. I pointed to it, feeling like the sharp pin poking a happily floating balloon. "Eighteen thirty-seven. The birth year doesn't match the census that links him to Jonathan."

Brad groaned. "Dead end." He scooped up his hat, tapped it on his knee. "Unless the genealogy is wrong. It's someone else's research—they could have screwed up."

"Or maybe we have two different Allen Kilroys."

Brad donned his hat, wiggled it so it fit snug, then stuck his pencil in the side. "Still pretty cool to actually find a Gregory that might be related to me. Hard work, but way cool."

I agreed.

We gathered up our things, put the genealogies away, thanked the woman who had helped us initially, and went down in the elevator.

"So," Brad began, "it's my family—of course I think it's neat. Is it boring you?"

"Are you kidding? I'm invested now. There's a story behind the ring in that poem, and I really hope it's yours."

"Ours." He caught my gaze with his own, greener than fresh-cut grass on an early June afternoon. The elevator slowed and brought us back to the ground level. My stomach flipped. "Whether or not the ring I gave you is Liberty Gregory's, we're both part of this story now."

I opened my mouth, then closed it, unable to think of an appropriate response to his words. But that didn't mean I didn't like the sound of them.

We exited the elevator and then the building, zipping our jackets against the cool wind as we turned right on Newbury Street. When we got to Clarendon, he paused instead of turning right, back to Commonwealth.

"Still some light left. Up for a walk?"

Something like a shield went up around my heart. The way he'd paused when we were supposed to turn right, the way his eyes almost pleaded with me. "Where?"

He stepped closer to me, and for the first time since we met, I wanted to move away from him instead of toward him. "Do you think you could make it to the finish line with me?"

There was so much I wanted to read in that one question, filled with something akin to desire but laced with hesitancy. I hadn't thought about ever going back to the finish line. I never wanted to get close to the place of that horrid day, to risk reliving the memories I ran from every night.

"I can't, Brad."

"You *can*. You won't."

I ground my teeth, turned my back to him, and started walking toward Commonwealth. A woman with a stroller walked by and I got a crazy feeling that I needed to protect her—protect her child—from Brad. From the man who wanted to bring me back. I ignored the preposterous feeling and moved on. Maybe I needed to go back to see my shrink.

I felt Brad beside me, keeping up with my fast pace. "You ran this morning, Annie. You didn't think you could do that. Going back to the finish line might be good for you."

I whirled on him. "Would going back to Iraq be good for *you*? Would reliving whatever made you jump a mile when that car backfired be beneficial for *your* emotional health?"

He blinked, mouth open slightly. I had caught him off guard, and my words had come out harsher than I intended, but I wouldn't take them back.

Something flashed across his face. Acceptance? Defeat? He held his hands up. "You're right. I'm sorry."

"Listen, I appreciate you helping me—you *have* helped me. But I'm not some run-down house that needs fixing. You can't just demolish me and then put me back together." I shoved my hands in the pockets of my jacket, looked at the retreating back of the woman with the stroller. "You're just pushing too much right now. We still don't know each other that well, and healing . . . well, it takes time."

His lips drew straight and I redirected my gaze to his work boots, standing on a crack in the concrete. Wordlessly,

I started back toward the Common. Brad followed, silence widening the gap between us.

When we crossed to the Public Garden, he said, "Please, Annie. Don't be mad. I said I'm sorry."

"Forget about it." And deep inside, I knew I should take my own advice. A part of me even thought to apologize for being such a whack job, but I didn't. I couldn't. It was who I was, apparently, and if Brad couldn't understand that much, then maybe we didn't need to be pursuing whatever this was between us.

CHAPTER 14
Liberty

The babe lay solid in my arms, nursing at my breast with tiny gulps. I looked down upon him, at his sweet face scrunched from the birth canal, his little nose pressed against my skin. Mere moments before, Midwife Louisa had rubbed the first breath from my newborn babe. It came out strong and gasping, ending in a hearty, bonny cry.

Midwife Louisa scurried around my bedroom, cleaning up the mess of labor. "'Tis not hard to love your son after all, is it?"

How utterly absurd to cast the father's sin upon the babe's shoulders. The child could not be more innocent or unaware of the events surrounding his conception. And to think I had almost chosen to end his life. . . .

A tear dribbled down my cheek. Midwife Louisa came beside me, put a hand on my arm. "He is a healthy eater, I'd say."

I looked up at her. "Thank you." She knew what my gratitude was for—the delivery, yes, I would always be thankful for that. But more, I thanked her for this child's life.

She waved her hand as if to swat a fly. "You are most welcome, my dear. Though I am the one who has been blessed these past months. Now, what will his name be?"

"James. After my brother." Though my son had a British officer's blood coursing through him, he would never know it, for he bore the name of a Patriot.

"Very well, then." She nodded once, as if to solidify the choosing of the name. To her credit, she didn't ask if I would keep the babe. She seemed to know.

Though keeping him would not be easy. While I was not well known in the town, people knew of me—mostly by way of my brother. I'd hidden myself away from everyone these past months, declining the Mortons' more recent dinner invitations. In keeping the babe, I would risk doing the very thing I feared most: disgracing my brother's honored name.

The bell above the door of the shop rang out, familiar to my ears by now. While I had attended Boston's cases of worms and common distempers, salved their burns, and even lanced abscesses in the early days of my pregnancy, I found myself in the shop more often than not the past six months. I stood from writing notes in the ledger to greet the person at the door.

"Mr. Gregory. Good day, sir."

"Good day, Miss Liberty."

"Out of tea already?" It seemed Mr. Gregory's sister was fonder of her tea than all of Boston.

Mr. Gregory smiled. It was not an unpleasant smile, only a bit worn around the edges. Its familiarity had brought comfort over the last several months. "I'm afraid I'm here for me this time. I have a toothache I'm hoping you can help me with."

"Certainly." I turned to Midwife Louisa's well-stocked shelves, searching for the cloves and catnip. Unbidden, my mind recalled the lieutenant as he sat at the breakfast table many months ago, his face pinched in pain. I thought of him often. Too often. Every night I sought to go back in my dreams and redo the moment when I took his ring. Again and again I pondered throwing it in the harbor to rid myself of the guilt. I pondered selling it at the public vendue, but never followed through, knowing if I did either of these I would never be able to return it. If that were ever possible. Not a redcoat was in sight in Boston's streets. I might never see the lieutenant again.

The thought should not sadden me so.

"I'm glad to see you are better, though you look to have lost some weight with your bout of sickness."

"Um . . . yes." I took up our customary fiction—one which Mr. Gregory had initiated when it became increasingly clear to him that my state of health would not be a proper topic of conversation. "Midwife Louisa took good care of me. I am feeling quite well now." I gathered his purchase, directed him in how to use it. When he leaned over the counter, the smell of leather and wood surrounded me. He handed me a few coins, but not before a tiny piercing cry lit the air.

James, waking from his nap.

Mr. Gregory mercifully pretended not to hear, though it was all my mother's heart could do not to run up the stairs and soothe my son. "Farewell, Mr. Gregory."

He looked up the stairs, then at me.

To his credit, as usual, he spoke not a word. "Farewell, Miss Liberty."

"You can't hide him away forever, child. You must make a decision." Midwife Louisa's eyes pierced me as we sat beside the fireplace, its heat warming the chill from the December night.

I stared at the orange flames. "I'm not giving him away." I patted James's cloth bottom as he squirmed in his sleep.

"Liberty, I do not expect you to. But will you hide him in this house until he's grown?" She paused from her work of grinding purple coneflower in her bowl. Its sweet, honeyed scent belied the bitterness of the herb.

"I fear I will have to leave come spring."

"Child."

I wiped the corner of my eye on my free arm. "I do not wish to. Midwife Louisa, you are the closest to family I have. But I will be scorned, shamed. And so will my son. I would be a fool to stay and suffer it."

Midwife Louisa cleared her throat. She stared at the floor at my feet.

"Speak your mind. Please."

She continued her rocking. The flames of the fire played off the pockmarks of her face. "I have spoken to Mr. Gregory of your circumstances."

The words sunk in slowly, thickening my thoughts to molasses. I must have heard incorrectly. "Pardon?"

"Do not be angry with me. His brother is married to a midwife from Lexington. Last he spoke of them, the woman sought help. I thought it may be an answer to your prayers."

I stood, James tight in the crook of my arm. "I trusted you. You told him . . . everything?" I had given many of my secrets to Midwife Louisa. I could not fathom her betrayal.

"He asked me, child. Told me he suspected you needed help, and he would not judge but be happy to oblige in any manner." The older woman smacked her dry lips, cracked with age and the heat of the ever-present fire. "I believe he's smitten with you, Liberty."

"And so I should cast myself upon the mercy of a stranger? Trust him, as I wrongly did you?"

"Forgive me, child. I only wished to help. I did not tell him all, only that you were mistreated by someone."

I paced the tattered rug before the fireplace, breaths

heaving. Mr. Gregory could assume nearly anything from what Midwife Louisa had said. "You told him nothing more?"

"Nothing."

I lowered myself into the rocking chair, let James's weight—no heavier than a lump of cheese hung to strain in a cloth—relax against me. I would do anything for this child. Anything. Move far away, tell many a lie—perhaps even kill—for my son.

"Mr. Gregory is willing to take you to his brother's family. They have a large house out in the country. No one will recognize you there. No one will look for you, and yet you will not be so far away that you cannot visit every now and then. He believes the roads are still passable. As keenly as I will feel your loss, a fresh start would be just the thing for both you and James."

"What will he tell his brother's family?" I whispered.

"Whatever you wish. But I think the closer to the truth, the better."

I might as well stay in Boston if I was to raise James beneath the ugly truth.

"Mr. Gregory is to pay us a visit tomorrow. I will speak to him if you are not interested. If you are . . . then I think it best you discuss the matter yourself."

I closed my eyes, the sound of a horse's hooves on cobblestones echoing outside. I needed a fresh beginning. Perhaps God was speaking after months of silence. Perhaps this was His way of opening a door for me.

"I will speak to him. Thank you, Midwife Louisa."

CHAPTER 15
Anaya

I ADJUSTED MY ear-warmer over my head and increased my stride to keep up with Grace's fast walking pace. The brisk wind nipped at my skin, which was unaccustomed to the still-cold outside temperatures. I tried to discreetly look at her prosthesis out of the corner of my eye.

Caught. She stopped walking, balanced on one foot to lift it up. "Pretty cool, right? I only use it for running. It's called a blade." It was metal, and she didn't wear a sneaker with it. Instead, the metal curved, meeting the ground with what seemed to be little resistance.

"Very cool," I agreed.

Grace smiled and put her leg down. We continued

walking. Her long, thin ponytail slapped her back with every step she took.

"I hope you realize how out of shape I am. I've kind of boycotted exercise for some time now."

"Were you scared to run again?" she asked.

"Were you scared . . ." As if it were all in the past. As if it were no longer an issue.

I'd lost too much time. I couldn't afford any half truths here. If I wanted to do things right, it would begin now, with honesty.

"I'm still scared."

Her pace stilled for no more than a second before she continued. "What are you scared of?"

Good question. "I'm not sure. Going back, I guess. Reliving that day. Even these past months." My breathing quickened, whether from the walking or the topic of conversation, I couldn't tell. "Maybe I'm punishing myself for copping out on you guys."

Grace's mouth thinned to a straight line. "So, like, why did you cop out?"

Here it goes. I'd known the time would come when we'd have to talk this through.

"There's no excuse for my actions." But I could at least try to explain myself . . . what I understood of myself, anyway. I sniffed, ordered the emotion in the pit of my stomach not to come up, no matter what. We continued walking, and somehow it was easier, having to focus on something besides Grace and my words. "I felt guilty. For asking you guys to be there, for encouraging you to want to run with me. I felt guilty that I hadn't come in at a faster pace like I'd wanted. Grace, if only I'd known that finishing two minutes faster—one minute, heck, thirty seconds faster—would have saved you from all this, I would have. But I didn't. I didn't give it my all."

She didn't say anything, so I continued, breathless from both the walk and the words rushing from my mouth. "When you transferred to Spaulding and I got cleared to go home, the guilt continued. What if I had gone just a little faster? What if I had fought through the discomfort and pain? What if I just waited another three years so you could run with me? What if you two were somewhere else in that crowd—anywhere else? Why couldn't God give us that?" I swiped at my runny nose, my vow not to get emotional wavering.

"At Spaulding, it really sank in that this is forever for you. Life would never be normal. Do you remember the last time I saw you?"

"Sure . . . I was at Spaulding, like you said."

I nodded. "You were with a speech therapist. She was asking you to remember words, do some math equations. When I realized they were checking you for brain damage, something inside me snapped. I left. I know it was selfish, and as the months went by, I convinced myself you guys were better off without me. That you didn't need me around, reminding you of that day, of my part in it. But it was the coward's way out. Just like in the race, when things got tough, I took the easy way out. And I know I missed a lot of your struggle. But Grace, please believe me when I say I am so sorry."

And I was. I realized that now. This wasn't all about me. I'd hurt this niece I loved. I'd hurt my sister.

Grace stared at the sidewalk for a long time. The sound of birds and someone running a vacuum to clean their car punctuated the silence.

"What if you hadn't found out we might be moving? What then? How long were you going to stay away, anyway?"

Oh, boy. I wiggled my fidgety fingers, suddenly bursting to expend energy. "In my head I was always going to give your mom a call next week, next month . . . sometime soon. But when the time came, I'd stop short of dialing that last number. When I heard you guys might be moving across the ocean—that if I didn't act right away, I might never see you all again—well, it pushed me to do what I should have done the whole time."

The swish of Grace's pants cut through the air; then her fingers inched toward mine. She squeezed my hand. "I'm glad you're here now. Maybe we could think of this as our next journey. You know, kind of the beginning of our healing?"

She made it sound so simple. I thought of Lydia, wondered if she'd be at the house when we returned. "Our next journey. I like that."

"Ready, then?"

I nodded and propelled myself into a slow jog. We finished up the block as Grace chatted about playing guitar and singing in the church worship band.

Through puffing breaths, I told her about Brad, the ring, and the genealogical society. I left out the part about our shaky departure in Boston the day before. Though I had thought to call him last night, I hadn't. Maybe for now, it was wise to give each other space. After all, I couldn't be as brave as he wanted me to be. And quite possibly, he couldn't be as understanding as I needed him to be.

"He gave you a ring the day of the bombing and you, like, just found him?"

So she didn't know anything—about my hazy hero, the ring, or the card her mother had had in her possession all this time. But of course she didn't. She'd been going through an amputation and rehab. Why should she care about some ring a guy had given her aunt?

"Yeah. Wild, huh?"

We picked up our pace as we passed my sister's house, completing a block. I noted the vacant spot for her car in the garage. We settled into a comfortable rhythm, and our chatting quieted. My feet pounded the pavement. My body jiggled. My breaths came out loud, filling the silence in between the sound of Grace's prosthesis hitting the road. She seemed hardly winded. When we passed the house again and Grace asked if I was up for another lap, I agreed, even though my lungs pinched in my chest. When we finished that, we slowed to a walk and, baby that I was, I fought tears from spilling onto my cheeks.

I wanted to thank Grace, but I knew if I did, I would cry. Instead, I felt comforted by a warm peace surrounding me in the cold sunshine. As if someone was trying to show me that life was wild. Crazy. That it couldn't be controlled. Junk happened, but sometimes . . . good could come out of it.

We walked a final lap, and I gestured to Grace's leg, finally able to work up the courage to ask. "Does it . . . does it hurt?"

"Not so much anymore. At first it did, like crazy. Turned out I didn't have a right socket fit. But now it's just normal for me. Like anything else, I guess. If I get lazy and don't exercise, it hurts when I start up again."

I rubbed my burning thighs. "Gotcha." Though did I really? Could I truly pretend to understand all she'd been through?

We approached her house for the final time. "Mom's home. I'll go in and get us some water. Want to stretch out here?"

"Sure." I flopped onto the pavement of their driveway and flung one leg out, the other crooked in a triangle.

The storm door shut behind Grace. The stillness of their quiet road allowed me to hear voices from inside. I recognized a particularly strident one as my sister's. I switched the position of my stretch, contemplated grabbing the bottle of water from Grace and beelining it to my car for cover.

Instead, a moment later, Grace came outside, followed by a rather docile-looking Lydia.

"Hey," I said to my sister.

"Hey. Good run?"

"This girl whipped me, but it feels good. Yeah." I wondered if she resented the time I spent with Grace. I wondered why, after she told me she had a family to protect, she allowed Grace to initiate and maintain contact with me.

I placed my palms on the pavement in a downward dog yoga position to stretch my calves.

"Do you want to stay for supper?" Lydia said.

My locked elbows threatened to give. I craned my neck to look up at where my sister stood on the grass. "Me?"

"No, the lamppost, you ding-dong." She scrunched up her nose. "Of course, you."

Lydia . . . joking with me? I pushed myself to a standing position. Bits of gravel stuck to my sweaty palms, and I brushed them off, leaving indents in my skin. "Um, I'd love to, though I'm not certain if you'll be able to stand the smell of me."

"You can shower if you want, Auntie. I bet Mom has some extra sweats." Grace practically bounced up and down in her place by her mother.

Did Lydia look miffed, or was that just my imagination?

"Yeah, sure. You know where the bathroom is. Towels in the closet. Help yourself."

"Thanks."

I followed them inside, feeling fifteen different kinds of out-of-place. Grace led me upstairs to the bathroom that she and Joel used, fetched me some clothes from Lydia's room. When I came out, I heard Joel and Roger talking downstairs. I hadn't seen my nephew or brother-in-law yet. A twinge of something akin to homesickness squeezed my insides.

I walked down the hardwood stairs, my socks slipping

slightly against the polished wood. I saw Joel first. He knelt at the coffee table, a grass-stained knee planted on the burgundy area rug. He looked for a Lego piece in the bucket before him, then to the building instructions at his side, then back to the bucket. His tongue stuck out, signaling his high level of concentration.

I moved toward him, stood at his peripheral vision so as not to startle him. I looked at the half-built plastic blocks. A plane? Or a tractor? I decided to keep it safe with a simple "That looks great."

He startled for a minute and looked at me, then back to his Legos. "Thanks."

He continued building. I thought to ask if he remembered me or not. I mean, the kid was only five two years ago. But I'd been around enough when he was young. Surely he remembered me.

For a fleeting second, I quelled a stirring sensation of anger. Hadn't Lydia prepared her son? She should be here in this room with us, to help work out the kinks. Surely her bitterness couldn't be enough that she would leave Joel to be surprised alone by my sudden appearance.

I sat on the couch across from him. Pans sounded from the kitchen, and the scents of chicken and cooking wine wafted into the living room.

"Do you remember me, Joel?" The quiet words drifted between us.

He jiggled a plastic windshield onto the front of the vehicle he built. He nodded, slightly.

I continued. "I'm sorry I haven't been around so much, but I'd like that to change, if it's all right with you. Maybe we could go out for ice cream sometime, or see a movie if your mom says it's okay?"

Nice. Bribe the kid, Annie.

A small smile tipped one corner of his mouth. I performed a mental Rocky victory stance, grinning at the inside joke Brad and I had shared the day before.

Brad. Nope, I didn't need to go there right now. I shook my head to clear it of both Brad and Sylvester Stallone.

"What's your favorite movie?" I asked.

"*The Lego Movie.* I like Emmet. He uses his head as a wheel."

"Really?" I had no idea what he was talking about. My confused expression must have shown, because Joel took one of his Lego people—a construction worker from the looks of it—and popped off his head. I feigned horror by clapping my hand over my mouth. "You decapitated him," I croaked.

He giggled. "It's okay, Auntie Annie. It doesn't hurt him."

I blinked back tears at the sound of my name rolling easily off his lips after all these months. Whether or not my sister could forgive me, she'd raised some incredible kids. They could throw off the past so effortlessly. Was it who they were or the fact that they hadn't yet been marred by the cruelty of the world? And yet I couldn't say that for Grace. She had been marred. The world had shown her the ugliest it had. She had every right to be bitter. But she chose to live up to her name. She clung to grace and enjoyed life with a gusto I admired. I envied her.

Joel took a Lego wheel and attached it to the construction worker's body. "See?" He grasped the man's legs and rolled his wheel-head along the wood of the coffee table. "That's how he did it. Well, actually, he didn't really take off his *whole* head; he just took off his hat. But this works good too."

Grace came into the room. "What do you want to drink, Auntie? We have lemonade or iced tea."

"Lemonade would be great." I stood. "Thanks for showing me that trick, Joel. I think I'll see if your mom and sister need any help."

"Okay." Joel went back to his Legos and I followed Grace to the kitchen.

Lydia stood at the counter, cutting cucumbers.

"He sure got big," I said.

Lydia cut a cucumber piece particularly hard. The knife hit the cutting board with a sharp thwack.

"Can I help?" I clasped my fidgety hands in front of me.

"You can set the table," Grace offered. She placed the plates on the counter, pointed to a drawer. "Utensils in there."

I remembered. I scooped the plates up and carried them to the table.

"While we were out, I invited Auntie to come hear me play at Chopps on Friday, Mom. We could pick her up, right?"

"Grace . . ."

I stole a glance at my sister. Her bottom lip trembled.

"I'd rather meet you there." I winked at Grace. "I work late on Fridays and the bank's not too far."

Grace carried a small selection of salad dressings to the table. "Okay, sure. No pressure, though, okay?"

"Deal."

The door to the garage opened. Roger entered, his tall form filling the doorway. "Oh, hey, Annie." Roger was always the strong, silent type; I hadn't thought much of how he would feel about my being here. We may have never been close, but I had hurt his family.

That's why I was surprised when he came over to me, giving me a quick hug. "It's good to see you."

"You too." My words got lost in the cotton shoulder of his shirt.

Lydia brushed past us, the salad bowl in her hand. "Dinner's ready, Joel!"

We sat down, me between Grace and Joel. When they held my hands for a prayer before the meal, Grace squeezed my fingers, feeding me much-needed reassurance.

I sliced into the chicken marsala, moist as ever. What didn't my sister do well? Whether it was school, raising fantastic kids, keeping a pristine house, nursing, or cooking, everything seemed to come easy for Lydia.

Except patience, perhaps. I remembered how frustrated she'd get trying to help me with my homework. English, of course. Never math—I deserved to be better than her at one thing, after all.

I remembered sitting at my desk in the room we shared,

a bright purple My Little Pony looking down at the eraser marks on the first line of my paper. Mom called to me, asked how I was doing. I shrugged. I heard her whisper to Lydia, urging her to come help me. My body tensed. I wanted Mom to come help me for once, but cooking, gardening, paint or dance class, chatting on the phone, church social events, whatever—all took priority over spending time with her daughters. Or so it seemed to me, anyway.

"Another book report?" Lydia put her hands on her hips. I nodded.

"I told you—think of three things you want to say. What did the book teach you? Why did you like it?"

I crossed my arms over my chest. "I didn't like it. It didn't teach me nothing."

"*Anything*. But it did. Even crappy books have a lesson in them somewhere."

"Fine. It taught me to not read any more books."

"There you go, then." Lydia walked away. I knew she didn't really care what I wrote. And I knew if I did turn in something snarky, Mrs. Wells would give me a bad grade. I sulked at my desk for another thirty minutes. Mom didn't check on me again. I heard her laughing on the phone, oblivious to her daughter's struggle. I wished for Daddy to come home, but he wouldn't be back from St. Louis for another three days. I finally pushed out a mediocre paper that earned a C. Average enough not to be noticed. Average enough to get by.

"So can she, Mom?" Joel's voice broke into my reminiscing.

I blinked, looked at Lydia, who all but glared at me over the spinach leaves on her fork. "Annie, you should have talked to me first."

"It's just ice cream, Lyd. I'm sure—"

"Roger . . ." My sister put down her fork of spinach, rubbed her temples. When she dropped her hands, she flashed a perfect smile around the table. "Grace, tell me about your day. How did the chem test go?"

Grace stared at her food, seemed to vacillate between pretending the little blip in the conversation didn't happen—like her mother did—or addressing it. She stuck a tine at the end of her fork into a marsala-drenched mushroom. "I think I did well."

Joel didn't get it. "So can I? Dad?"

"We'll talk about it later, Joel," Roger said.

The rest of the dinner was tainted. And the worst part was, Lydia was right. Again. I should have spoken to her first. I kept pretending I would be accepted back into their lives, but I was still an outsider. I'd lost the privilege.

And it looked like Lydia would never stop reminding me.

CHAPTER 16
Liberty

Midwife Louisa's footsteps sounded above my head as she paced with James on the second floor. Before me sat Mr. Gregory, his hat crumpled in his hands between splayed legs, the snow from his boots melting on the throw rug.

I opened my mouth, then closed it. How to begin such a conversation?

"I don't wish to pry, Miss Liberty. You needn't tell me anything you choose not to. I only wish to help. I can bring you to Lexington if you'd like. My sister-in-law is seeking aid in the running of her home and as a midwife. The house is a full one—six children underfoot—but she would be much obliged for any help."

"And she and her husband are willing to feed two more mouths?" There, I acknowledged I had a child.

Mr. Gregory didn't flinch. "Yes, ma'am. My brother is out in the fields come warmer weather. And he isn't keen on Cora—his wife—riding to her patients alone in the winter months. The little ones need tending to. Lexington is growing. More families, more babies."

I clasped my hands together. "I understand Midwife Louisa told you some about . . . about my past circumstances. I do not wish—"

"I have not told my brother anything except that you are a kindhearted woman in need of a place for you and your son. What you wish them to know is yours to tell."

For some reason his words made my eyes prick with tears. They seemed sincere. And yet . . . "You needn't pity me, Mr. Gregory."

"It is not pity that inspires my actions." His eyes met mine with an intensity that struck me to the core—not in an altogether unpleasant way.

If not pity, then what was it that motivated him? I did not ask for fear of his answer. For fear of those eyes, suddenly intimate. "I do not have means to pay you."

"Helping my brother and his family would be payment enough."

I swallowed any remaining doubts. "Then it is settled. When should I plan to bid farewell to Midwife Louisa?"

Midwife Louisa pressed her lips to James's head, just below his knitted cap. "I will certainly be missing you both." Her hand reached down to squeeze mine. Streaks of sunshine fell warm through the dusty window onto my shoulders. Outside, Mr. Gregory checked the wagon.

"And I you." I clasped her hand back. "Thank you for everything. And please, forgive me for being angry with you over Mr. Gregory. As I should have realized, it seems you knew best after all." I clung to the woman to whom I would forever owe a debt of gratitude for my son's life. How different things might have been had I not met her.

"You are forgiven a hundred times over, child."

My throat grew tight at the absolution. It seemed this woman could read my very heart, and still she loved me. I clung tighter to her hand.

She squeezed back. "Just remember: do not be frightened of the truth or of your past. The Lord can work powerfully through it."

I nodded acknowledgment. Perhaps I didn't doubt that God could work; rather I assumed He wouldn't choose to employ a cursed, weak individual like myself.

Midwife Louisa took up a package wrapped in brown paper and pressed it into my hands. "Some supplies to get you started. Don't be a stranger now."

I promised I wouldn't, dragged in a breath, and opened the door to start my new life.

Before me, in linen breeches and a heavy cape, Mr. Gregory stood beside his wagon, my valise situated behind the seats.

I handed James to Midwife Louisa so I could board the wagon. Mr. Gregory placed his large hands at my waist and helped me up, not keeping them there a second longer than necessary, which I appreciated. While I felt comfortable with Mr. Gregory after his many visits to Midwife Louisa's, it struck me now what a vulnerable situation I put myself in. I hadn't been alone with a man since the incident with the captain. And here I was, entrusting myself entirely to Mr. Gregory's care, alone on a country road.

Beneath my thick stockings, my legs began to tremble. I reached for James, found myself meeting Midwife Louisa's gaze and pleading with her for reassurance. She placed a hand on my arm, looked at me directly. "All is well, Liberty. I would trust Mr. Gregory with my life." Her words were solid, firm, and I believed them. Once again the older woman had given me what I needed.

Mr. Gregory settled the lap blanket around me, and I counted the fact that I did not flinch at his closeness a victory. "Rest assured, Midwife Louisa, I will die before I let anything happen to either of these two." Such a bold proclamation, and yet I felt the weight of its sincerity. He sat beside me, his cloak brushing against my own, the scent of soap and leather wafting in my direction.

"Godspeed!" Midwife Louisa called. I blew her a kiss, committing her image to memory.

Mr. Gregory waved and slapped the reins against the horse's back, steering us toward the town gates on the Neck.

Due to the rhythmic bumping and rocking of the wagon, James slept longer than usual. By the time he woke, we were well past the crowded streets of Boston, packed with men and women in their market-day frippery, small boys with brooms and rags trying to catch the next chimney to sweep, vendors selling everything from coffee to Seneca oil. We were past the gallows on the Neck and the graves of suicides that sent shivers through my body.

Now the quiet soothed me. No haggling people quibbling over necessary goods, no church bells, no music. Just the sound of the churning wagon wheels on the ground, thawing slightly in the bright sunshine, and James's tiny breaths puffing out into the air. Mr. Gregory and I made trite conversation, him speaking of his childhood in Lexington or me admiring the country landscape. When James woke, I pondered how to nurse him in the small confines.

"Mr. Gregory, might we stop so I may feed him?"

He raised his eyebrows at me, shifted slightly in his seat. I could feel his discomfort at the mention of something so personal. "Can you not manage in the wagon? If we stop every time . . . we may not make it before dark."

Despite the cool weather, hot blood rushed to my face. "I suppose if I must."

"You need not fear, Miss Liberty. I will keep my—you need not fear."

I cleared my throat, arranged my cloak over James's head. "Thank you for doing this." I spoke to cover up the sound of my son's tiny gulps, in case they could be heard above the ruckus of the wagon.

"'Tis no trouble. I am due for a visit with my brother anyhow."

For the first time I wondered about this man, who lived with his sister, who had never started a family. While not considered old, it seemed he would have taken a wife by now.

"I look forward to meeting them."

"Little Rebekah will take to you and James like no other. The rest are older and mind themselves overall. Though Thomas—he's seven—has some trouble minding himself very well."

I laughed. "Sounds like it will never be dull."

Mr. Gregory let out a laugh that bellowed out beyond the landscape. "Dull is one thing my brother's house could never be accused of."

"Why did you move to Boston?"

"More opportunities for building work. And then there was Edwina."

My interest perked. "Edwina?"

"My wife. I met her on one of my trips into Boston. She died during childbirth, as did our babe. It's been four years already."

"I'm so sorry."

Mr. Gregory's eyes remained on the road. "I miss her every day, but time does heal in its way. The Lord gives and the Lord takes. I'm trusting He has a plan in all of this."

My silence ate up the open conversation faster than the wheels ate up the dirt road.

"For you, too, Miss Liberty."

"Pardon?"

"I believe the Lord has a plan for you, too."

I didn't bother hiding the snort that escaped. James began to cry, and I adjusted my clothing, put him over my shoulder, and patted his back.

"You don't believe in the Lord's sovereignty?"

Not since Grandmother had I known someone to speak of God in such a blatant manner. True, most Bostonians went to church and touted their Christian character, but few spoke of such matters. I shifted in my seat. An air bubble traversed James's body, culminating in a loud belch.

"It's not that I doubt God's sovereignty." I tucked the blanket around James, began rubbing his back. "I suppose it's His goodness and willingness to work in my own life that I doubt."

Mr. Gregory met my gaze, a smile on his face.

"Am I amusing?" I asked.

"Not at all." He turned his eyes again to the horses. "Rather, I find your honesty refreshing."

"So glad I've refreshed you." I glanced sideways at him, one side of my mouth pulled up tight to convey my sarcasm.

"Aren't you going to spout Bible verses at me or tell me I'm wrong to doubt my Creator?"

He continued looking at the road, his body swaying with the movement of the wagon. "No."

"You're going to leave me here believing God doesn't care a whit about me?"

His turn for the sarcastic look. "I think you already know all the answers, don't you, Miss Liberty?"

Did I? What had Grandmother said? *We are never so far away from God that He can't reach His hand out to grasp us.* No matter the transgressions between us. All we had to do was turn and be healed.

It sounded so simple, but what if the trust simply wasn't there?

I finished nursing James, ignoring Mr. Gregory's question. My son fell asleep at my breast, and after I arranged him in the crook of my arm, I dug in the basket for a couple pieces of bread and cheese I'd packed that morning. I offered one to Mr. Gregory, which he took.

I never did answer his question. Perhaps because I didn't know the answer all that well myself.

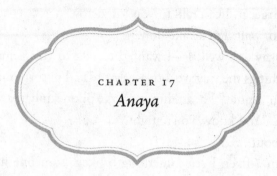

CHAPTER 17
Anaya

I DRAGGED MY EYES open at the tune of "Gonna Fly Now." It lit up my phone in the darkness of my bedroom. I rubbed my eyes awake.

"Feelin' strong now . . ."

"Won't be long now . . ."

Brad.

I sat up straight, adrenaline rushing through my limbs, my mouth dry. He was calling. I shouldn't care so much, but I did.

I rolled over and grabbed my phone before the song closed out with lyrics about flying. "Hello?"

"Aww, Annie, I woke you up."

"It's okay. I have to open tomorrow, so I tried to make it an early night." I glanced at the time on my screen: 10:04. "I think I already got in an hour. What's up?"

"Forget it. I can talk to you tomorrow."

"No, wait. I'm awake now."

"Okay . . . well, I—I wanted to talk to you. I just can't leave things the way we did last Saturday. I'm sorry for pushing you, Annie." I heard him shift the phone, inhale a wobbly breath. "You know, you're right."

"About . . . ?"

"I'm a fixer. I see something broken, someone hurting, I want to fix them. Including myself. Slap some duct tape on and plow through the pain. But I've been thinking . . . maybe being broken isn't always such a bad thing."

I snorted. "Really? In whose world?"

"Well, maybe being broken can bring us together, you know? Like it has a higher purpose. Maybe it's how we help one another, look for meaning in this botched-up life."

I rolled his words around in my head, tried not to brush them off as idealistic. Like it or not, they poked at the shell I tried to erect around my heart, the one that assured me Brad could never understand. I thought of probing him further about his own ghosts, about his time in Iraq, but feared shutting him down and pushing him away. I much preferred this—him, back in my life, talking to me—than the silence of the last couple days. "I'm sorry too. For spazzing out on you."

"Forgiven. In a heartbeat. Now when can I see you again?"

Warmth sprouted in my belly. He'd glimpsed my demons and hadn't turned tail and run. I leaned back against the headboard, relishing the feeling of acceptance. "Why don't you let me cook you dinner tomorrow night? If you're free, that is."

"And afterward, if you're still interested, we could look over something I found."

I kicked my covers off. "Something on Liberty?"

"Not on Liberty, but on Thomas. The one we found at the society the other day that's married to Amelia Gregory. I found another clue that confirms it. He *was* Granddad's great-great-grandfather."

I looked over Brad's shoulder at my laptop. The scent of my homemade meatballs lingered in the air, our sauce-splattered plates sitting in soapy dishwater in the sink.

The tension from our last time together wore off over dinner, relaxing into comfortable conversation. I listened to accounts of his work, about a house built in 1795 that he and his team were redoing, about the many specifications for restoration required to keep a house "historical." It felt . . . different to have Brad in my house, to cook for him, to hear about his workweek. Different, and rather nice. Maybe even natural.

Brad clicked on a heading that read, *Massachusetts Marriage Records, 1840–1915.* The record was for Allen

Kilroy. "It shows he married in 1853 to a Madelyn Warren of Boston. It also shows his parents' names—Thomas and Amelia." He clicked over to another page. "I found the birth records for a Jonathan Kilroy of Lexington. His parents were Allen and Madelyn."

I searched the screen for a date. "The birth year checks out and everything."

"All the dots connect. I do have ancestors by the name of Gregory."

I squeezed his shoulder. "Good work, Mr. Kilroy." I opened my notebook and started scribbling down information. "So now we switch over to Amelia's side, right? Try to find out who her parents were?"

He nodded, opened another tab on my laptop. "I think I found something on her last night." He gave me a sheepish grin. "I stayed up until one."

"Wow."

His fingers flew over the keys. "I searched her for two hours. The records are definitely slim once we start heading back to the early nineteenth century, but I did find something on Amelia Gregory in the society news. Only again, there's no way to be sure it's in fact our Amelia, but it's a perfect match for the information we have so far."

I skimmed over the digital picture of a rather worn newspaper clipping from the *Boston Gazette*, March 1834. The article told of a dance at Munroe Tavern. It spoke of dance cards, a practical joke repeated from a dance some twenty years earlier, and an Amelia Gregory who insisted on relieving an ill Negro servant woman of her duties. When a patron made a fuss that without the sick woman, they would not be served, Miss Gregory stepped in and served the drinks herself, much to the dismay of the young beaus named on her dance card.

"And look, I found a book of Lexington's history online, with a copy of Amelia's dance card."

I squinted at the computer. "Thomas K.'s name on half the spots on her card."

"It must be him, and this must be his future wife, my four-times-great-grandmother. I think we should go back to the society, search for some clues in their microform. Or maybe the Massachusetts Archives in Dorchester. There's only so much we can find online, especially now that we're so far back."

I grabbed up our water glasses and added them to the sudsy dishwater. "Seems you've done pretty well. Sure you need me?" I kept my tone light but avoided his gaze.

The chair scraped against the linoleum and I felt his presence behind me, smelled soap mixed with spicy cologne and, always, a hint of wood. I stilled at a touch on my elbow. "You're not mad I found things on my own, are you?"

I shrugged and turned, surprised by the solid wall of Brad that stood less than a foot from me. "Not mad. Maybe a little disappointed. Selfish, I know."

Here I was again, revealing more of my unflattering self to this guy I was fast becoming attached to. I was surprised when he stepped closer. I inhaled a shaky breath, my heart dancing beneath my lungs.

"I feel like I'm the one who keeps letting you down." His Adam's apple bobbed. "I know I don't measure up, Annie. . . ."

I wondered if he was thinking the same about me. My fingers touched his sweatshirt, hesitant. I wouldn't lie to him. He didn't measure up. I'd pictured an athletic-looking, lean man. Maybe a runner who'd finished the race an hour before me. A doctor who cheered on a friend. A Red Sox fan, of course. But not an emotionally scarred ex-soldier. Not a tattooed contractor who resembled a lumberjack more than a marathon runner.

"No, you don't."

He gave me a sad smile, started to pull away. I held on to his sweatshirt, made a bold move of stepping in closer. "But there is no one else I'd rather be standing here with right now. Fantasy . . . or real."

The words were out, in the air between us before I fully thought them through. I checked . . . and discovered they were sincere, which caught me off guard—maybe as much as what Brad's closeness was doing to my body.

Those green eyes came alive with a request so potent I couldn't look away. He lowered his lips to mine in a kiss that drew me with its promise but held me with its sweetness. A kiss that shattered me, and then pulled me back together.

When we finally parted he tugged me in for a long hug, pressed his mouth to the top of my head. An intense longing

HEIDI CHIAVAROLI

to never let him go—to confess feelings I hadn't yet had time
to explore—overtook me. I kept them at bay. I hadn't ever
felt such a strong connection to another person before.

"I'm really glad we found each other, Anaya."

"Me too."

"And I promise not to do any more searching without
you."

"Thank you."

He lifted a hand to the hollow at my neck. His fingers
brushed my throat and he pulled the chain until the ring
was above my sweater. He ran his thumb over the stones, the
inscription. "You are strong, Annie. And I'm hoping to prove
it to you one of these days."

I guided his hands away from the ring. It was time I
revealed a deeper part of myself to him. "Brad . . ."

He waited.

"There's something I think I should tell you."

Whether or not he would admit it, I saw his guard go up.
I saw it in the way his body tensed, the way his jaw tightened ever so slightly. And after a statement like that, why
shouldn't it?

"Okay . . ."

My middle trembled, and I breathed through my nose
to settle the feeling. "I'm not proud of my actions these past
couple of years. I abandoned my sister and niece for more
than twenty months because I couldn't face reality. I'm a coward, Brad." Warm tears gathered in my eyes. "And I can't let
you stand there thinking I'm some strong heroine or even a

strong victim. I'm a horrible person. Rather than pushing through the pain and sticking with the people I care about, I ran out on them. It's only fair I warn you."

He studied me and I wanted to turn away from his pressing stare. "Annie, I have no illusions of you being perfect."

"Phew, glad that's cleared up."

"And I'm sure you don't have any imaginings about me being so either."

I shrugged.

"You know, last night, when I was searching around on the computer about the ring—which of course, will be my last time ever doing *that* . . ." We laughed. "I tried to find out about the crest of the ring too. I think there might be more to it than we've thought about."

"Like what?"

"For you and me, the marathon bombing hits close to home, right? But my research got me thinking that throughout history people have always had moments of deep suffering: school shootings, the Holocaust, loved ones lost at war. We just have a hard time relating when it was a long time ago or far away. I read about first-century Christians who were brutally tortured. I mean, these guys were thrown in with the lions, burned at the stake. I read an account about Nero using them as human torches. They hid out in catacombs beneath the city. And you know what symbol they often used to encourage one another?"

I shook my head.

"They used an anchor similar to the one on our ring. And

the other symbol—the horn. It stands for God's strength. They put their faith in something bigger than themselves." He lifted a hand, let it fall back to his thigh. "I don't know, Annie. I'm still thinking I can save you myself—help you see how strong you are. That we can escape our past by overcoming it. But maybe . . ."

"What?"

"Maybe neither you or I can do it by ourselves. Maybe we both need someone stronger too."

CHAPTER 18
Liberty

"There." Mr. Gregory pointed to a large two-story home that shared a common with a meetinghouse, a tavern, a belfry, and another grand home. The sun set behind the house, giving it the image of a safe haven. A new beginning. Perhaps even a resting place.

He directed the horses toward the barn, where he dismounted. A boy of about twelve walked out. "Uncle!" He dropped his pitchfork and launched himself into Mr. Gregory's arms, then, as if remembering his age and that he was nearly a man, pulled back and adjusted his hat. "'Tis good to see you. I can take your horse in."

Mr. Gregory tousled the boy's hair. I watched the tender exchange from where I perched on the wagon seat.

When Mr. Gregory had helped me down, he introduced me to his nephew, Michael, and grabbed my valise.

The door of the house opened, and a gaggle of children piled out, followed by a man whose solid build resembled Mr. Gregory's. "Brother. You are here at last. The children have not stopped hounding me since we told them of your impending arrival." The glint in the man's eye told me he did not mind the hounding all too much. He turned to me. "And you must be Miss Liberty. I'm Graham Gregory. It's a pleasure to meet you. My wife is much obliged for your help."

"The pleasure is all mine, Mr. Gregory." I said, pulling out my etiquette lessons from Grandmother. If I wanted this new beginning to work for James and me, I would have to make a decent impression.

"And who is this?" he asked, gesturing to James.

I'd practiced a number of answers to this question a thousand times over the last couple of days and with each turn of the carriage wheel on the way here. There would be no getting around the fact that James was my child. I could only hope the Gregory family would presume me a widow from the simple words I would give, or perhaps that I'd been abandoned by my husband. Either conclusion would be more flattering than the truth.

"This is James. My—my son. His father is . . . no longer with us."

Graham smacked his hands together and rubbed them,

not questioning me further, for which I was grateful. "Let's get you two warmed up inside. Cora's busy with supper. Prepared a feast for you two, she has."

We entered the house, the scent of roast mutton teasing my nostrils and the pleasant undulating sound of a spinet relaxing my senses further. A slender woman turned from sliding a pot of beans into the oven. She wiped her soot-blackened hands on her apron before hugging her brother-in-law. "At last! And you have brought my salvation!"

Graham Gregory shook his head, put his hands up in the air. "There's no taming her, I tell you. Miss Liberty, this is my wife, Cora."

Around a pack of children who begged for Mr. Gregory's attention, I offered Mrs. Gregory a small curtsy, but she swatted it away and gave me a hug, her mobcap falling off her glistening forehead. "Pleasure to meet you, dear. And look at this bundle. A wee one, isn't he? You settle yourselves, why don't you? Rebekah here will show you your room. Nathaniel, grab her things, please."

"Thank you, ma'am. I appreciate your inviting me."

"And we'll scoot you right back outside that door if you start calling me ma'am, hear?" She winked at me. "Please, call me Cora."

I followed Rebekah and Nathaniel up the narrow stairs. Rebekah looked back at me when she reached the top, a piece of maple sugar Mr. Gregory had slipped her tight in hand. I guessed her to be about eight, blue eyes brighter than a robin's egg. "I can change him if you want. I'm real good with babies."

"Perhaps you could help me?"

She smiled, revealing a missing front tooth. "Cilla moved in with the girls this morning so you could have this room. I'm hoping she doesn't wiggle around as much as Annabel." Her eyes grew wide and she slapped her hands over her mouth. "Oops. I'm not supposed to complain."

I laughed, bent near her. "Don't worry, your secret's safe with me."

Nathaniel came out of the corner room, hands empty. By far the oldest, he shared his father's and uncle's wide form and strapping shoulders. I guessed him to be sixteen, at least. We were not so very far apart in age, but the heaviness of the past year combined with the weight of my son in my arms confirmed that I was far older in the ways of the world.

"I put your valise in there for when you're ready," he said.

I thanked him, and Rebekah led me to the room. Ropes hung from the ceiling, supporting a bedtick made up with a homespun coverlet. Alongside it stood a chest of drawers and a small table with an earthenware pitcher and bowl. Two windows looked out onto the common. I hadn't expected such a lavish area.

"Will it do?" Rebekah asked, hesitation in her voice.

"Oh, child, it will more than do. I feel so . . . so blessed to be with you all."

She smiled and dragged a small cradle from the far wall. "James can sleep in here." She then opened the top drawer. "Changing cloths. Babies need lots of those."

"They certainly do." I laid James on the bed, took the knit hat from his head, where a tuft of soft hair stuck up.

Rebekah sat beside him. "Mama's real glad you're here. Daddy don't want her midwifing so much anymore. Says Dr. Richards been spreading gossip about Mama being a—" she lowered her voice—"a *w-i-t-c-h*." She laughed. "That's the maddest thing I ever heard. Daddy says he's just after her patients."

Blood rushed to my head. "Oh my." I tried to keep my voice level, though I couldn't deny the news rattled me. "I thought we were long past such things."

Rebekah swatted a hand at me, much like her mother had done downstairs when I curtsied. "Oh, don't worry, Miss Liberty. Mama's no witch. That's nonsense talking. People are just afraid of what they don't understand, right? And Mama heals good. Real good. Better'n Dr. Richards. He keeps saying people should be storing away their concealment boxes to ward off evil spirits and witches like Mama. Nothing God-honoring about that."

It seemed the family had an adversary in town. Had I brought myself and James under that same enmity?

I pinned James's fresh changing cloth and sat down to nurse him, but not before feeling for the silver and ring, still sewn within the folds of my traveling dress. Their hard round edges afforded me a measure of peace. If I sensed trouble brewing for me and my son, I would find another way for us. If the Lord didn't provide a way, the sterling and the ring most certainly would.

I glanced at the empty dish before me, not a crumb of apple tart left on the plate, my belly satisfied for the first time in months. I leaned against the straight-back cherry chair. James lay in his cradle beside the fire, eyes closed in sleep, seeming equally content.

Graham pressed a kiss to his wife's temple. "Thank you for dinner, Mother. It was a delight as usual."

We all echoed our gratitude. Graham and Nathaniel broke out a chessboard. Michael bundled up to go milk the cow and fetch some cordwood. I sipped the last of my "swamp tea," attempting to keep my dislike of it from my face.

Cora didn't miss my reluctance. "A first for you, is it?"

"'Tis good. I think it will only take some getting accustomed to. Labrador, is it not?" The yellow color and rancid taste were nothing like the tea from England.

Cora smiled. "You do know your herbs, then. We do what we can. Nonimportation tea is a start. We also have chocolate if you prefer."

I shook my head, not wanting to cause any trouble. "I will certainly grow accustomed to it in no time."

Mr. Gregory stood. "Miss Liberty, might I steal you away for a walk around the green?"

"I am not certain that would be—"

"Go on now." Cora brought a dish from the sideboard to the basin. "We'll watch James. And don't worry, you can put in your share of the work starting tomorrow."

I didn't see a way out. I only wished to be thought on well, not to be shirking my responsibilities for a walk in the dark with a man on my first night with these kind people.

I grabbed my cloak and muff, and we slid out the back door. The candles from the tavern across the way lit up a good portion of the common. The tin lantern Mr. Gregory carried shone light before our steps. The cold air chilled my nose, and I burrowed further into my cloak.

"I will be leaving tomorrow, early in the morn. I wished to speak with you privately, make certain you are content with the situation here."

"I most certainly am. Though I wonder if I should fear very much of being accused a witch."

Silence.

"Mr. Gregory, if I could see the tips of your ears, I would wager they are red as a ripe tomato."

He laughed, a bellowing, joyful sound. We walked behind the three-story meetinghouse, its shadow blocking the light from the tavern. "Please, Miss Liberty. You must call me Hugh. And as for the witch nonsense, I do not take the doctor's blustering all that seriously."

"Perhaps that is because you are not an unwed mother who practices midwifery, Mr. Gregory."

"Hugh."

I sighed, not wishing to provoke the discourse, to be thought of as a tease, or worse . . . as the captain had thought of me—a common camp girl with whom he could take his pleasure.

"Mr. Gregory, it is not accusations of witchcraft that truly concern me. I think Massachusetts Bay Colony has had its share of excitement with the coming and going of the king's troops, as have I. But I do wonder what your brother's family thinks of me." I walked a few more steps, the rocky soil crunching frozen beneath my boots. "I wonder what you must think of me."

It needed to be out in the open before us. If he was smitten with me as Midwife Louisa inferred and as I sensed, if he planned to court me, I could not keep the truth of James's lineage from him.

"I only think of you what I see. You are a loving mother, a gifted healer, and a pleasant traveling companion. I would be lying if I didn't say I've noticed what a bonny lass you are."

I cleared my throat. I did not have much experience in the manner of courtship. Did I even wish to? How, after the liberties the captain took, could I ever trust a man—whether Patriot or redcoat—again? And yet how wonderful would it be for me and James to have a provider and a protector, someone to shelter and watch over us? I would no longer feel the need to pretend if Mr. Gregory was willing to take James as a son and me as a wife.

And yet part of me could not forget that last night with Alexander by the fire, the lilt and sway of his voice caressing words of poetry. How he had confessed his affection for me.

"Mr. Gregory, just so we are clear . . . James's father was—is—an officer in the King's Army."

A tight silence stretched between us before he responded.

"Midwife Louisa hinted as much. And I can see how this fact would upset you. The night of your brother's death, I saw how dearly you loved him." We walked on. "If it is not too bold of me to say, I would not fear that you have disappointed him. You haven't the slightest need for shame. It is not as if you were associating with those blackguards or putting yourself in a foolish position. I am certain your brother would be proud of you."

His words, meant to soothe, cut deep. For I *had* associated with those blackguards. I *had* put myself in a foolish position.

"Thank you," I croaked.

"I only must ask, and forgive me if I intrude . . . but why was this officer not tried for his crimes? Even the Crown has a standard and does not allow for its officers accosting innocent young lasses."

His words stirred up a desire in me to cling to the belief that I had been an innocent young lass. I had been taken advantage of. The fault for my transgressions lay entirely on the captain's head, not my own. Yes, I had lived in their home, but that did not give one call to do what was done to me.

Yes, this path of thinking pleased me. Mr. Gregory might assume I'd merely been walking down a back alley or the dark common, couldn't imagine me working for the enemy or falling in love with a soldier of the Crown. What he saw in my being was enough to draw me to that imaginary girl. I wanted to be that innocent maiden. And perhaps if Mr.

Gregory saw me as such, and I convinced myself, the guilt would not be so very painful. Perhaps I could eventually forget Alexander altogether.

"If I sought justice, the officer would know of James . . . and I do not wish him to know of my son's existence." The honest words were a start, perhaps a cornerstone in building a satisfying life for myself and my son.

We continued walking, turned left so the tavern was in front of us. "I can't say I fault you for that."

I breathed around the emotion lodged in my throat. His sympathy—though couched in a slight half-truth—was a resting place for my burdened heart. "Thank you . . . Hugh."

He reached out and laid his fingers upon my arm, just above where my hands rested in my muff. I thought of the last time a man had reached out to me with such tenderness. Alexander, by the fire, with that ring gleaming upon his finger, and my heart thumping more wildly for his touch than it did now, for Mr. Gregory's.

"Miss Liberty?"

"Hmm?"

"I was saying I thought to ask if I might write you after I leave?"

There were worse things than a solid man's interest. I may prefer to be alone, but the well-being of my son was at stake. James's future would prove much more prosperous with a man in his life.

And so my decision was made. Even if all went well with Graham Gregory and his family, they would not wish me with them forever. Writing Hugh, perhaps opening up my heart to him, was a keen path for a single mother. Anyone would expect it. And as I made my answer, a stir of anticipation rippled in my chest. There was hope of me having a family yet.

"I would like that very much, Hugh."

CHAPTER 19
Anaya

BRAD TUGGED AT a strand of my hair as we took the elevator of the genealogical society up to the fourth floor. "You're tired."

We'd spent the morning searching the gravestones at two old Lexington cemeteries, with no recognizable name match. After that, we went to the Massachusetts Archives. Within the first hour of our search, we found a birth record for Amelia Gregory—born in 1815 to a Michael and Ava Gregory. Our initial excitement dwindled after three subsequent hours of finding nothing more. We grabbed lunch and decided on another trip to the society, though now I battled exhaustion and defeat.

Even if we did find Liberty's name, how would we find the story behind the ring? The poem would probably be our only clue, and what we could draw from that could never be more than conjecture.

"How many miles did you run this morning?"

"Just shy of three." I'd woken up in the predawn hours to squeeze in the run before our trip to the archives. "I'm feeling it now, though. Hey—Grace gave me my sponsor sheet. Think you could swing twenty bucks?"

"To see you run? I'll swing way more than twenty."

I laughed, felt some of my vigor return. "I wasn't inviting you to the race, that's for sure."

"Come on, you think I wouldn't be there?"

A thin sweat broke over my skin as the elevator door opened. "No, really. I don't want you to come."

He scrunched his eyebrows, shook his head, as if to say, *Why the heck not?*

He didn't say it, though, and I stepped off the elevator first. It took several moments for my eyes to adjust to the dim light of the microform room. The whirring of microfilm sounded to our left.

We spoke with a woman at the reference desk who suggested we begin searching in the Middlesex County records.

We signed up for a microform machine, found an index book marked *A–L*, and settled at a circular table beside machine number seven.

"So why don't you want me at the race?" Brad whispered in a voice that carried to the other desks around us.

"Forget it," I said in an equally loud whisper as I flipped open the book to the *G*s.

"I'm coming."

"No. You're not."

"Yes. I am."

"Do you want to get us kicked out of this place?" I ran my finger down the list of Gregorys, searched for any with the names we'd come up with. The woman at the desk had also said searching Lexington alone could give us clues.

"Don't think you're off the hook, woman."

We giggled like high school sweethearts misbehaving in the library.

"Come on, help me look."

Brad ran a calloused pointer finger down the alphabetical page. "No Liberty, or Amelia, or Michael, or Ava."

"We came all the way here. Let's just look at a few. They might give us a clue. Here." I pointed to the first name on the list. "Beatrice Gregory, elopement notice." I wrote down the number of the microfilm and we went to the back wall to find it. After a brief search we slid the film into machine number seven.

It was an elopement notice from 1786, stating that a Beatrice Gregory had run off with a man who was not her husband. Apparently Benjamin Gregory wished to notify the public that he was no longer accountable for her debts. No other names were given.

Brad rewound the reel and slid it out. "Two more, then we find some chow. Deal?"

I agreed. Hitting roadblocks had a way of wearing on our hope.

The next name in the book was a Constance Gregory of Lexington. We put back Beatrice's microfilm and picked up Constance's. It was a society news page from 1828 stating that Constance Gregory would be vacationing in Philadelphia for the summer with her aunt.

Brad replaced the film while I wrote down the file number of the next Gregory from Lexington in the book. Cora Gregory, journal, 1770–1776. I went to the back wall to get the film box.

This was much longer than the previous microfilms and appeared to be a record of midwife attendances. We skimmed through the first few, straining our eyes to read the old writing. Record after record of delivering babies, nursing children through a dysentery epidemic, salving burns, treating cases of worms. My stomach began to churn and I was about to suggest we call it quits early when a name caught my eye in an entry of spring 1771. The record looked like all the others, except at the top, written in Cora's meticulous hand, was the heading, *Assisted by Liberty Caldwell.*

"Brad, look."

He squinted at the screen. "Do you think that could be her?"

"Maybe. She's living at the right time. Her first name isn't a common one in the eighteenth century."

We scrolled forward. More often than not, the name

Liberty Caldwell appeared at the top of the page. Near the end of 1773, many entries listed her name as the *Sole Midwife.*

"It looks like Cora took Liberty under her wing to train her, and eventually Liberty went out by herself." I continued to scroll forward. A sudden time lapse appeared in mid-April 1775.

"The war," Brad said. "Begun at Lexington. Though people would still need a midwife. I wonder why there's a break."

The next entry picked up in November 1775. A labor and delivery with Cora Gregory listed as midwife. And below her name, next to *Assisted by,* the woman we'd been hoping to find.

Liberty Gregory.

CHAPTER 20
Liberty

10 DECEMBER 1773

Dearest Liberty,

*In the years I have been writing you, I have not once
confessed my deep feelings. Some may say I am slow
to act, or a coward to write you in this way instead of
speaking them in person, but I sense your need for space,
your need to find your way as a mother . . . alone.*

*Yet the onset of this cold winter and the biting wind
whipping off the harbor release a burden in my soul.*

I miss you, Liberty. I do not wish for our relationship to be only through paper and an occasional visit. Soon James will be old enough to realize he has no father like other boys.

Liberty, I wish to be his father. I can think of no better pleasure than to hear him call me "Father," except perhaps to hear you call me "Husband." I make my intentions plain here so you may consider this request in the privacy of your oft-guarded heart. Don't fret, my dear. I cannot imagine you any other way. Though if you accept my proposal, I do plan to tear down those walls bit by bit. Because, my love, your heart is my goal.

See what you have done to a grown man! I doubt if I ever talked so foolishly to even Edwina. You do indeed make me a fool, dearest Liberty. And I believe I am a better man for it.

I await your reply with an eager heart. There is much informal business to be done here in Boston.

Should I hear from you with favor, I will plan to build a homestead in Lexington. I long for the country and farm life . . . and you. My sister's recent marriage has proven well for her soul, and there is nothing to keep me tied to Boston. Does Lexington suit you? I pray it is so. Farewell, my love.

With eager anticipation,
Hugh

Dearest Hugh,

Though I fear you are not fully aware what you heap upon your head, I must selfishly accept your proposal. Come as soon as you can, my dear. James has been asking for you.

The Reverend Clark's wife is due for her tenth child any day now, and I am to help her deliver the child myself. Little by little, Cora is releasing the midwifing to me. Her instruction is faultless. I have learned much—both in midwifing and in the managing of a household. Still, I feel I should persuade you to seek out another. And yet greedily, I pray you don't.

I long to be the wife you deserve, my dear. I will try my very hardest in honoring you and our family.

I hope your business in the town has not been too dangerous, and I pray you were not involved with those frightful Mohawks in the dumping of the tea in the harbor. Imagine—Mohawks romping about in Boston. You are indeed safer here in Lexington. When I think of all you work for, I am reminded of my brother and all that he died for. 'Tis not in vain, my love. I will be glad to have you near soon.

With fondest thoughts and sincerest regards,
Liberty

CHAPTER 21
Anaya

"THERE SHE IS!" Brad stood up straight and hit his head on the microform machine. He rubbed his crown. "That has to be her. She must have gotten married sometime between April and November."

I couldn't deny the thrill of finding Liberty. We had discovered her maiden name, that she had a career as a midwife, that she had lived in Lexington. These details made her all the more real to me.

My fingers shook as I pushed the forward button, the entries one hundred times more interesting now that they had led us to the possible owner of the ring. I told myself this shouldn't matter so much to me. None of it. Brad's family, the ring, the poem, Liberty. None of it should matter at all. And yet it did matter, so very much. The bombing, the ring, Brad, Liberty . . . they were each becoming a part of my own story.

Brad put his hands on my shoulders and gave them a squeeze. "The chances have to be about one in a million that there would be another Liberty Gregory from the area who lived in this time period. She must be the author of the poem."

"And maybe your ancestor."

"If we didn't already have the line from the poem matching the inscription on the ring, I'd say it's a long shot. But now I'm thinking it must be true. We just don't have solid proof that connects Michael Gregory to Liberty. Maybe if we find her marriage license? Based on the journal entries, we know she was married after the battle but before the end of 1775."

I continued forward on the reel. We didn't see anything new, a few entries with either Cora Gregory or Liberty Gregory. "Liberty most likely married into Cora's family. If we can find Liberty's husband's name and then match his and Liberty's names to a birth record for Michael, we'd have the proof we need."

Brad pulled the reel out of the machine and we scanned the frames we needed and downloaded them to his thumb drive. We went to the computer and Brad clicked on a website I hadn't seen yet, then on *Massachusetts Town Marriage Records, 1620–1850.* He typed as much information as he had in the search box, and the first result was a hit.

Hugh Gregory. Spouse—Liberty Caldwell. Marriage

date—July 8, 1775. Marriage place—Lexington. I scribbled the information in my notebook. "We're getting there, Brad."

Brad's fingers flew over the keys as he searched for records on the birth of Michael Gregory. We landed five birth record results, but none of them listed parents as Liberty or Hugh.

"Where is he? Don't tell me we're going to hit a wall now. He should be here."

The horrible feeling that we'd missed a step in our research washed over me. I looked at the sketch of Brad's family tree. "Unless we're missing a generation. Liberty and Hugh were married in 1775. Amelia was born in 1815. That's forty years. Enough for another generation if they had their babies young enough. Maybe Liberty is Amelia's great-grandmother, not her grandmother."

I didn't state the other possibility: that there was no connection between Brad's family and Liberty Gregory. If so, our search ended here.

Brad raked his hand through his hair. "We spent the whole morning looking for something on Michael and found nothing." I could sense his desperation, and I couldn't resist humming the *Rocky* theme song.

He groaned. "I get it, I get it. I'm not giving up; don't worry. We may not have found Michael, but we found Liberty Gregory, and that's even more exciting." He closed his eyes, opened them. "We can always continue looking online at home. We only have an hour left before they close. I saw another book on Middlesex County on the back wall. I'll go get it."

My stomach rumbled as Brad left and came back with a red book titled *Index to the Probate Records of Middlesex County Massachusetts, 1674–1871*. He flipped to the Gs.

"Plenty of Gregorys again. No Liberty."

"How about Michael? Or Amelia?"

"One Michael from Lexington. A will from 1864. If the Michael we're looking for was born shortly after Liberty and Hugh got married, that would make the guy almost ninety years old. Did people live that long back then?"

I bit my lip. "I suppose it's possible, right? Any other Michaels?"

Brad shook his head. "Not from Lexington. Might as well look." He said the microfilm number to himself two times before going to the back wall again.

When the reel was in the microform machine, he fast-forwarded to the correct number. The second page held Michael's name; his date of birth—November 12, 1796; the date of death—October 16, 1864; and the probate date—November 7, 1864, along with the name of the person who had read the will.

Brad returned to the first page, which began the will. We read.

I, Michael Gregory, resident of the Town of Lexington, County of Middlesex, State of Massachusetts, being of sound disposing mind and memory, and conscious of my own mortality, do make this my last will and testament. First of all I

bequeath my precious soul into the hands of God,
trusting in the merits of Jesus Christ for salvation.
My temporal and worthy estate I give and desire of
in the following manner. My will is that all my debts
and financial charges be first paid out of my estate by
my esquire. I give and bequeath unto my daughter,
Amelia Kilroy of Lexington, together with her
husband, Thomas, the house built by the loving
hands of my father, Hugh Gregory.

"There!" I squeezed Brad's arm. "That's it. The connection, Brad."

"It has to be . . ."

I looked at him, his face drawn tight at the desk where the film reflected the picture. "What's wrong, then?" I followed his gaze to the last sentence before what looked like a lengthy list of Michael's items began, along with to whom they were to be dispensed.

Also to my daughter, Amelia, I leave one gold signet
ring with the name of *Smythe*, given to me at the
death of my mother, Liberty, and engraved with the
anchor and horn of Christ, inscribed with the words
Qui fortis salutem tribute.

"I can't believe it," I whispered. "We found her."

Brad continued staring at the image. "I—she really is my ancestor."

A solemn silence spread over us like a warm blanket. It was an almost-holy experience, this finding of information that connected us with the past, with the family of the man who now sat beside me. It reminded me of my own mortality, of the fragility and beauty of life. I breathed it in as we sat with the picture, communing with history's memories—a history I could no longer separate from myself.

In a way, now, it belonged to me as much as Brad. So much more than it had when I woke in the hospital with my rescuer's—Liberty's—ring in my hand. More than when I'd discovered Brad's card in Lydia's living room. Nothing about this history was make-believe. The poem, Liberty, the ring, Brad . . . they were all swirling around me, catching me up in their whirlwind, inviting me to be a part of something bigger than myself.

After a few minutes passed, Brad scrolled to the next screen, a continuing list of Michael's smaller possessions and monetary disbursements.

Brad flipped to the family tree I'd sketched. "According to the will, Michael Gregory was born in 1796, a year after Liberty wrote the poem. Gee, it took Hugh and Liberty twenty-one years to have a child. They must have been in their early forties, at least."

We scanned the images onto the flash drive, thanked the reference genealogists, signed out, and left the building.

Brad slipped his hand into mine. "That . . . was so cool."

We walked half a block before I spoke. "Thank you."

He cocked his head to the side, swung his arm with mine. "For what?"

"For letting me be a part of that little bit of magic. I know it's your family, but I feel like . . ." *Like I'm a part of it. Like it belongs to me, too.* But I couldn't finish the sentence, didn't want to force myself into something so intimate.

Brad dragged me toward a building, off the main part of the sidewalk. He pulled me close, wrapped his arms around me. "Like it's your history too?"

I shrugged. "Kind of."

"It is your history, Anaya." He dipped his head to mine in a kiss as sweet as double-churned ice cream. When he pulled away, he lifted the ring off my sweater and bounced it gently in the palm of his hand. "This ring has a pretty neat past, and part of its past is you. I don't regret giving it to you that day. In fact, my life has gotten a heck of a lot more exciting since you came into it. So don't you dare apologize any more for sharing this journey with me, okay? Because, Annie, I'm having the time of my life."

His emerald eyes cut to my core, and I felt myself slipping—falling—into a heady web of feelings I couldn't quite piece together or pull apart.

Again I caught a glimpse of the good that had come from that horrible day. The world might always contain evil, but somewhere in the last month I'd found a hope that out of darkness, something good—something that knew love more powerfully than hate—could be born.

CHAPTER 22
Liberty

MAY 1774

"Confound that King George, and confound the Regulars!" Graham slapped his copy of the *Boston Gazette* on the wood plank table, startling me from the letter I penned to Midwife Louisa.

Nathaniel and Michael eyed the paper, waiting for their father to give them a nod signaling they could snatch it up.

Rebekah stood from her spot on the floor where she played with James. She laid a gentle hand on Graham's massive arm, soothing the political beast within. "What is it, Papa?"

His expression softened little. "Oh, only that the high and mighty in London have ruled that the Port of Boston is to be closed." He picked up the paper. "The House of Commons calls us a 'nest of locusts.' Not one ship may enter, not one may leave, except His Majesty's warships and transports, until every farthing of tea is paid for." Graham rubbed his eyes. "'Tis a good thing you left when you did, Hugh. Half of Boston will starve beneath such an order."

Over his pipe, Hugh's steady gaze settled on me, and not for the first time, I wondered if I was the only one of us who held secrets. Yes, he'd left to come build a home for our future, but had his reasons for leaving Boston been twofold? How involved had he been in the treasonous acts in Boston, in the circular letters flying about the colonies? The scent of dinner—fish stew and corn bread—lingered heavy in the air.

"I take it the troops are back in town, then?" Hugh looked at James, playing on the floor with three wooden blocks, curls thick at the nape of his neck.

Graham nodded, slid the paper to his boys.

My chest grew tight. The thought of the captain—or the lieutenant—back on the mainland stirred up a long-forgotten panic within me. Yet certainly neither would seek me out over a bit of silver and a ring. . . .

Later that night, as I changed into my dressing gown and settled into my bed, James already sleeping snug on his straw-tick mattress on the floor, a soft knock came at the door of my chambers.

I sat up. "Who's there?" I said in a loud whisper.

"Hugh."

I gathered the blankets to my chest, called through the closed door, "I am settled for the night."

"Please, Liberty. May I come in?"

I sat up, adjusted the coverlet around me. "Very well."

His familiar form, still clad in work clothes, stood at the threshold. He left the door slightly ajar.

I wondered what being married to this man in just another month would be like. I knew I didn't deserve him. I knew I should tell him the complete truth surrounding the events of James's conception, and yet I could not risk losing him—losing the safety and comfort he provided.

Quiet steps. Candlelight on the nightstand, flickering against the wall. The sound of James's heavy breathing, content in sleep.

"Forgive me for this impropriety, but I must speak with you, my dear." The floorboard creaked as he approached and knelt beside my bed, though he did not touch the coverlet with as much as a pinkie. The scent of soap and leather and fresh-cut hay wound around me, and his breath smelled of mint leaves.

Warmth radiated through my body. I wanted him close, and I didn't. I longed for his embrace at the same time that I feared it. Would the intimacies of marriage bring forth fresh memories of the captain's crimes? Would I ever be able to find rest in a husband's arms?

His teeth glowed white in the light of the candle. "The news of the Regulars—how does it sit with you?"

I sat up, tucking the covers around my upper half. "How do you suppose it sits with me?"

"Liberty, now is not the time to take offense. I—I only wonder if we should marry sooner. I want to protect you and James. While I don't believe James's father would come looking for the girl he accosted, we can't be certain. You have never told me exactly what happened that night."

His words pinched my heart, and I thought perhaps I should be out with it. Tell him I had worked for the Crown. I had used King George's money to survive. I had cared for an enemy soldier.

Then his words from a long-ago December night came to me, replaying in my mind as they often did when I entertained telling Hugh the truth.

"You haven't the slightest need for shame. It is not as if you were associating with those blackguards or putting yourself in a foolish position."

No, Hugh could never know the reality of my unpatriotic transgressions.

"I do hope you will feel safe enough with me to tell me one day. I only want to know how best to keep you secure."

"You would hate me if I told you the truth." My bottom lip quivered.

A flicker of something foreign passed over Hugh's features—doubt? "Why? Were you parading yourself about on the Common like a camp girl?" He laughed to dispel the crazy idea.

"No, of course not." Yet his reaction confirmed my fear. If I had sunk so low as to consort with the enemy, then he could possibly hate me. Consider me below him, even. The thought pricked my eyes with tears, and I turned my back to him and lay down to hide my emotion.

"Forgive me, Liberty. That was crude of me." His fingers found my braided hair, and relief filled me when I did not flinch at his touch. "Please say you'll forgive me."

He had naught to ask forgiveness for. It was I who was buried in disloyalty and transgressions as deep as the tea in Boston Harbor. And yet the best I could do was move forward beneath Hugh's love, beneath the hope of giving my son a future. No good could come from Hugh knowing the truth at this point.

I turned to him, finding his face closer to mine than it had been before. "Of course I forgive you. And will you forgive me for not being able to share with you all of my past? Can we rest in the promise of a future together?"

He leaned in slightly, and I thought he would kiss me, almost wanted him to. But he stopped short, ever the perfect gentleman, his fingers hovering above the coverlet. "I wish you would say we had reason to marry right away."

With one word from me, we could be wed the next day. Why did I hesitate, then? Was it the truth that I kept from him, the fear I had of leaving Graham and Cora, or was it more?

"I think we should stay with our original intentions. Besides, the banns must still be read." I could only pray the banns read in nearby towns would not reach the ears of the captain. I prayed they would not incriminate me. "Also, our home is not yet complete. Cora still depends on my help. Another month will hurt nothing."

He groaned, pressed a whiskery, glancing kiss to my cheek. "I'm not so certain about that, but I am certain you know what is best. I've waited for you this long; I suppose I can wait a bit longer."

We bid good night, and he left my chambers, closing the door tight behind him.

I fell asleep, confident I had chosen a good man to spend the rest of my life with. Why, then, did I dawdle at the opportunity to wed him sooner?

The sight of the scarlet coats bubbled and simmered within me. I hadn't expected those coats in Lexington—Boston, yes, but what business did they have here?

They arrived without much show on the common. Eight of them upon horses. No doubt they could feel the hatred targeted at them. I'd been sweeping the front stoop, and the bristles of my broom froze on the hard rock slab, my breaths shallow as I watched the redcoats tether their horses and enter Buckman's Tavern, muskets at their sides.

At some level I'd been able to fool myself into thinking

all the events in Boston had been a bad dream. This life—the life I clung to and anticipated with Hugh, the one in Lexington—was real and true. Yes, we spent our nights grinding saltpeter, sulfur, and charcoal into a paste that would serve as gunpowder. We sent casks of olive oil, cured sides of meats, and bushels of corn and flour to smuggle past the gates of Boston, where our fellow men were being starved into submission. We gobbled up the *Boston Gazette* like piglets hungry for a meal, and the men signed their names on papers vowing they would mobilize at a minute's notice. But while we rallied behind our Cause, at the same time it seemed unreal. Far away. I could pretend it was some illusion.

But the sight of the harsh sunlight gleaming upon the epaulets against crimson coats made me doubt my fantasy. It brought reality screaming before me, mouth wide open and appearing like a child about to tantrum.

I quickly finished sweeping the ledge, something akin to curdled milk in my belly. I opened the keeping room window, strained my ears to hear across the green, but I couldn't make out anything of sense. Only men's voices. Certainly the Regulars were only passing through. Certainly they didn't have business here. Certainly they wouldn't avail themselves of the newly prolonged Quartering Act, forcing entry into our houses to take our beds and food.

I kept busy in the house the rest of the morning. The children were at school, Graham was in the fields, and Cora was visiting two patients. I usually loved days like this—days when it was only me and James and the wash and perhaps a poem or two. But today I didn't care a pig's tooth to be in the house alone with my son, every sound on the green making me jump, every passing clop of a horse making me contemplate a spot to hide.

After I fed James his noon meal, I tucked him upstairs for a nap, grabbed the clean wet wash sitting in the bucket in the backyard, and began the task of hanging it up to dry. The scent of lye mixed with that of Cora's herb garden. I stooped to pick up one of Michael's socks and pinned it to the line.

Then, a knock. It echoed in my head before plunging downward into my chest, reverberating around my insides until it produced nausea. I thought to run upstairs to fetch James and come back down to hide in the barn. Yet the notion was surely a silly one. The knock could be any number of people—was not the wigmaker supposed to come today to powder Graham's wig? And how many a message boy happened upon our house bringing news of a person in need of a midwife?

Still, I pretended not to hear the door, continued to hang the laundry with a rhythm I didn't normally practice.

Bend and clip.

Bend and clip.

Bend and clip.

Images of Captain Philips at the door, demanding I return his sterling, caused me to pick up my pace. He'd be mad with anger that I'd stolen from him. And I could only give him a few pounds back—the rest had been spent. I imagined him forcing me in the house, punishing me in some obscene way.

I imagined James waking to see his mother hurt, confusion and panic in his eyes.

No.

I wouldn't allow it. I'd scream for help or . . . my eyes landed on a sharp ax beside the shed. Well, I'd do what I must to protect my son.

I continued my rhythm, praying whoever continued their incessant knocking would eventually leave. How I regretted not accepting Hugh's offer to marry me sooner now. I was a fool to think I could test fate—test the Regulars. They'd killed my brother, stolen my innocence, and now I thought they would change their intent?

"Good day! I'm sorry to trouble you, but I'm looking for someone."

I froze at the sound of the man's voice, joyful and familiar. I fumbled with a pin at the line, let it drop to the muddied ground at my feet.

Then I turned.

The lieutenant stood tall in his shiny boots, the only difference since I'd last seen him being a ruddier complexion and an extra spattering of lines around his eyes. His epaulets signaled he'd been promoted. The insignia glinted against the sun.

With quaking hands, I fumbled with my skirt, searching in my deep pocket for the ring, which I always kept on my person, along with the last few pounds of the purloined sterling silver. Something about the weight of the ring and the money brought me comfort, reminded me of the means

I had to provide for myself if all suddenly went wrong as it had on that long-ago March night.

Neither brought me any consolation now.

In my desperation, I dug farther, feeling for the metal, tearing stitches in my haste. I needed him to leave. Now. He could not be here. In this moment, he frightened me more than Captain Philips ever could, for the sight of him shook up long-buried forbidden feelings.

"Miss Liberty . . . it is good to see you."

I clawed at the fabric, desperate to give him back what I owed, desperate for him to take it and leave. My fingers found a deep corner, where they brushed the sought-for metal, or was it the captain's sterling?

He took a step toward me and I ordered my fingers to cooperate.

"Are you—quite all right?"

I pushed my fingers into my pocket, stitches tore at the side of my dress, but not before my fingers grasped the contents I pursued and pulled them forth. In my trembling hands, Alexander's ring spilled on the ground, alongside the coin. I practically crawled to the spot where the signet ring lay faceup beside a mud puddle, a brown splatter on its otherwise-flawless surface. I scooped it up and thrust it at the officer.

"Forgive me. Take it and go. Not a day has gone by that I didn't wish I had passed it over."

He looked at the ring, clutched in my muddy fingers, through squinted eyes. Then he reached up a hand, folded my fingers over the heirloom.

I wished I could summon a cringe at his touch. I had sworn to myself—to James's memory—never again to cross this line. But the tender gesture gave me no reason to cower—it only made me want to cry. Standing before me was the only man who knew the struggles I'd gone through, and here, he treated me as though I were more than a victim, more than a common thief, with a single touch.

I pushed my hand at him, his still wrapped around mine in a warm embrace of fingers. "Please, sir. Forgive me."

"Liberty." He spoke my name in a brush of a whisper, slight admonishment in his tone. Exactly as I had always pictured Jesus speaking Mary Magdalene's name after He rose from the grave.

A tear eased out of my eye and I silently cursed it. Why should I cry now?

He squeezed my fingers. "I do not want the ring back. 'Tis not why I came."

"Please, please take it. I only feel guilt when I think on it." I stopped. "If you didn't come to secure the ring, why have you come?" To retrieve the money? Did he know of my child?

"I wished to be certain you fared well." He swallowed, his throat muscles bobbing in one smooth motion. "I have often thought of you since we left for Castle Island. You are not the only one to feel guilt these past years. Every day I've wished I had changed the course of things."

My bottom lip trembled. "Concern yourself no longer. What is done is done."

He released my hand; his eyes wandered briefly over the

stray chickens in the backyard. "I also want to tell you that Captain Philips . . . he is back in England."

The words took a few minutes to sink in, but when they did, relief flooded my veins.

"I did file a complaint against him for his actions in Boston . . . for what he did to you, but as you can imagine, it did not gain much credit. Yet when he requested to serve the king in London, it was granted."

I swallowed around the dryness in my mouth. "Thank you."

"I have come to ask your forgiveness, Miss Liberty. For underestimating the evil he was capable of. For not reaching you in time . . . that day."

I turned back to the wash, my mind still fuzzy from his presence, the ring still tight in my hand. I did not wish to talk about that day, to relive my humiliation in front of this man.

"Please. I feel responsible. Many are the nights when I long to turn back time, when my guilt consumes me. I haven't even the right to ask, I know. But will you forgive me?"

The blood boiled hot beneath my skin and I whirled on him. "There is naught to forgive! Did I not willfully return to the house that day? Did I not raise that candlestick to his head? Did I not have a choice to steal from you? I'm sorry if you feel guilt, but I cannot forgive a crime where none has been committed."

His bottom lip shook. "The man who pointed me to you—Dr. Richards over at the tavern—he said you have a son. A son but no husband."

Heat crept up my neck to my face. I didn't answer. Curse that Dr. Richards. While most assumed I was a widow, Dr. Richards seemed always willing to discredit me or Cora in any way that might gain him a patient or two. Even if that patient was a redcoat.

I spun back to my laundry, feigning not to hear the question. Or statement, rather. The heat of his gaze seared my shoulders, and for some mad reason I wanted to turn toward him and tell him all. How I hated all the Regulars—even him—with a passion that scared me. How I held the horrible secret of my disloyalty from everyone—even my intended. How I hated myself now for even wanting to confess these things to him—the enemy.

His footsteps from behind. Then a feather-light touch on my elbow.

"Sir . . ."

"Please, Liberty. You've called me Alexander once before." His intimate tone caused a not-unpleasant shiver to scurry up my spine.

I shook my head, my face still at the clothesline. "You were right about something that night. I was young. I am wiser now, and I think—I think you should leave."

And I hated myself for wanting him to stay. I conjured up images of my brother's bleeding body in the snow on that early March night, tried to pin the blame on the lieutenant as I had when I'd stolen his ring, but all I could see was him standing up to Captain Philips for my safety that same night, the sheen in his eyes and a hatchet in his hand after the captain had left my chambers that last horrible day.

I stooped to pick up a pair of Graham's breeches. Alexander gently tugged them from me. "Do you know how many dreams I've had taking me back to that day? Every time—every dream—I chop down that door in time to stop him from that unspeakable act." Raw pain consumed those green eyes, and I didn't doubt for a moment that he told the truth.

I broke the connection. "'Tis not your fault. *Please.* You must leave." Whereas before I was frightened for my own life and that of my son, now I wanted him to leave for an altogether different reason. This man—enemy or not—was on my side. I couldn't bring myself to hate him so, and yet he was still very much the enemy. And I was a traitor.

He clasped my hand in one smooth motion, and I prayed Cora wouldn't happen upon me in such a state. A state which I had to continually remind myself I was *not* enjoying in the least.

His thumb rubbed a small circle on the inside of my wrist, and though it should have felt presumptuous, it did not. "Since my return to Boston, I've been set on finding you. You are a bit of a tough chase, too."

"You shouldn't have bothered."

His thumb went still at the spot where my pulse thrummed up a rapid, disloyal beat. "I've come to ask your hand in marriage."

I blinked, mind numb. I couldn't have heard right, and yet his hands, his eyes, his posture, left me knowing I indeed heard him correctly. "That is the most preposterous thing I have ever heard."

He straightened. "I do not see that it is so very silly. I could bring you beneath my protection. Help you raise your son, even. I could find you a place up north, perhaps. I care for you, Liberty. I have not stopped thinking about you these past years."

"You hardly know me. No doubt you have dreamed me into a fanciful damsel in distress. You only feel needless guilt, and it is causing you to make rash and unwise decisions."

"What is unwise about marriage to a woman I care for, to a woman whose life will forever be hard because of my poor choices?"

"And I suppose you'd have me raise my son a Tory?" I spat the words.

"No. No, this has naught to do with political matters. I realize it won't be easy, but I would do whatever it took."

His words lingered between us. Was I fancying the idea, or did he hint at desertion? Would he leave the Crown for me? I cast the idea aside. Ludicrous. No sane officer would entertain such a notion.

I closed my eyes, took a deep breath. "Alexander."

I felt his fingers along the smoothness of my cheek, and I leaned into them, shame erupting in my belly, the scent of cedar familiar. I opened my eyes to see his face close to mine.

"Yes?" he said.

"Alexander, I am betrothed."

His hand dropped. "I see."

"Surely you see this is for the better. You can be released of your guilt without having to marry an American. Isn't that right?"

"Liberty, I care not what side of the Crown you fall on." He laughed—a short, humorless sound. "You never saw yourself for who you truly are."

"I know who I am." A traitor. A thief. Though Hugh made me feel far apart from all of those ugly words. Of course with him, I would always be hiding truth in the shadows. With him, I would always be a liar.

Alexander's shoulders drooped, and he shook his head. "You were always like an angel to me."

I wanted to climb inside his thoughts and view myself the way he claimed to view me. What did he see that was so incredibly good?

"You are happy with this man, then?"

Foolish question. Marriages were not about happiness. They were about a mutual need requiring fulfillment. A safe and nurturing environment in which to rear children. "I am content, yes."

"Might you be more content with me?"

I folded my arms in front of me. "You are entirely too bold to ask such a question." And I was a fool to even think on the answer.

He smiled, but it quickly melted off his lips. "You will never see past this red coat, will you?"

I shook my head, heard James babbling upstairs to himself. "I think not."

He pressed his mouth into a thin line. "May I at least see you one more time before I go back to Boston? It is the least you could do for me, no? I have made up an outrageous lie to take my troops down here as it is. I am staying at Buckman's Tavern. Will you meet me tonight? Just so I may say good-bye to you for good?"

"I don't think—"

"Please, Liberty. I wish no regrets when we part this time."

I couldn't say no. Did I not owe him this much? "Very well."

Once again he smiled, revealing the dimple in his left cheek. I'd forgotten about that pleasant dip of skin.

He lifted my hand in his to graze my knuckles with his mouth. "Thank you. You have—"

"Here now! What are you about?" A deep clearing of a throat sounded from behind me, followed by the cock of a pistol. "Step away from her now, you lobsterback, or I'll blow your head to bloody bits."

I'd never heard such hard words come from Hugh Gregory's mouth.

CHAPTER 23
Anaya

I LOOKED AT Brad over the center console of his Accord. "Ready?"

He turned onto Lydia's street. "Gee, I kind of feel like a kid who's about to meet my date's parents."

I clutched the bowl of marshmallow salad in my lap. "Am I that bad? Sorry, it's just that Lydia asking me—and you—over is a big step." Or rather, Lydia agreeing to Grace's suggestion that they have us over. Still a big step.

On Easter, no less. A time of new birth, new beginnings. I'd attended church with Lydia's family that morning—again at Grace's invitation. Grace had sung and strummed her guitar to a song called "Cornerstone," and I felt something foreign stir within. As soft as a whisper, as strong as a solid oath. I didn't evaluate it too much for fear of scaring it away. I thought on Brad's proposition from a while back that we depend on someone stronger than ourselves. Words from the song replayed in my mind, drawn out by reminders of the ring.

> *Weak made strong in the Savior's love . . .*
> *I rest on His unchanging grace . . .*
> *My anchor holds within the veil . . .*

I couldn't even pretend to understand what they all meant, but whether it was emotion or the holiday, I glimpsed victory in that song and rested in the words.

At least I had in church, during the sermon. And even when I'd gone home to make the marshmallow salad. But now, on my sister's street, I wrestled with them, wanting to retake control.

"So, Lydia and I, we haven't talked about her meeting you in the hospital. She doesn't know I took your card from her Bible."

"Okay . . ."

"I was kind of hoping you could, like, go along with her if she pretends she never met you before. I don't know how much Grace has told her about you." I tapped a fingernail on the glass of the marshmallow salad bowl. Petty of me to even ask. But Lydia meeting Brad could really mess things up. I felt our journey to reconciliation was going smooth.

Slower than a snail on wet plaster, but smooth. I wasn't ready to confront her about Brad's card, or anything to do with the time after the bombing. We were okay, going along at our own pace, for the most part ignoring the past.

"I'm not going to be dishonest, Annie."

"I'm not asking you to lie. Just, you know, don't bring up that day at the hospital."

"It's not like I was going to come right out and ask her why she didn't give you my card."

"Great. Thank you."

"I was going to wait until after dinner at least."

I flicked his arm.

He laughed. "No worries, I'll play it cool. But really, don't you think you should talk to her about all this?"

I shrugged. "I'm waiting on her timing. I don't want to push too hard, you know? I'm the one who made the decision to stay away, to ignore phone calls and texts. I'm here now, offering myself back into their family. The ball's in her court."

He didn't say anything, and we turned into Lydia's driveway.

The sun made its weary descent behind the still-bare maple in front of my sister's house. I knocked on the door and Lydia opened it, surprising me with what looked like a genuine smile and a "Happy Easter." I wanted to hug her as we would have done in the past, especially on holidays, but she didn't offer her arms and I sensed such a gesture wouldn't be appreciated. I'd settle for the smile and the welcome, however forced it may or may not be. Scents of baked ham and green beans beckoned us into the warmth of the house.

Lydia reached for Brad's hand as I introduced them. I tried to brush off the tension thick in the air. Had Lydia noticed the card missing from her Bible?

"Nice to see you again." Brad smiled warmly. A part of me admired that he refused to be dishonest for even a second. Another part of me could have strangled him for adding the word *again* to his greeting.

Joel sauntered over, stuck his hand out to Brad in a very grown-up manner. "Hey. Heard you build things." He shoved his hands in his pockets and rocked back on his heels, much as I'd seen Roger do in the past.

"I sure do. You a builder too?"

He bobbed his head, his mouth pressed in a serious line. "Legos mostly. But I helped Dad build a shed last summer. We finished it in one week."

Brad whistled. "That's some pretty serious building. I'd love to see it."

Without taking his hands out of his pockets, Joel jerked his head toward the backyard. "Come on. Dad's out there now."

"Grab your coat, young man. It's not spring yet, despite what the calendar says." Lydia closed the door behind me and rolled her eyes. "I caught him out there after church in a T-shirt."

I placed the marshmallow salad into Lydia's waiting hands and shed my own coat, hanging it on the rack in the foyer.

Lydia started to the kitchen. "I'm just finishing up the sweet potato and green bean casseroles."

I placed a gentle hand on her elbow. "Thank you. For inviting me—us—today."

Lydia smiled but pulled away slightly from my touch. "We're glad to have you."

I ignored her likely unintentional move from me and concentrated instead on her genuine tone. I wanted to ask her if she was thinking the same thing I was when we were in church this morning. That new beginnings were always possible. That maybe God could help us repair our broken relationship. Wouldn't that be small beans compared to bursting forth from a sealed grave?

But I didn't want to scare her.

"Brad seems nice." She put the marshmallow salad in a fridge full of cheesecakes and pies.

"He is." I stood at the corner of the kitchen island. Remembered how Brad encouraged me to be straight with Lydia. Honest. "He's the guy who gave me the ring the day of the bombing."

She poured milk into a glass casserole dish and whisked it together with the cream of mushroom soup. Her gaze flicked to me, and I thought I saw something in it. Recognition? Guilt? "No way."

"Yeah, he said he saw—"

"You know what?" The interruption, perfectly timed, couldn't have been more clear. She didn't want to talk. Not about the day of the bombing, not about Brad's card, and probably not about breaking down that wall between us. "Grace is upstairs. She's been up there awhile. Do you mind checking on her?"

If it hadn't been an excuse to get me out of the kitchen and away from her, I would have taken her trusting me with a small task that involved Grace as a step forward in our healing—a stone removed from the barrier before us.

I looked at her back, her body shaking slightly with the furious whisking of milk and mushroom soup. "Sure . . . I'll head up there."

I shook off the feeling of defeat and jogged up the stairs, the muscles of my thighs protesting and feeling every foot of the four-mile run I'd completed early that morning. While it was beyond hard to lift my head off the pillow, swig down some juice, pull on my running clothes, and push myself out into the cold weather, my waistline—and my overall demeanor— was thanking me. How had I gone so long without this fuel?

I thought of Brad, of our discovery the week before, of our evenings together the past several days. Instead of trying to find further pieces of the story of the ring, we'd simply enjoyed the find. We'd watched the Red Sox take on the Phillies, we visited the Boston Marathon exhibit at Faneuil Hall Marketplace, cuddled on my couch watching *Rocky* movies, played wall ball with my landlord's daughter, Emilia, and made up our own stories of how Liberty came into possession of the ring—a ring that was important enough to her family that it was left to the sons and daughters of nine generations.

I didn't voice the thought, but I wanted a spectacular story for the ring. I think Brad did too. It was likely the reason we weren't rushing to find any more answers right away.

I did know one thing. Somewhere in the past few weeks, I'd started living again. It was akin to flying, and I couldn't get enough of it.

I took a right down the hall, knocked on Grace's half-open door.

"Come in."

I peered around her door. Grace's little-girl pink walls had been done over in muted shades of green and blue, reminding me of a spring day. Posters of mountains and lakes adorned her wall. A *Boston Strong* T-shirt hung in a large frame above her desk. Avoiding it, I looked at another poster—a single green tree growing tilted from a bare, hard-rocked cliff, with text underneath: "Winners are committed to hang in there long enough to win."

I almost missed Grace, lying supine on her bed. Her hair lay wet, soaking the pillow, her eyes closed. She wore flannel shorts. And no prosthetic.

I tried not to stare at the stump of her leg, about three inches below the hem of her shorts. It surprised me with its smoothness, pulled tight at the end in one long scar.

I lowered myself on the bed beside her. "You okay, kiddo?"

Her eyelids fluttered open. "Oh, hey. Thought you were Mom." She smiled. "I took a shower after my run. Sometimes the hot water and exercise swells my leg and it won't fit into the socket. I just have to wait a bit for the swelling to go down."

"I—I didn't realize—"

She squeezed my hand. "It's okay, Auntie. Really. It happens."

I didn't have a clue about half her struggles. And here I was, thinking I was ready for new beginnings. Grace would never get a new beginning. A new limb. Her hurts were forever.

I pressed her hand back. Above her bed was a snapshot of a group of people beside Boston Public Library—near the finish line of the Boston Marathon. I spotted Grace at the front, searched the other faces, recognized a few from news interviews.

"All the amputees, right?"

Grace smiled. "Yeah. We kind of bonded, you know? We encourage each other. Sympathize with the struggles, the bad days."

While I didn't want to dwell here, especially on Easter, I had to know. "Will the trial being over bring you closure?"

It was a question I'd been asked myself. I still didn't have an answer, but I couldn't help wondering what Grace's would be. She drew in a breath and her stomach rose. "A lot of those people in the picture with me . . . they think it will. A lot of them are for the death penalty, though not all of them."

She quieted.

"What do you think, Grace?"

She swallowed, took her hand from mine to clasp hers together. "I think evil's in the world. And one trial, like, isn't going to change that. But I think justice needs to be served.

Death . . . I'm not so certain. I wouldn't want to be responsible for sending anyone to their death, even someone others may consider the worst of sinners."

She lifted her residual limb up, then lowered it in what I assumed was a sort of physical therapy exercise she could probably do in her sleep. "You know the apostle Paul? He called himself the worst of sinners. He persecuted people. Imprisoned a lot of Christians, condoned their murders, even. It was pure evil. And to save him, he only looked to one person."

"Christ," I whispered.

Grace smiled, her straight teeth perfect against her flawless skin. "A guilty charge or the death penalty isn't enough to wipe out the evil done on that day two years ago. I get that the courts have to do their job—that's a good thing. And who knows, maybe it will provide some closure. All I know is for me, the healing didn't begin until I let God take over." She sat up, reached for her prosthetic cover, and slipped it over her limb.

I didn't want to go downstairs. I wanted to mull over Grace's words, ask her more questions, soak up her peace. But she was already rolling the liner of her regular prosthesis over her leg, and Lydia called to us that dinner was ready.

"Hey, kiddo?"

She looked up from squirting a mixture labeled *rubbing alcohol/water* into her prosthesis.

"Thank you. For accepting me back into the family. For forgiving me."

She pushed me gently. "Auntie, you're crying. Stop it. Of course you're a part of our family. That didn't go away just because you did." She stood and pushed her residual limb into the socket, creating a whooshing sound of air. "Don't worry. Mom will get there. I only had to forgive you for myself. I think . . . when you're a mother, it's different, you know. Like Mom feels if she forgives you, she's saying it's okay that you hurt me—hurt our family."

I nodded, ordered the truth of the words not to bring more tears to my eyes.

"I could, like, talk to her for you."

I shook my head. "Your mom and I need to tear down our own walls. You've already done more than you know, Grace."

We started downstairs. "She'll come around. You'll see."

CHAPTER 24
Liberty

MAY 1774

"You deaf and dumb? I said step away from her." Hugh's voice was hard. I scarce recognized it.

Alexander dropped my hand and backed away from me. I moved my mouth to try and assure Hugh that Alexander had meant no harm, but no words came out. What could I say to explain why he was here? Why he was in such close proximity to me? His marriage proposal would sound more absurd coming from me as an explanation than it had coming from Alexander himself.

Hugh came closer, his breaths heavy beneath a sweat-drenched shirt, the pistol still aimed at Alexander.

"I'm well, Hugh. No harm is done."

He ignored me. "If I see you on this property again, I will shoot you without warning. Is that understood?"

Any other British officer would stand up to a colonist with a pitiful pistol, tell him that he was threatening the king himself, that he stood to go to the town gallows that very night. And how would he like to hang beside the graves of suicides, alongside other hopeless riffraff just like him? But Alexander nodded, looked at me one last time—which I sensed further enraged Hugh—turned, and walked around the house and out of the backyard.

Hugh's rapid breathing didn't cease, his eyes wild with unfettered fury. He lowered the pistol.

Upstairs, James called for me.

"You knew him."

It wasn't a question.

The sun dipped behind a cloud, and I scooped up Graham's breeches—the pair Alexander had taken from me not minutes before—and went back to clipping them to the line. "Yes." I tried to sound nonchalant. As if that were that, and now it was time to tend to my laundry.

James called for me again. I brushed my hands against my skirt, realized my left hand still held tight to the ring.

"Your dress. It's ripped. Did he—"

"No, Hugh! No. I simply tore it."

He grasped my arms, the muscles in his fingers pinning me tighter than the tension in the clothesline. "So help me, Liberty Caldwell. Tell me the truth now, or I will round up the militia and drive that man out of town on account of him accosting you."

I shook off his hands, feeling as if I were a child being scolded by her father. "He did not accost me, and that is the truth of it."

Hugh rubbed the muscles in the back of his neck. My heart went out to him with the single gesture. He was working hard building a home for us. Working hard to provide for James and me. He acted this way out of love. Should I blame him? Yet Alexander meant no harm.

I reached my hand out to Hugh, let my fingers flutter just enough to graze the hair plastered to his skin. "I am well, darling. Please do not fret."

"Was that James's father?" He whispered the words, bound in tangible fear.

Again, James called to me.

I forced out an awkward laugh. "Don't be foolish." Yet there was nothing so very foolish about it. "Now excuse me; I must go see to my son." Something about how my words came out sounded divisive. *My son.* As if in a few short weeks Hugh wouldn't offer up paternity to James out of love for me, as if he didn't love my son already.

Nevertheless, I didn't rescind them. I needed distance between us, or Hugh would push me for answers I couldn't give.

I scurried up the stairs to James, thankful Hugh didn't follow. When I reached my son, I pulled him close, buried my face in his precious brown locks, so like my brother's, and inhaled the scent of lye soap that clung to his clean clothes.

I thought of my brother while holding his namesake. "I am so sorry, James," I whispered.

If I was to honor my brother, if I was to honor my husband-to-be, I could not see Alexander this night. Or ever again.

My son stayed still beneath my affections and played with my mud-crusted fingers until he pried out the ring, holding it in chubby fingers.

It was just as bright as a newly minted shilling. I could still remember it on Alexander's hand the night he read me *The Odyssey*.

I let the fact sink in that Captain Philips was an ocean away, that he would likely never come back to the colonies, that James and I were free of him forever.

In my thoughts, I replayed Alexander's sincere marriage proposal and tried to convince myself that I should risk meeting him tonight, at the very least to thank him for seeking me out, to thank him for his offer of protection. To return the ring.

Of course, I would never be able to share all of this with Hugh. And I would never be able to forgive myself for letting Alexander leave without a proper farewell.

From where he sat on my lap, James dropped the ring. It clattered to the wood planks of the floor where it spun around in circles and finally settled, its golden brilliance gleaming from where the sun shone through the window.

And the guilt returned. For no matter which decisions I

made, the fact remained—Hugh could never know of my involvement in Boston at the officers' house. He could never share in my shame. He could never know how I had fallen in love with one of the king's Regulars.

Bored on my lap, James slid to the floor, then stuck his bottom up in the air to push himself to a walking position. He lifted the ring and studied it, as if trying to figure out its sordid history. He held it out to me. "What's this, Mama? What's this?"

As I looked at my son, together with the ring, a knowing settled over me. I would marry Hugh. He was an honorable man, and the best fit for a secure future for James. And while my heart may not thrum for him as it did—traitor that I was—for a certain red-coated man, I would do all in my power to love him as I should, to honor him as a wife and lover.

And I would throw myself into this very role first thing tomorrow morning. After I put the past behind me forever. After I said farewell and insisted Alexander take his ring back for good.

I stole across the green in the shadow of night, the press of time tight upon me. I did not have long. James would sleep through my absence, no doubt. Rebekah would tend to him if he woke to find me gone, as she had the many times I'd been out into the early hours of morning.

No, James was not my worry.

I thought of Hugh, asleep in his brother's house, his body weary from a long day of building our home, tending to fledgling fields, seeing that he donated some to the starving people of Boston. His mind likely full of unrest at the crimson-coated visitor. I felt I played the part of the unfaithful wife, three weeks away from marriage. I should turn around, steal away to my safe bed, keep the ring tucked in the pocket of my dress for all of time, and forget about Alexander.

And how would my guilt play out then? To know that I had shunned the only man who knew the full extent of my sins—who had nevertheless accepted me and wanted me as his wife. No, my attachment to Alexander was a moot point. When it came down to it, this meeting was the decent thing to do. Returning the ring was the decent thing to do. With all my past disgrace taunting me, I was ready to act honorably. Even if my husband-to-be didn't agree with my actions.

The tavern whispered of sleeping inhabitants, of dirty dishes waiting until morning, of old fires and whiskey aged to a strong tang. I idled beneath a maple for a short time, wondering how Alexander could possibly know of my presence. More likely than not, I'd go home without our farewell. The thought both relieved and disappointed me. I had tried. And yet I wouldn't risk my fool of a heart any more shame.

And then the door of the tavern opened, and his familiar shadow stepped out. As he came closer to me, the light of the moon showed his uniform absent of a red coat. He was only a man. Not a coldhearted killer or even the pawn of a king. He was a man. A man who cared for me.

As he walked to me, his shoulders back and profile regal, it was as if an invisible force drew me to him. And I knew all at once it had been a mistake to come. I should have borne the guilt of not saying good-bye. Of not attempting to return the ring once more. I should have risked this small remorse to honor my husband-to-be.

He ducked beneath the tree, clasped my shaking hands in his own. "Thank you for coming."

"I've done so against my better judgment." I inhaled the scent of cedar and soap, did not resist when he stepped a bit closer.

"Tell me you love him, Liberty, and I won't beg you to come away with me. I won't profess my own feelings for you. If you tell me such now, I will turn and go back into the tavern a happy enough man knowing you are happy."

My head swam with his words, with his presence sucking the air from the night, with his tall form hovering over me, his warm breath washing me in a dream.

My hesitation seemed answer enough. For when Alexander pulled me closer and lowered his mouth to mine, I did not resist. I allowed myself to become caught up in the pleasant heat emanating from him, allowed my body to shamelessly press along his.

He tamed his lips against mine. I could feel how he restrained himself, and I teased him, begging him with my own hungry mouth, relishing the slight taste of salt upon his tongue.

He gave in easily, his arms coming around me in hasty pleasure, his lean muscles strong yet tender against my sides. I melted into him, forgetting. Forgetting what should be done, forgetting my responsibilities to a husband-to-be.

I could allow this man to love me. I could love him back. Things could be . . . just like this. Behind the curtain of passion and ardor, anything seemed possible. A life in the mountains, away from the town and redcoats and a starving Boston. Alexander being a father to—

I pulled away, reality coming to a halting crash on my moment of indiscretion. I put my hands on his chest, pressed him back slightly. "I shouldn't have—"

He quieted my words by dipping his mouth back to mine. "You care for me, Liberty. I feel it in your kiss." Another sweet taste of him. "Please don't deny it. We can be together."

I thought of running. I thought of staying. My mind scrambled for a way to make everything right. Everyone happy. In the end, it always came down to what was best for James. At one pitifully low point, I even tried to convince myself that what was best for James was what was best for his mother. Me. And running away with Alexander was what was best.

Yet running away where? To a hovel in the woods? What happened when Alexander was found and shot on the common for desertion? What happened when he was ridiculed for who he was—loyal to the Crown? Would he stand by us?

Could I stand by him? What sort of legacy of honor was I bringing my child up into—my child, the namesake of my dear brother who had died for freedom?

With final determination, I pushed Alexander away. Hard. "I—I do care for you, Alexander. More than I dare admit. But we can't be together. My son . . . Hugh . . . the Crown. There are too many reasons to count."

"I love you, Liberty. It is more than enough to come up against your other reasons."

"You are a sentimentalist."

"You must be so also to kiss me as you did."

I knew he wouldn't back off easily. It came to me then how to dissuade him. Lord, forgive me. But my cruelty would hurt less for him in the end, I was certain.

I breathed deep, forced the ugly words from my mouth— the same mouth that not moments before had been upon this man in a show of passion. I schooled my voice to exhibit sincerity, sorrow. "Alexander, you are not listening to me. A kiss is only a kiss. Many times have I kissed Captain Philips with similar show."

I watched the slow shock on his face in the patches of moonlight that filtered through the trees. "You lie."

I forced my gaze to remain on his. "I do not. I'm sorry, Alexander, but I was not as innocent as you presumed me to be."

"I don't believe it." Yet his wary gaze showed his doubts, which hurt ten times worse than the words I spoke. Did he really think me capable of giving away kisses to the captain while I fell in love with him?

"And, Liberty Caldwell, do you kiss this Hugh—your betrothed—in the same manner?"

Oh, that I should feel such an overwhelming need to kiss Hugh that way. Why could not my passion be directed in such a fashion? I looked away from Alexander's intense gaze. "Yes," I whispered.

I wanted to hear him call me a disloyal whore, to anger him with my betrayal, to prove to him my sinful heart. Instead, he backed away a step. "Do you love him?"

"Yes." And I did, didn't I? Who would be so foolish as to not love a man who would take me as his wife, who would take my son as his own without knowing my history?

A small smile tilted Alexander's sweet mouth, which even now called to me. "You are pushing me away, dear one. And yet it is not my place to beg you. Know, though, that I will always love you, my sweet lass. How many times have I replayed that night in my mind, when we were together by the fire? How many times have I stopped Philips from his indecency? And now, how many times will I fall asleep, knowing you are in another's bed, wishing very much that my life were his?"

His words caused a tear to seep out of my eye. "You go too far, Alexander. Even if we were to be together, you would be sorely mistaken when you realized I am not the sweet lass you claim me to be. You should leave this town as quickly as possible."

He brought his hand to my chin. "Would you set him against me, Liberty? Would you rally Lexington's minutemen so that they hunt me down and do away with me forever? Is that what your heart desires?"

No! No, it was not what it desired at all. I stood on my tiptoes, pressed a last kiss to his cheek. "Farewell, Alexander. Do not ever regret this night, and I will try very hard not to either." I searched the ring from the pocket of my cloak, pressed it into his warm palm, and ducked out from beneath the tree before he could protest. I scurried across the green to the house where Hugh slept, perhaps dreaming of me.

Whom did I fool? I already regretted this night. For instead of hiding one secret from the man I was to marry, I now hid two. And how much worse was the second sin of my heart, committed three weeks away from the bond of marriage?

CHAPTER 25

Anaya

"YOU'RE GOING TO have to roll me up the stairs to my apartment." I placed a hand over my stomach as Brad and I made our way up. "I have to remember that just because I'm running a little now does not mean I can pig out on my sister's carrot cake."

Brad laughed, offered his arm. "It sure was good. And she's not at all the tyrant you made her out to be, either."

I stopped midstep. "I never said that."

He scrunched up his face. "You implied she might be hard to get along with. . . ."

"I told you she was having trouble forgiving me. That's a lot different than hard to get along with. And for your

255

information, I tried to bring up the hospital, your card and all that, and she totally changed the topic."

"Just give her time."

I slid my key in the door. "Whose side are you on anyway?"

"Annie . . . yours, of course. Always. I'm trying to encourage you. And if you keep thinking you two are on different sides, you'll never get to where you want to be with her."

We stepped in, closed the door behind us. He was right. I put my keys on the hook beside the door. "Maybe I've read *Little Women* too many times. I've just always felt that sisters were supposed to be close. But why? Because we come from the same womb?" Yes, I'd done a horrible thing. But I'd apologized. *I* wanted to start new. What more could I do?

"You grew up together. Things will fall into place, you'll see." Brad wrapped his arms around me, started kissing my temple, then trailed his mouth down my cheekbone. He let out a sound of frustration. "Six comes early on a Monday. I should go; it's late."

I tilted my face up toward him. "Too late for *Rocky V*?"

He groaned. "Pulling out the big guns, huh?"

I giggled. "I've just had such an amazing week with you. I don't want it to end."

He nudged my cheek with his nose. "You have the day off tomorrow, right?"

"Right."

"If the inspector comes to the job site first thing like he's supposed to, how 'bout I cut out early and we be tourists on the Freedom Trail?"

I turned into his lips. "I can't think of a better way to spend my day."

He pulled away to see my face. "Me neither. In fact, you're starting to scare me a little, Anaya."

"How so?"

"I—I've never felt about anybody the way I feel about you. It seems like what's happening, like it's some sort of fast, exhilarating ride that I never want to get off of."

He'd grown serious, and I found myself doing the same. Hoppy toads—the little fast kind—jumped around in my stomach. I inhaled that spicy wood scent I'd come to associate with him alone. I ran my tongue over my teeth, avoided his deliberate gaze. "I know what you mean."

His breaths played against my forehead and I leaned into them. Closer, closer still. "Do you think we've separated ourselves from it yet?"

"It?"

"You know, the whole trauma thing around our first meeting. Let's face it—you wouldn't have given me a second glance if you hadn't found out I was the one who gave you the ring that day."

"That's not true." Not completely anyway. The hoppy toads settled in my stomach. Was it true? There was no denying that the force that drew me to Brad was his role as my hero that day. Since I'd met him, the anxious, sweat-producing, nightmare fairy-tale dreams had nearly stopped. I felt myself healing. "Okay, maybe it is a little true. But so what? We're together now and I'm not looking to turn back, so what does it matter?"

He shrugged. "I guess I'm scared you have a sort of tunnel vision when it comes to me. Like you're going to wake up one day and realize I'm not the hero you thought I was. I'm not perfect, Annie. And yes, there are things about me you don't know."

"Tell me, then. I want to know everything." I grasped his face between my hands. "The good and the bad, Brad. We all have things in our past we're not proud of. It's a part of you. I think I can take it."

He looked at the space behind me and his eyes grew dark. It scared me. He was always so open and honest.

I stroked his slightly stubbled cheek with my finger. "It's the war—I know it is. Won't you share your burden with me?"

He ran his hands up my arms until our fingers were entwined. Then he led my hands away from his face, clasped them to his chest. "Annie, I—I love you. And because I do, this is one burden I have to bear alone."

If I could have thought on his words longer, I would have disagreed with him. Love shared all burdens, didn't it? But I was so caught up in his confession of love, I couldn't think straight enough to argue. My brain grew fuzzy and I leaned against him, suddenly not strong or sturdy enough to hold myself up.

"I think I love you, too," I whispered. He lowered his mouth to mine to capture my lips in a gentle kiss that made every one of my nerve endings tingle. He tasted of peppermint and new beginnings. Of Christmas mornings and steamy summer nights. He deepened the kiss, and I leaned into him farther. Ran my hand over the back of his hair—not much longer than the Marines would have allowed—then his neck. We sunk into each other, and while my heart thrummed out a crazy melody and I longed for more, I also felt a foreign feeling of contentment settle over me. Like this—this was how it was supposed to be. This was the man I was supposed to be with.

And Brad was right: it was a little scary.

Frighteningly, awfully scary.

In a really good way.

"Man, I can't get enough of this stuff." Brad pointed at Paul Revere's engraving of the Boston Massacre. It sat just below the large front window of the Old State House. Behind the redcoats pictured firing into a crowd of colonists was a depiction of the same State House we stood in. A red circle had been drawn around the window in the engraving, connected to the letters *You Are Here.*

"Me neither," I admitted.

"If only we had a DeLorean and a flux capacitor."

I rolled my eyes. "If only."

He bumped my side with his arm. "Well, don't you? It would make figuring out this whole story a walk in the park."

We'd taken both an Old State House tour and a Boston

Massacre tour, hoping to glean some new insight into that tragic winter night 245 years ago, hoping to come to a better understanding of Liberty's poem. But while we'd taken in a bunch of amazing history, none of it seemed to bring us closer to learning more about Liberty and the ring.

We exited the building and headed southwest along the path of bricks that signaled the Freedom Trail.

I imagined living during the Revolution, befriending a girl named Liberty who loved a British soldier. What was she like? Did he love her, too? How did they meet? And had their love been doomed from the start?

We toured the Old South Meeting House and walked past the said-to-be-haunted Omni Parker House hotel, a historic meeting place of writers Henry David Thoreau, Henry Wadsworth Longfellow, and Ralph Waldo Emerson. We explored King's Chapel Burying Ground, then walked up the stone steps to the Old Granary Burying Ground—the final resting place of John Hancock, Sam Adams, and Paul Revere.

We turned right and stood in front of Samuel Adams's grave. Beside him was a large headstone listing the five victims of the Boston Massacre, above the name of a twelve-year-old boy, a victim of the first struggles between the Patriots and the Crown.

"Hey." Brad pointed to the grave. "James Caldwell. That's Liberty's maiden name, right?"

I nodded. "You don't think . . ."

"Caldwell's a pretty common name, but it's worth a check." Brad pulled out his phone and punched in one of the websites we'd used the past few weeks. He did a search for James Caldwell, date of death March 5, 1770 in Boston. Two records came up. He clicked on the first, *Deaths Registered in the City of Boston*. It listed James's name, date of death, cause of death, where he was buried, and finally, under the *Family* heading, one name.

Sister: Liberty Caldwell

CHAPTER 26
Liberty

MAY 1774

I slipped into the keeping room with utmost care, stepping out of my muddy boots and allowing my stocking-clad feet to smooth out any noise the door made.

A movement from the corner of the room, where Graham's chair was kept, echoed through the quiet house. "So help me, Liberty, I consider myself a patient man." My heart skidded to a halt at the sound of Hugh's voice.

"Hugh, I—you gave me a fright."

"Where have you been?"

I didn't think the lie through; I only told it. "To aid in a birth. The call came late. I thought not to wake Cora but to—"

A hard slam—his fist on the nearby table. "You lie!"

My future—James's future—crumbled before me with the two words, and I scrambled to make him believe my story. "'Twas a girl of—"

"I saw you." Hugh's soft words barely made it past my frantic ones.

"What?"

"I saw you outside the tavern. With him."

"Hugh, you must believe me. He is not James's father—"

"Who then is he, Liberty? For you seemed all too familiar with him beneath the tree."

I collapsed under the weight of the truth. With a single decision I'd ruined my son's future. Now there was naught to do but allow honesty to prevail. "I—when I came to Boston to find my brother, I had given the last of my money to a farmer for a ride. It was November. I was on the streets, accosted by a group of young men. An officer helped me. He offered me an employ in his home—one he shared with another officer. He was always kind, never inde—"

"You loved him." He spoke the words calmly.

I was grateful for the dark of the house, so I could spare myself a bit of shame.

"He is not James's father. It was the other officer who forced himself on me. I know I should not have worked for them, but I had little choice. The streets or—"

"There is always a choice, Liberty!"

A stretch of silence. Footsteps on the stairs. "Brother, is all well?" Graham.

A groan from Hugh. "No. But please, go back to bed."
The footsteps receded.

I took tentative steps in Hugh's direction, reached for him in the dark. "Please, Hugh. I regret my choices every day. But I did not ask to be an unwed mother. I did nothing indecent. You must believe me. You never demanded the truth from me, and I have been grateful for that."

He snapped his hand away from mine. "All you have done is lie, Liberty. How can we base a marriage on that? Every time you have a call in the middle of the night, I will remember this night—remember how you ran to another, a lobster, no less."

I fought the urge to shush him, for it did indeed sound horrible. "I told him farewell this very night, told him I loved you."

A derisive snort. How I much preferred his sweet words to me over this show of unbelief and hatred. "And do you, Liberty? Do you love me?"

I knew if I were to break through to him at all I would have to be honest, beginning this moment. I swallowed down the urge to tell him yes, of course I loved the man I was to wed. Instead, I forced the truth through parted lips. "I care for you very much, Hugh. I *want* to love you."

"And you love *him*?"

I shook my head. "I feel . . . strongly for him. He was with me during that horrible time—"

"And did nothing to stop it."

I opened my mouth to defend the lieutenant, to tell

Hugh that Alexander had tried with all his might to get to me that horrid afternoon, but what use would it be? Painting Alexander in a favorable light would do nothing to soften Hugh's heart toward me now.

He sucked in a shaking breath, the sound cutting through the dark. "I didn't realize how young you were when I asked for your hand in marriage, Liberty. You are but a girl, not so much in age perhaps, but in your fanciful thoughts. You flit back and forth in your desires. You tell lies to gain a secure future. I thought I saw something honorable in you. I see now that I was wrong."

The words stung me, more than I would have expected.

"And now you will be the one to leave when I truly need you?" I whispered.

"Did you not truly have need of me before this night, then? I have offered myself to you, given you many chances, rose above my own doubts. But I can no longer ignore them, Liberty. A marriage is built on trust, and I fear there is no mending that between us."

My bottom lip trembled at the thought of my life without him. It trembled at the words, sharp as arrows, that left his lips to pierce my heart. If only they weren't true, they would not have the power to pierce as they did.

I thought to beg but couldn't leave my pride to do so. And flitting though I was, I knew I could run back to Alexander, that he would make a way for us and for my son if Hugh wouldn't.

"I suppose that is all there is to say between us, then." I

crossed my arms in front of me, trying to contain the shudder that rose within.

"There is something on the table. I think it belongs to you."

I reached my hand out, saw several small objects in the light of a flickering candle. The cool metal met the tips of my fingers.

I closed my eyes in defeat, remembered the captain's sterling tumbling to the ground beside my basket of laundry earlier that day. Hugh would wonder how I had come by such a sum, why there was money in the midst of what had transpired between Alexander and me.

An apology itched my lips, but I did not stoop to satisfy it. Not once had I begged Hugh to court me. Not once had I pursued him. He came to me—an unwed mother. He knew I held secrets yet did not press me. Did he truly think my past was only honorable?

As much as I tried to shift the blame of our failed relationship onto him, I knew I only scratched the surface of the problem—not so much my past as what I had done this day. Tell untruths. Seek another's arms. Dishonor the wedding vows I intended to take in a few short weeks.

I dropped the coins into my pocket and left him to go to my room, alone in the dark. A quiet sort of stifle—certainly not weeping?—chased me up the stairs.

The next morning I took James to Buckman's Tavern to speak with Alexander about his proposition. Mrs. Buckman told me the Regular detachment had left at daybreak.

When I returned to Graham and Cora's house, trying to accept the fact that I would likely never see Alexander again, that I was indeed the flighty woman Hugh blamed me to be, my accuser stood on the front step, his gaze intense and sad. My face burned with embarrassment as I realized Hugh had watched me steal away to the tavern again. He did not scold me or make any cutting remarks. Instead, he nodded once, picked up a threadbare pillowcase stuffed with clothes, and walked in the direction of what was to have been our new homestead.

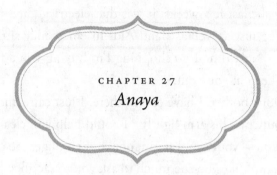

CHAPTER 27
Anaya

I LEANED BACK in the patio chair and looked at Brad beside me, studying Liberty's poem on his phone. His hat shadowed his profile, and I traced his outline with my gaze. I didn't even try to hide the fact that I stared. Sitting here with him now, on such a perfect spring day, felt so natural. So right. I couldn't imagine Brad not being in my life anymore. This Brad—the real one, not the imaginary Red Sox Sweatshirt hero. Yet him not being a part of my existence—that's just what would be if the bombing hadn't occurred. That's just what would be if I hadn't found his card in Lydia's house that day.

I caught a glimpse of his finger wrapped in black electrical tape. "You cut yourself again?"

His face reddened. "Utility knife got away from me."

I shook my head. If I'd learned one thing from Brad Kilroy the last few weeks, it was that electrical tape stopped bleeding just as well as Band-Aids in emergency situations. Gross. "Next time I go shopping I'm buying you a first aid kit to keep in your van."

"Don't bother. I have one in there. I just can't find it."

I punched his arm lightly. "I could help you clean it out sometime—your van, I mean, not your cut. I get too queasy."

"Naw, I like you too much to ask you to sacrifice yourself like that." He leaned over, kissed me soundly on my lips, but pulled away all too soon.

I sighed, content, and sipped my iced coffee, straightening out my legs in the late-afternoon sunshine. One of the things I loved about my apartment was the small patio on the side of the garage, below my residence. With the stubborn winter holding on to New England with a frosty grip, I hadn't had much time to enjoy it. But now the days stretched longer, the arrival of early April causing the trees to turn pink with new buds.

I gestured to Brad's phone. "Back to business. So Liberty's brother . . . he died on the fifth of March, right?"

Brad nodded.

"And it had something to do with her British soldier. Do you think he was the one who shot James?"

Brad looked at the phone between us and read, as we had a hundred times before.

Bitterness and betrayal won,
on that fifth of March the fight begun.
Sorrow and secrets I bore alone,
for guilt and remorse left unatoned.
The ring not mine, but yours, I know;
untold grief was mine to sow.

"Could be, but Annie, we could make up a million possible stories around this poem. Unless we find historical facts, we're going nowhere with this."

I rubbed my forehead. "I know, I know. But we've exhausted the listings for Liberty, Hugh, and Michael. Is this it, then?"

Brad took his hat off and tossed it on the ground, along with his pencil, which landed on the inside of the darkened brim. "Maybe there's nothing more to find. Maybe we stop here. This chase has brought us together . . . maybe that's enough of a story."

"You're giving up? Just like that?"

"No, not just like that. It's only that I don't see any more avenues. We've been looking at the same documents over and over. We know there's the ring—maybe Liberty stole it; maybe he gave it to her. And we know he died doing something for her, but what? And when? Where else is there to look?"

I unclasped the ring from my neck, let the sun catch the brilliance of the bloodstones.

Qui fortis salutem tribute.

Victory belongs to the one who is strong.

I ran my fingernail along the slight grooves of the anchor and the horn. I wondered if the previous owners of this ring had rested in God's strength, not their own. Perhaps that was to be the lesson I learned from it. Perhaps Brad was right. Maybe it was enough that we had found the connection between the ring and Liberty. Maybe it was enough that it had brought us together, that it had pointed us to the beliefs of those who had come before us. Maybe I needed to spend more time exploring those beliefs instead of trying to unbury a story that didn't want to be unearthed.

I slid the ring—much too big—onto my finger, then slid it off, wiggling it over my knuckles. The name *Smythe* flashed back and forth in my line of vision. We'd tried looking up the name at the genealogical society, had even searched in the England and Wales Birth Index. But without more information, finding the correct Smythe was like trying to find one of Willy Wonka's golden tickets.

I remembered running the marathon on Patriots' Day two years earlier. My legs had felt as if they were on fire. My toe throbbed, and I thought perhaps my nail would fall off before the end of the race. I longed to sit and down a sports drink. Normally, I would remind myself that the pain was temporary, that reaching my goals was what mattered.

But I chose to give up. It hurt too much. I didn't feel like thinking positive, or proving myself, or clinging to hope. What did it matter if I came in at a slow time?

I gave up.

I wasn't going to do the same now, when the story of the ring could be right beneath our noses. I stared at the engraved surname on the ring, so obviously English. I thought of Lydia's family's possible move across the ocean. I hadn't heard any update from Grace, though I hadn't asked either, too frightened to hear the decision that had the potential to rip my sister and her family out of my life permanently.

"England."

Brad looked up from his phone. "Come again?"

"We could try to contact someone at the National Archives in England."

Brad shook his head slowly.

"They would have better records of the King's Army, right? If we could find a Smythe whose regiment was in Boston on the date of the massacre and at Lexington in April 1775, we'd have some more missing pieces to Liberty's story. Maybe we could hire a genealogist to do some legwork for us."

Brad stared at his sneakers, nodded. "Could work. Might be expensive, though. I saw an advertisement online—it was close to a hundred dollars an hour to hire one of those guys."

I pressed my lips together. How much was Liberty's story worth to us? It seemed callous to put a price on it. And yet . . . I groaned. This was one thing I did *not* want to quit on.

"What if we put a cap on it? What would you think about each of us pitching in a hundred bucks for a couple hours of research, see what they find? If there was a Smythe in Boston and Lexington on those dates, I'd think a professional would be able to find it easy enough, right?"

"And if they don't come up with anything?"

"We let it rest, accept that the story of Liberty's ring was meant to die with her."

Brad's lips pressed into a thin line. "Yeah. Yeah, that sounds reasonable to me. I'm in."

He held his hand out for me to shake, but when I did he pulled me in for a kiss. A car door shut, and then the sound of little feet on pavement scurried close. Brad and I parted to see Emilia staring at us, her thin legs clad in leopard leggings and her face wearing a smile that said, *I saw what you two were doing.*

"Hey, Emilia." Brad stood and gave her a grand bow. She giggled. "You up for a game of wall ball?"

"Yes!" She jumped up and down. "I just love having a tent!"

We giggled and I pulled her pigtail. "Tenant, honey."

She continued bouncing. "Okay, I *love* having a tenant! Annie, do you want to play?"

I waved to my landlord, Cara, carrying a bag of groceries into the house. "I'd love to, sweetie, but I was just about to head in and make some lunch. I'm running a few miles tomorrow with my niece, and I need to store up my energy."

"When's your race?" Emilia kicked at the grass, flattening the green blades beneath her cowgirl boots.

"A few more weeks."

"Are you going, Brad?"

"You betcha. Wouldn't miss it for the world."

"Brad . . ." My warning tone couldn't have been clearer, but apparently Emilia missed it entirely.

"Can you take me, Brad? I want to see Annie run too."

"If your mom says it's okay."

I panicked beneath Emilia's brightening face. "No. I'm sorry, Emilia. But that won't work."

"Why not?"

Brad turned to me, his hands stuffed in his pockets, thumbs sticking out. "Yeah. Why not?"

"I don't want anyone watching me, okay?" I sipped the dregs of my iced coffee, sugar sliding up the straw. "No biggie. We'll plan something next Saturday. A picnic, maybe, and kite-flying."

"But I want to see the race—"

"And I'm cheering for you whether you like it or not." Brad stood his ground. "She says she went last year. I don't see—"

"She's *not* coming to the race." I didn't recognize the force in my voice, the slight waver of my words. They were quickly followed by wetness at the corners of my eyes. I knelt beside Emilia. "I'm sorry, sweetie, but this is something that's really important to me. Can you understand that, you think?"

She stuck her bottom lip out. "I guess so."

"Thank you." I chucked her chin. "Now give Brad a good game for me, will ya?"

Her expression didn't cheer as much as I'd wished. "Sure. I'll go change into my sneaks."

She headed back to the main house and went inside, her cowgirl boots dragging along the sprouts of new grass.

Brad and I looked after her. I turned and climbed up to my apartment, heaving deep breaths as I took the stairs. I shouldn't be angry at Brad. He was trying to support me. But I'd already told him I didn't want him at the race, and I certainly didn't want Emilia coming. Couldn't he respect that?

I heard footsteps behind me. I left the door ajar, opened the fridge, and pulled out a loaf of bread.

The storm door shut softly in its frame. I felt his gaze heavy upon me. I ground my teeth, tried to control the unrestrained fury that boiled in my chest.

"You can't keep living in fear."

"Well if that isn't the pot calling the kettle black . . ." I wasn't in the mood for nice. He had no right to judge me.

"What's that suppose to mean?"

I threw the bread tie on the counter, turned to face him, ready for a fight. "I notice, you know. When a dump truck unloads and its back end slams. A closing door. Crackling fire. That time near the Public Garden when that car backfired. You cover it well. But I can see it still sets you off. You're ready to jump into action. So don't tell me I need to stop living in fear, because, Brad, I don't think you've stopped living in it either."

I watched his jaw clench, the muscles in his face tighten. He squeezed his fists by his sides. I cared for this man. Why did I insist on goading him?

The temporary pleasure I felt while putting him in his

place quickly fled. I grabbed some turkey and cheese from the deli drawer.

"I'm going to play ball with Emilia." He left the kitchen without waiting for a reply.

For the next twenty minutes, the echo of the tennis ball against the side of the garage and Brad and Emilia's laughter played through the open window. My chest ached with a longing I couldn't pin down.

When Brad came in, he asked if we could wrap up the sandwiches to go.

Once in Brad's Accord we headed east. Traffic ran light, and he eased us into the parking lot of Revere Beach. The waves dove beneath the foamy surface, breaking into a million droplets of chaos that flowed up onto the sand and then ebbed back into the constant, beautiful turmoil.

I was about to ask if he wanted to get out and walk when he finally pulled the key from the ignition. The bright sun beat through the windows, warming the seats and the interior of the Accord.

He tossed the keys in the center console, leaned back in his seat, sighed long and heavy.

"The rules of engagement in Iraq were . . . sketchy. I was under a command whose unspoken view on ROE was to go with your gut. Expect an attack from insurgents. Expect them to use women, even children to get to you. Fire first, ask questions later."

I held my breath, suddenly uncertain if I was ready to hear this part of Brad's story.

"We were still reeling from September 11. Still on fire for what was done to our country. I thought taking up the fight was a good thing. A noble thing. But it messed me up royally. You know soldiers, they can become immune to killing. But not death. Not the fear of their own death. That's what propelled us. Defend ourselves. At the lowest of times, that's what it boiled down to. Kill or be killed. In those moments, I wasn't thinking about what was best for my country, or best for Iraq. I was saving my buddies. Saving my own backside. I was lower than a street rat."

He cracked the window. Salty sea air wrapped around us as Brad's hands began to tremble. I inched out my own to hold his quaking fingers but he wrenched them away, his mind light-years distant in another place. Another time.

"It was a woman. She had a large bag—a backpack—strapped to her. She didn't stop when we asked her to. We were on edge after two Humvees ran over IEDs the day before. Three of my buddies had died. I was running on an hour of sleep." He swiped a frustrated hand in the air. "Forget the excuses. I was the one behind the Mark 19." He looked at me, his eyes tortured. "Annie, we—I—thought for certain she had a bomb strapped to her. But when the smoke and dust finally cleared, beans and scattered produce lay on the ground. She'd been bringing us groceries."

Silence swallowed up the car as I allowed his words to sink in. "Brad . . . I'm so sorry." I reached for his hand again, but it remained motionless, cold.

"I still battle demons, Annie. And that day—the day of

the bombing—hasn't made it any easier. But I was able to get to you so quickly because of my experiences in Iraq. I didn't think. I acted. Only this time I saved a life—yours—instead of taking one."

I squelched the burning emotion in my throat.

He finally squeezed my hand back, the edges of the electrical tape on his wounded finger sticking to my skin. "My dad sent the ring and a letter to me a month after I shot . . . after the woman. It filled a hole inside of me. Made me look up instead of in. I knew my only chance of living out this cracked life was to give everything over to God. So that's what I did. Only somewhere in the last decade, I wrestled back the control, stopped reminding myself that the work was done." He swiped the back of his hand across his nose. "These last few weeks, learning about Liberty's ring, it's like my dad reminding me what's important all over again. What my heritage is. And I don't want to lose that hope again. God took the worst and healed me. Far from perfect this side of heaven, and yeah, you're right—I still live in fear sometimes. But I get through it by making a conscious choice not to be afraid. Not to make decisions out of fear."

Brad let silence fill the car before he broke it again. "Emilia should be able to come to the race."

"I'm not there yet, Brad. You're strong. Your faith—it's strong. Mine's not."

"That's the thing, though. This isn't about you. Or me. Or even our faith—as weak or strong as it may be. Jesus is strong enough for us. We can't keep looking back."

"I think my faith has a rearview mirror."

"Tear it off, then. Because after all we've been through together, I'm thinking that as much as I want to, I can't finish my own healing, or yours. I'm beginning to believe there's only one way to freedom."

"What's that?"

He hooked a finger beneath the chain at my neck, slid it down to the ring. "Trusting His power. Not ours."

CHAPTER 28
Liberty

JUNE 1774–APRIL 1775

Hugh did not visit his brother's home often after our falling-out. Graham and Cora agreed to keep me on, claiming they were happy for my help. Apparently Hugh had not tainted my reputation by telling them of my transgressions.

I saw him every Sunday at worship. I tried to contain my jealousy when I saw him leave with the young and pretty Widow Johnson more than once, their forms visible beyond the wooden belfry beside the meetinghouse, where she no doubt enticed him playfully. Late at night, I would pour my confusion onto paper in a scramble of words I wouldn't dare call poetry. I gleaned no strength from them.

James continued to grow, as did political tensions. New Whig families came to Lexington to plant their kin away from the chaos in Boston, away from the inundation of King George's soldiers beneath the command of General Gage. I wondered often about this commander, whose wife made no secret of her alliance with the Americans. I wondered if their marriage was doomed, if they felt free to speak to one another at all of their beliefs. Upon thinking of them, I often convinced myself it was better that Alexander and I would never be together. For certainly a Regular and an American could never survive what I felt in my blood was to come.

Graham and the boys made bullets each night while I kept busy with my needlework, and Cora maintained her meticulous records of our patients' ailments. Patriots gathered to drill on the green—Graham, Hugh, Nathaniel, even Michael among them.

It didn't take long for Gage to realize that the people of Massachusetts were not the country bumpkins he assumed them to be. The first week of September, after Gage had sent men to remove large supplies of gunpowder from the Provincial Powder House, six miles north of Boston, the people rioted against the homes of leading Tories in Cambridge, chasing them out of their dwellings. It seemed no secret that Gage feared the people would storm the town of Boston.

I was in the keeping room salting and peppering lumps of butter to put in a clam pie when Graham rushed into the house on the tenth of April, his breath expelled in one loud sigh, as if he hadn't breathed in a space of five minutes. "Sam Adams has arrived. He's staying with the reverend. I have invited Mr. Hancock, along with Mr. Adams and the reverend, to dine with us tomorrow night. Is that enough notice for you, Cora?"

To her credit, Cora appeared flustered for only a moment. "Of course, Graham. But I must admit, such esteemed company in my home—I will be a knot of worry."

I am certain I read through her words as well as Graham did. By *esteemed* she meant *targeted*. There was only one reason both John Hancock and Sam Adams had fled from Boston to Lexington. Doubtless, Gage was no longer content to permit Patriot leaders in the town he commanded, soaking up precious information, wagging their tongues to the ears of the American countrymen gearing for battle.

With each passing day, it became more and more apparent that I hadn't escaped the turmoil in Boston by coming to Lexington. Years later, it had followed me.

The next evening, Rebekah stayed upstairs with the younger children while Cora, Priscilla, Annabel, and I served a fine feast of Indian pudding followed by a veal roast, beans, and Cora's potatoes. The men—including Hugh—ate with fervor. It was not until I brought Mr. Adams's plate to the sideboard to fill it with one of Cora's famed tarts that he addressed me, his palsied fingers crippled worse than I remembered them five years earlier. "Miss Caldwell, won't you tell me how you fare?"

Graham cleared his throat to come to my rescue. "Miss Liberty stays with us to help with my Cora's midwifery. She is very skilled indeed, both in her occupation and in the kitchen."

I smiled my thanks and turned to Mr. Adams. "I am well, Mr. Adams. A day does not go by that I do not miss my brother, but I must admit you were correct when I spoke with you after the shooting."

Mr. Adams cocked his head. I glanced at Hugh, remembering how he shared that dreadful March night with me. "At the time, I confess I did not note my brother's sacrifice a most worthy one. But as I watch the struggle for our freedom play out, as I wonder with fear and anticipation where our country is headed, I admit—I am proud of him. He would have wanted nothing more than to be sitting at this table with you, planning the next step toward our freedom."

A small smile tipped Mr. Adams's mouth. Mr. Hancock raised his glass. "To James Caldwell, then, and to his sister, Liberty."

The others raised their glasses, and while I couldn't claim to do many things right, I felt that I had done something in that moment. I felt it in the unshed tears pressing at my eyes. I felt it in the way Hugh stared back at me, something akin to pride on his features.

If only we could have stayed just so. If only our town—our worlds—as we had known them did not have to bear such a very heavy brunt for freedom. I had given enough in

the death of my brother. I could not fathom God asking me
to give more.

APRIL 19, 1775
1 A.M.

The steady, methodic tolling from the belfry on the green
woke me out of a deep sleep, rousing instant panic in the pit
of my stomach. Instinct told me it wasn't a fire that needed
putting out this night. All knew that at one point this entire
fracas would come to a head. I just wished it didn't have to
be here, where my son slept.

I opened the window of my bedroom, craned my neck.

"To arms! To arms!" called Captain John Parker, commander of Lexington's militia. "The Regulars are coming!
The Regulars are coming!"

I shut the window, thankful James still lay sleeping. I
donned my petticoats, dress, and mobcap, then opened the
door of my chambers. Cora stood in the hall. She grasped
my hand and led me downstairs to the keeping room. "We
must gather the extra muskets, anything Graham and the
boys aren't—"

"The boys? Cora, surely you aren't letting Michael go?"

"It is Graham's decision. And Michael's. He wishes to go,
to do his part. He is nearly a man and has not drilled for
nothing. I trust Graham won't allow anything to happen to
him."

"Where will they go?"

"Buckman's. Hurry now, all the muskets. We will hide them beneath the mattresses. Many women will be in labor tonight."

The cold metal of a musket was shoved into my hand as I tried to comprehend Cora's words. "The tavern? But here—in Lexington?"

"The Regulars are on their way to Concord. Military stores are there—provisions, cannons, gunpowder. They must be stopped. This is where a stand will be made."

Hugh . . . Graham . . . Nathaniel . . . Michael. They would all be in harm's way. What would this day bring? I did not have time to dwell on it. I watched Cora press a kiss to her husband's and two sons' cheeks and send them off to battle the unknown. I hid extra weapons in barrels of feathers in the barn and under my mattress. If a Regular invaded our home, I would lock myself in my bedroom and, if needed, mimic the sounds of a woman in labor. Cora would claim to be my midwife, which was not so very much of a stretch. We were confident no redcoat would press the matter to search within the room, where the weapons would be safely stored.

"Are we secure here, with the children?" I strained my ears to hear the telling sound of drums—the Regulars would not come quietly or stealthily. They always came with show. I pictured Alexander in their lines, marching steadily toward our town. The thought of seeing him again, under such unpleasant circumstances, was reason enough to make me want to hide in the woods with my son.

Cora put a cool hand to my cheek, the first motherly gesture I ever received from her—the first time I likely would have welcomed it. "None of us are safe. But my husband and two of my sons may need assistance I can give them—not to mention the other men. Being a midwife is not about safety. It's about putting others before ourselves. Though I admit, I cannot imagine the Regulars would harm women and children. They are men with hearts, red-coated or not."

Though I knew the truth of her statement, I certainly had need of the reminder at the moment. Would I flee in the face of trouble when I was needed? Or would I do my part in this fight for freedom? Would I be able to tell my son a tale that would make him proud?

I swallowed my fears. "We should have the girls confine the children upstairs. Priscilla could be on the lookout to free us to tend to the men."

Cora smiled, the crow's-feet heavy at her eyes. "That is a brilliant plan."

Once downstairs, we looked over our supplies—tinctures of honey and camphor, juniper, balsam, poultices, and our prepared tea of yarrow, catnip, and mint for fevers. Even a bit of brandy to administer before giving stitches. Cora paced the room, wringing her hands, then held them out to me. "Pray with me, dear?"

We knelt on the hard planks of the floor in the midst of our supplies and poured our hearts out to our Creator. There, with Cora, I felt my spirit open to the presence of God. Perhaps it was the act of beseeching the Lord with another soul, perhaps it was the sincere openness of our prayers, or perhaps it was Cora's certainty that God loved us enough to carry out our good and His glory this morning.

I felt the cleansing of my spirit as surely as I had heard the tolling in the belfry on the green. I didn't want to leave that place of peace, that place of prayer and healing and power and strength, that place of intimate communion with Christ, and yet Cora closed out the prayer, handed me a handkerchief for my tears, and gently urged me to my feet.

We were quiet after that, organizing already-tidy supplies in the keeping room, slipping out onto the front stoop now and then to listen. The peace I felt while praying with Cora lingered, a faithful companion. The night wore on in silence, with no sign of the king's regiments.

It appeared the warning had been misunderstood or, perhaps, wrong altogether. The crowd of men at Buckman's Tavern slowly dispersed to go home to their own beds. Just shy of three in the morning, the Gregory men returned home as well. Cora and I sent the girls back to bed and lay down ourselves. And I praised God for answering Cora's prayer that no one would be forced into battle this night.

CHAPTER 29
Anaya

As APRIL SETTLED IN to rouse us with thoughts of warm weather and new beginnings, Grace and I became more and more a team. With her help—competing, urging, encouraging—I remembered my running legs, and with some hard work on my own during the week, we ran together on weekends, pushing one another in a way that brought us closer together.

While we increased our distance, any topic of conversation came up for grabs. Her social life, mine. The past—her struggles, mine. I better understood my sister's pain by hearing of Grace's many doctors' appointments, how she finally came to accept that living with a fake leg would be her life.

She lamented over the fact that she'd never be one of the cute girls in a bikini on the beach. She shared her fears over living alone at college in a couple short years. She told me of dreams where she could run without pulling on a prosthetic. And I tried not to feel the guilt all over again.

Brad and I chiseled at the poem daily, each time coming up with half a story, half a mystery that might never be known. We waited patiently for word from the genealogist we had hired in London. And at night I pondered Brad's words from the beach, wondered over the strong, inexplicable way I felt tied to Liberty. Whether or not I knew her entire story, I could deduce the majors from her poem. She'd known suffering. Guilt. Love.

She had clung to a God I gave new pieces of my life to with each rising sun.

I was on my lunch break, walking along the brick pavers of downtown Lexington, when I caught the news in the passing conversation of two men in business suits. I ducked into Panera Bread and opened the newsfeed on my phone. Sure enough, a CNN report confirmed it.

I stood huddled in the corner of the lunchtime rush, feeling little more than numb.

The first part of the trial had ended, *guilty* stamped on the soul of the younger brother who chose to put a pressure-cooker bomb in a backpack behind a group of spectators that included children.

The rest of the workday went by in a blur of accounts opened, checks scanned, drawers balancing. All I could think about was getting to Grace and Lydia. When I arrived at their house in my workout clothes, Grace met me at the door.

We clasped one another in an embrace. Her tears wet my shirt. When we pulled apart, she swiped at them, apologized, then suggested we not wait any longer to go for our run.

We didn't speak much but rather let the pounding of our sneakers—and her blade—on pavement, the heavy breaths, the beads of sweat, do the talking for us.

When we returned, Lydia waited on the porch. She sat on the front steps, her arms clasped around her knees, her gaze straight ahead. She looked so small sitting there, guard down for once.

When we approached, I hung back. She broke her intense focus to look at me as she stood.

Then she hugged me. A good hug—the squeeze kind. I felt a thousand unspoken words in the gesture. I sobbed—partly from shock, partly from relief—into her shoulder, inhaling the chamomile scent of her hair. My body trembled and hiccuped against hers as I tried to speak through my weeping. "I'm sorry, Lydia. I'm s-so sorry. I wish I could go back and do it over."

She didn't speak, didn't shed tears of her own, but she did hug me a little bit tighter.

A piece of the wall between us came down with that hug. While it wasn't exactly a pardon or an acknowledgment of forgiveness, I clung to it and the hope of which it whispered.

APRIL 19, 1775

I startled awake at the sound of far-off drums and fifes. Sitting halfway up in bed, I squinted at the pink light of dawn just reaching past the thin gauze of my curtains. I sat still, exhaustion causing me to wonder whether the drums were a product of dream—nightmare, rather—or reality.

The steady thrum and sickeningly jolly tune entered my being, where they rattled around, creating a rift of fear larger than the span of Boston Harbor. With a horrified sense of betrayal, I realized God's plan had not been to deter the red-coats after all. They were coming.

The belfry on the green sounded the next moment, and

I scooped up a sleeping James, pressed a kiss to his matted head, and scrambled out of my room to where Cora ushered Cilla and Annabel into her chambers along with the rest of the children. The boots of Graham and his two sons echoed down the stairs. A moment later, the door closed.

"Stay in this room and keep away from the windows. You mustn't leave until we come fetch you. Do you understand?" Cora's calm voice smoothed my frayed nerves. Cilla, Annabel, Rebekah, and Thomas nodded, their eyes now wide and cleared of sleep.

James tugged at my arm. "Momma?" He no doubt sensed the fear in the room. Though he was almost too heavy to hold, I lifted his warm little-boy body in my arms, breathed a prayer for every child in the room. I handed him off to Rebekah, who was his favorite, and left the room without looking back.

The drums and fifes grew louder, closer still. Cora hummed "A Mighty Fortress Is Our God" to mask the sound, but soon it overpowered her hymn. We gathered at the window and pushed aside the drapes with trembling hands to watch what would become of our men.

The militia had dwindled throughout the night to a mere seventy, maybe eighty men. They lined themselves along the green, straight and proud, their own young drummer boy among them. I saw brother beside brother in both Graham and Hugh, Nathaniel and Michael. A well of pride erupted in me but quickly diminished at the first sight of crimson coats against the foggy, red horizon.

The mass of red floated as far as the eye could see. Like little red ants—the light infantry along with the drummers and fife players, followed by the tall grenadiers with their intimidating bearskin caps. Some held flags with yellow borders, their regiment numbers proudly displayed on a red shield encircled with thistles and roses. I wondered if Alexander was among the throng.

They drew closer. Muskets clanked. Boots stamped. The giant wooden wheels of wagons protested beneath the weight of their six-pounder field guns.

Our militia looked pitiful against the King's Army, and no doubt, with their beaver hats and old flintlocks, they felt it. Yet they stood firm—unshaking—against the Regulars, against King George III himself.

My hands trembled on the painted sill as the Regulars gathered in perfect formation on the green and the drums let out one last loud rap.

Then, silence.

One of the commanders came forth, shouted at the militia. "Lay down your arms, you rebels, and disperse!"

My pulse pounded within my veins, my heart pumping blood to every inch of my body. A thin layer of sweat blanketed my skin, then cooled quick enough to create a chill.

"I say, lay down your arms, you rebels, and disperse!" I didn't think the words could have been spoken with more force, but the commander managed it. They brooked no refusal. He was speaking on behalf of the king himself.

Our militia wavered beneath the regal mandate, beginning

with the drummer boy. A few filed back. The Gregory men held their position. Others filed off to a stone wall on the right flank of the Regulars, the redcoats on their heels, weapons poised.

Then, though I couldn't tell whether it came from Patriot or Regular, a shot echoed through the still morning.

I gasped, shrank back from the window. I hadn't expected it, truly. Even with all the pomp and show, even with both sides at the ready, even having witnessed my own brother's lifeblood seep from him in a much smaller confrontation five years earlier, I wasn't prepared for the moment of that first shot. My stomach revolted and I swallowed the bitter bile stewing in the back of my throat even as more musket fire lit the air.

It came from behind the stone walls where some of the Patriots had taken cover, from the Brown Bess muskets of the Regulars. Smoke filled the pink haze of morning. The rotten stench of musket fire seeped beneath our door, haunting me with memories of that March night years earlier. All my mind's eye could see was scarlet blood on snow, stark red against white, and I grasped for the assurance I'd felt on my knees with Cora, just a short time earlier.

The militia retreated and the redcoats advanced, leaving behind a smattering of motionless Patriot bodies. I blinked, brought to life by Cora's muffled cries, her pleas to God mixed with the tears of a devoted wife, of a loving mother. I scooped up the waiting supplies and followed a trembling Cora out of the house and onto the green. Scattered musket fire sounded farther up on the common, but then, as quickly as it had begun, it was over, leaving behind only the stink of death mixed with the stench of gunpowder.

The Regulars resumed formation, let out a series of loud "Hip, hip, huzzahs," took up their fifes and drums, and without remorse, started up a jolly tune of "Yankee Doodle," mocking us in as complete a humiliation as could be found.

As they cleared the green, Cora and I ran to the wounded lumps. As I did, I searched frantically for Hugh's sturdy form among the standing militia, behind the stone walls, gathering near the tavern. I saw no sign of him, nor Graham nor Nathaniel nor Michael. I concentrated on tending to the wounded before me—the fate of the Gregory men would be known to me soon enough.

Cora went off to the left, I to the right. I bent beside a man who clutched his leg, but he waved me off to those more grievously wounded. Reverend Clark knelt beside one motionless man and recited a prayer.

An instinctive, guttural wail sounded from the other side of the green. When I looked, I recognized Nathaniel, his tall form bent over . . . ?

I ran toward him, my basket of supplies thumping my legs, the soles of my boots slipping on mud. Aware of the sound of Cora's retching, I saw Michael's too-small, still body beneath Nathaniel's. Out of my peripheral vision, I spotted another body, but I couldn't look. I couldn't bear to see which other brother had fallen. I collapsed to my knees beside Nathaniel, pushed at him to no avail, searched out Michael's wrist beneath his hysterical older brother.

I sought for a pulse, conscious of how young and tight Michael's skin felt beneath my fingers.

Nothing.

I fought my own tears, crawled on my knees to the body beside them, and finally looked at the face. Graham's. His eyes fluttered, lips moving. "Tell Cora . . . I'm sorry . . . I tried to . . . get . . . front of him . . ." He stared up into the dawn sky, took a crackling breath before his gaze froze, lids open, eyes lifeless.

No . . . Lord, no. It had all happened so quickly. Whatever feeling of peace I'd experienced just hours before while praying on the hardwood with Cora, I couldn't reconcile it with the hopeless feeling that overcame me now. I'd believed God would watch over us. I'd believed He'd had our good in mind. I'd believed . . .

Cora, wet vomit still on the corner of her mouth, crawled to her husband—then wavering, went to her son. I put my arms around her trembling body, the tune of "Yankee Doodle" growing faint as the redcoats continued their march to Concord.

Reverend Clark bent over Graham, said a prayer that would accompany him into eternity, then moved on to Michael. I willed my legs to hold me. There were others who needed help. I must tend to them. My knees lifted me inches, then failed me.

A shadow blocked out the rising of the sun. It spoke my name. "Liberty."

I lifted my head. Alexander stood before me in full uniform, but I couldn't comprehend his presence, why he should be here and not with his regiment. I wanted to seek his arms for comfort and I wanted to pound his chest for being part of such a thing. For the death of my benefactor and his son. My friend's husband and child. A part of me hated him in that moment, hated what he stood for. Blast the bloody Crown of England. Blast every last Regular imposing himself on us and our right to freedom. Their hearts—Alexander's heart—must be made of steel to inflict such pain and death. On one such as Michael, no less. A mere child.

He knelt beside me and laid a hand on my arm. "It should never have come to this. I—I am so sorry."

I wrested my arm from him and pinned him with the cruelest look I could muster beneath my tears. Just the sight of him made me grow hard inside. Cold. "Leave me now. I never wish to see you again."

"Liberty, I—"

"Leave!"

"They should have let us pass. They should not have fired upon—"

His words were cut short by a soft utterance of pain. His eyes widened in surprise, his lips parted. I didn't notice the tip of the bayonet in his side until he looked down to see it for himself, blood glinting on the metal. It disappeared, and his body jerked violently when he fell to his knees. Behind him stood Hugh, bloodied weapon in hand, eyes sad, defeated. He fell alongside Alexander, clutching his thigh, wet with crimson blood.

Black spots danced before my eyes. The last thought I remembered was trying to decide whom to tend to first.

Alexander or Hugh.

Alexander . . . or Hugh.

Alexander.

Or.

Hugh.

I never did make up my mind. And I'm still uncertain whether I swooned from the shock of seeing both the men I loved wounded . . .

Or the shock of realizing I very much loved both men.

The pungent scent of smelling salts whisked me awake. I pushed them away, breathed around the smell of ammonia. Mrs. Clark sat above me, her warm hand smoothing back my hair. "There, there, dear."

I pushed my upper body onto my elbows. "Hugh . . . Alexander. James."

She shushed me, placed the salts on a stand beside the bed. "Your son is being taken care of by Miriam White at the Gregory place. He is well. I called on them at the start of the hour."

I placed my hand upon my head. "Where am I? They must need help . . ."

"You're at Buckman's. Dr. Richards is in high demand, but I think he is rather enjoying the need. A rider has gone for Dr. Warren and Dr. Church. You must rest."

The image of Graham's lifeless body, of Michael's still form beneath his brother's, of two brothers alive—was Hugh alive?—and two dead. And Alexander. Oh, Alexander. A thousand regrets washed over me.

"Mr. Gregory is well. A minor wound to his leg is all. Dr. Richards says as long as infection doesn't set in, he will be walking within a fortnight."

My lungs relaxed as I breathed out, absorbing the news.

I wanted to ask of Alexander, but what would she know of a Regular? I ran my tongue over my dry lips. "Cora?"

Mrs. Clark's mouth turned downward. "She is grieving deeply, of course. She will need you now more than ever. Not as an apprentice but as a friend."

I nodded, feeling a sudden fierce loyalty to my grieving mentor. I wiggled my toes, set them on the solid surface of the floor. How dependable that floor was; how I appreciated such a small thing in that moment.

"I think I will see Mr. Gregory first. Is he at his brother's home?"

"He is here, in the next room. Please call on me if you need anything. I plan to bring a meal later."

My head swelled with pain, which then receded in what I knew would be a persistent headache. I thanked her, smoothed out my wrinkled skirt, picked up my basket of supplies, and prepared what I would say to Hugh beneath the fog of my thoughts.

He had lost a brother and a nephew this day. He had killed a man. A man I loved. The emotions I felt were too complicated to begin wading through. Perhaps none of them mattered. What mattered now was that Hugh knew I was there for him, that I cared for him—more than I realized. I may have failed him before, but I would resolutely stand by his side now.

I entered his room, the sunlight streaming onto the crimson quilt at his feet. I crept in with soft steps, my gaze on his closed eyes. Wet trails of shiny skin traveled from their corners to his ears, speaking quietly of his grief.

I crept closer, but a tight floorboard squealed of my presence. His eyes came open.

"I didn't mean to wake you." I pulled a chair to the side of his bed and sat, dizziness sweeping over me, the throbbing in my head obstinate.

Hugh stared at the ceiling. "I was not sleeping."

I longed to tell him how sorry I was, but such words didn't seem to do justice to the events of the day. Somehow *How could you?* didn't seem appropriate either.

"How is your leg?"

"It's there." Dry humor. Somehow fitting.

He sighed. "I should be dead also. I was alongside them. After I speared that lobster, they could have shot me. But he'd fallen behind. They didn't shoot me when they came for him, but they could have. I should be dead too."

That lobster . . .

Hugh didn't realize Alexander was the man I'd been talking to that spring day nearly a year earlier, in the backyard. He didn't realize Alexander was the Regular I'd run to that night. He'd been seeking revenge when he'd plunged the bayonet into his side, but he hadn't known the depth of my feelings for the man he aimed to kill.

Would it have made a difference? Would he have sought all the harder to do away with Alexander? Or would he have hesitated for my sake?

Hugh mumbled in delirium. "I should be dead. I should be dead."

My heart near split open at seeing him so distraught. Unbidden, fond memories came to my mind. Hugh's uncertainty the first time he stacked blocks with James on Graham and Cora's floor. His look of determination as he affixed two pieces of wood together—the first of what was to be our homestead. His smile as he came into Midwife Louisa's store, pretending to need more herbs for a sister who was no longer ailing.

His crumpled form in Graham's chair after seeing me run to Buckman's Tavern, to Alexander.

I didn't know how to comfort him. In the end, I chose to meet Hugh's helplessness with silence.

And when I reached for his hand, he did not pull away.

CHAPTER 31
Anaya

THE PACKAGE CAME earlier than I'd expected. A manila envelope adorned with a red-and-yellow Royal Mail stamp, it felt foreign in my hands. The distinct postage reminded me of the vast distance between Massachusetts and England. Grace had told me she'd overheard Lydia and Roger discussing possible living arrangements overseas. Though I knew the thought to be self-absorbed, deep inside I wondered if Lydia wanted to move away because of me, if she wanted to whisk her family from me once and for all.

I tightened my grip on the thin envelope, creasing it slightly. A sharp pang of isolation tore through me, and I picked up my phone.

He answered on the first ring. "Hey, beautiful."

I pressed the phone to my ear, leaning into Brad's voice. "Hey yourself."

"You up for watching the Sox tonight? They have to redeem themselves from Wednesday's game."

"Yeah, definitely."

In the background, I heard what sounded like a car door shut. "I'm in Cambridge. Want to grab something to eat?"

I clutched Liberty's ring in my palm, tugged the chain at my neck. "How about I make you dinner. Lasagna sound all right?"

"More than all right. Be there in an hour?"

I opened my mouth to tell him the package came, but the sound of a drill and hammering ruined the moment. We hung up, and I busied myself cooking the meat sauce for the lasagna, turning on the TV to a rerun of *I Love Lucy* to chase away the loneliness in my apartment.

When Brad walked in, the scents of tomato sauce and garlic filled the kitchen, the lasagna baking in the oven. Everything about the scene—him walking in without knocking, me cooking dinner for him—spoke of a warm normality, an exciting new kind of regular that I didn't know if I could ever live without, now that I'd experienced it.

I dried my hands on a dishcloth and turned into his embrace. I knocked his hat upward on his head and tapped the pencil at his temple so it didn't fall. He kissed me and I breathed in the scents of sawdust and spice and all things Brad.

"I missed you." He spoke into my hair.

"I just saw you last night." But I knew what he meant. "I missed you today too. How was work?"

"Good, got a lot done. I only wish—hey, is that what I think it is?" He let his arms fall from my sides. I followed his gaze to the envelope, the Royal Mail logo of a red-and-yellow crown on its upper corner.

"It is. I thought she might have e-mailed me some of what she found, but I guess not. Looks like that's it. I didn't want to open it without you."

"I should hope not." He gave me a wink and reached for the package, turning it in his hands much as I had first done when I received it—as if trying to imagine the contents within but frightened to tear it open and have our expectations dashed.

He placed it back on the counter, tapped his fingers at his thighs. "After supper?"

"I think that would be best. It's almost ready."

I forced down a small piece of lasagna and some salad as Brad ate with the hunger of a starving bear.

We shared bits and pieces of our day, but the distraction of the manila envelope remained in my peripheral vision. When we had finally cleared the table and loaded the dishwasher, there was nothing left to divert us.

Brad handed me the envelope. "Go ahead."

I shoved it back at him. "No, it's your family. You open it."

He shook his head and walked to the living room, where he turned on a lamp and sat on the couch. He patted the spot beside him. "We're making too much of this. It's not like any information in this envelope is going to tell us what did or didn't happen between Liberty and her British soldier. We probably know more about the story of the ring than any genealogist in London could ever find, what with the poem and all. I'm hoping for a name, though, you know? Something more we can go on."

I flopped onto the couch beside him, placed a hand on his knee. "You're right." I closed my eyes, listened to the gentle hum of the heat kicking on. "Let's see what's inside."

He tore the envelope open as carefully as he could and slid out a thin stack of computer papers. On the top sat a letter.

"You want me to read it out loud?" Brad scooted closer to me until our sides met. I leaned into his shoulder and nodded, reading along as his voice echoed in the quiet confines of my apartment.

11 APRIL 2015

Ms. Anaya David,

Thank you for allowing me the privilege of researching your family history.

Given the information you imparted to me, I believe I have found the soldier you are looking for. While there were two soldiers of the Royal Army possessing the surname Smythe in Boston in early March 1770, only one of those men was also present at the Battle of Lexington in April 1775.

Below, please find a summary of my findings, largely gleaned from muster rolls. Along with this letter, I have attached the details of my research, as well as their sources.

Name: Alexander Edward Smythe
Rank and Regiment as of March 1770 (in Boston): Lieutenant, 29th Regiment of Foot, British Army
Rank and Regiment as of April 1775 (in Boston and at Lexington Battle): Captain, 47th Regiment of Foot, British Army
Death: 19 April 1775, Lexington
    I wish you all the best in your continued research, Ms. David. Please contact me if I can be of any further assistance to you or your family in your genealogical quest.

                                    Sincerely,
                        Patricia Hurst, AGRA Genealogist

Brad tapped the papers on his knee. "Alexander Smythe. Do you think that's really him—Liberty's soldier?"

"He was the only Smythe around for both the massacre and the Lexington battle. It has to be him." I lifted the letter to see a slew of military records. "I guess he died at Lexington after all."

"Funny, I didn't think any Regulars died at Lexington. . . ."

"Can't deny the king's records."

Brad nodded. "Still can't figure it. Why would Liberty

hand down Alexander's ring to a son she had with Hugh . . . her husband? I would think Michael Gregory would have been ashamed to receive it, yet he made certain Amelia had it at his death."

I went into my bedroom, grabbed my laptop. "Okay, Kilroy. Work your magic with those websites. Let's see if anything for Alexander Smythe comes up."

An hour later, Red Sox game forgotten, we'd come up with a handful of Alexander Smythes, none of whom matched the time period and location we searched. I stifled a yawn. "He was an English citizen. It's not like we'd find any birth or death records, or even a census. There has to be something somewhere, though."

Brad set my laptop on the coffee table, put an arm around me, and pulled me onto his lap. "We'll have to take a look at the archives or NEHGS again. If a Regular did actually die at Lexington, someone must have written something about it somewhere."

I snuggled into him, soaking up his confidence, his solidness. I thought of our conversation at the beach—Brad's urging that I trust someone greater than myself. I thought of Alexander Smythe dying in battle, of Brad at war over in Iraq, of my recurring nightmares about the upcoming Patriots' Day race.

Silence hung over the room and Brad didn't move to put the Sox game on.

I reached for the ring, ran my finger over the engravings.

"So after Iraq . . . did you ever have dreams? You know, bad ones?"

He let out a long sigh, raked a hand through his hair. "I still do, once in a while. You having nightmares again?"

I nodded. "What are they like? Your nightmares."

"Sheesh, Annie, do you really want to know?"

I curled into him. "Yes." The whispered word hung in the air.

I felt his chest rise and fall beneath where my head lay. "For some reason I rarely dream about the woman with the groceries. I think about her all the time when I'm awake. I imagine going back over there, trying to find her family, telling them how sorry I am. I still think I'll try to one day."

The gentle swishing and humming of the dishwasher sounded through the apartment. "What *do* you dream about, then?"

I heard him swallow. Hesitate. Just when I thought he'd refuse to tell me, he spoke. "The woman with the groceries—that was the most horrible thing. That was my first tour. But there were other things that haunt me. Lots of them. One of—well . . . Annie, it's war. I don't think most people think about it, but someone had to . . . take care of—collect the dead bodies . . . the pieces of the soldiers blown apart by roadside bombs."

"Oh, Brad."

"I had a buddy who couldn't take it anymore. He went in a port-a-john, blew his head off." His words shook. "Peeling your friend's brains off a plastic port-a-john wall that's been baking in hundred-degree weather will make just about anyone go crazy."

I closed my eyes, shook my head. I thought of what I'd seen after the marathon bombing. The limbs, the blood.

"How do you get over something like that?"

He snorted. "Who said I'm over it?"

I slipped my hand in his.

"Those are the nightmares I have. Reliving that stuff. After I came back from that second tour in Iraq, I just wouldn't sleep. I was exhausted. Drank too much. I forgot all about the encouragement I got from the ring, from my dad's letter. Then I found someone—a buddy from high school who'd been in Iraq too. We'd talk about everything. We'd pray together, every day. It was intense, Annie. Almost like battle itself. But the worst of the nightmares stopped after that. Sleep came easier. So did living." He laid his chin on the top of my head. "The dreams come back now and then. I think they always will. It's a battle I'll probably fight until I die. But I don't have to fight it alone."

I didn't ask what he meant—I knew what he meant: that God was alongside him, a constant companion in a time of turmoil. I thought of the ring, how I had turned to it for comfort so many times after the bombing. Only it was a lifeless—albeit very cool—object, a piece of metal. How amazing would it be to have a living Savior beside me in my troubles?

"Thank you . . . for telling me." I knew it cost Brad something to open up this, the deepest part of his heart, to me. I didn't take it for granted.

"So what about you? You dream about the bombing a lot?"

I nodded. "The nightmares went away for a while after I met you, but as this race comes closer . . . I dream about that instead. About something happening. Stupid, huh?"

"Not stupid. Our fears can do crazy things to us." Then, "You want me to pray with you?"

I'm sure he felt me freeze in his arms. I was okay with Brad believing all this Jesus stuff. I knew it made him a better person, and that was fine by me. And maybe I'd pray on my own. Tonight. Alone. But with him? It just seemed too . . . weird.

"Maybe some other time, okay?"

He let the subject drop, and after a minute we turned on the Red Sox game, watching them win against the Orioles by one run.

When Brad turned off the TV, he poked a finger in my side. "So back to our friend. Alexander. I have to work all day Saturday, but how about another research trip sometime next week?"

Next week. After the race. By then, I'd either have made it through, with Grace by my side, or . . . I wouldn't.

"Yeah, that sounds like a plan."

CHAPTER 32
Liberty

APRIL 21, 1775

I woke to the sound of mumbling beside me, straightened myself from the hard chair on which I slept on the second floor of Buckman's Tavern.

"Graham, no . . . Michael . . ." A foul word, then, "Get away from her, you lobster . . . Liberty . . . my Liberty . . ."

My Liberty . . .

Those two words did confounding things to my heart.

He still cared for me. Though I had betrayed him, chosen the enemy over him, lied to him, and never even apologized for hurting him so, somewhere in the depths of his soul, he cared for me.

As my eyes adjusted to the dim room, I glimpsed Hugh's head toss back and forth, then settle. I rose from my crooked pose, rubbed the knot from my neck, and stepped closer to the bed.

My fingers sought the head of my patient. I released a long sigh of relief at its coolness.

I moved my hand to his temple, studying his face in sleep as he stilled beneath my touch. New lines etched his eyes and mouth. I knew I was the cause of more than one. How had I been so foolish as to spurn his love—to spurn an opportunity for a life with him, to spurn an opportunity for a family?

I allowed my hand to fall. There was too much misery and suffering in this life for one to bear alone. I thought of the peace I'd found before the battle, beside Cora and her prayers. Without thinking, I dropped to my knees alongside Hugh's bed and silently poured my heart out to my Creator. I continued this way until light streamed forth from the window and the sound of pans clattered in the kitchen below. I felt a hand on my head.

When I looked up, Hugh studied me.

"You needn't have stayed the night."

I straightened, took his hand from my head and held it, warm in my own fingers. "I wished to be certain you did not suffer a fever."

He stared at me then, so long I began to feel uncomfortable. I stood. "I'll need to remove your dressing today and apply fresh lint. Would you like me to do so now, or would you rather break your fast first?"

He shifted on the bed. "Best do it now."

I left the room to fill the pitcher with fresh water in which to wash my hands. I gathered my supplies and brought them to the bed. He removed the covers from his pale, wounded leg, pulling his white shirt as low as it could go without concealing the wound on his thigh.

"Perhaps I should fetch Mrs. Buckman to assist me. . . ."

He closed his eyes. "Whatever you wish."

I felt I had let him down by mentioning Mrs. Buckman. I did not truly need an assistant; I only wished to maintain propriety. Unbidden, the memory of kissing Alexander beneath the tree outside this very window, of Hugh watching us from across the common, came to me.

I swallowed the recollection along with my shame and focused on the task at hand. I sat on the chair beside his bed, my tray on the other side of his leg, and began to remove as much of the lint as possible without pulling at the exposed wound. "Does it hurt much?"

"No."

I continued working.

"How is Cora?"

I studied a piece of lint stuck in the open wound. When I pulled at it, Hugh flinched, and I left it alone. "She is grief-stricken, to be certain."

I smeared a tincture of honey and camphor on the wound, the ointment releasing an herbal scent into the air. I rinsed my hands, then dipped fresh lint in sweet oil—something Dr. Richards had neglected to do, or the old lint would have removed easier. I covered the wound with the lint, pulled his bedclothes up, and washed my hands.

I sat back in the chair. He did not look at me. "I am sorry, Hugh. For Graham, and Michael . . ." My eyelids grew hot, and I turned from him.

"Freedom—it comes at a cost."

Yes, I knew that all too well. "You heard news that the Regulars never obtained the stores at Concord?"

Hugh smiled. My breath caught.

"I heard we took them off guard on their way back to Boston."

"Yes." The Patriots had borrowed a rather unorthodox Indian warfare, shooting from behind fences and trees, stone walls, and windows, surprising the Crown with a victory.

Silence held us for a moment, and Hugh moved to a sitting position. He stared at the wall for a long time. "Why did you give your heart to him, Liberty?"

I placed a hand over my trembling chin. I wanted to claim that I hadn't willingly given my heart to Alexander, that he—the enemy—had stolen it. But I couldn't fault Alexander even for that.

"He . . . I was lonely when I worked at the officers' house. I was waiting for word of James; I had no family, no friend. Alexander—" Hugh winced, and I changed my words—"the lieutenant was kind to me."

"And James's father?"

"A scoundrel, I am sorry to say. The lieutenant blamed himself for—for what happened."

"As do I." Hugh exhaled loudly.

Tentatively, I sought his hand. He did not fight my

fingers, but neither did he seem to welcome them. "I am sorry I hurt you, Hugh. The lieutenant . . . yes, I loved him. But there is no future for us. We are enemies in this conflict, and I can no longer allow my heart to fancy that the battle doesn't matter. After the other morning . . . I see what is of utmost importance. When you fell, I—I couldn't bear to think I would lose you."

I couldn't pretend to understand the insanity of my heart, how I could possibly love two men at once. But here, now, I was putting Alexander behind me forever. I was choosing love that had proven selfless and sacrificial. I was choosing Hugh's love. If he would have me.

A thickness filled my throat. I knew what more I wanted to say to him, what genuine feeling swelled my heart, but what if my confession was rebuffed? What if I laid myself bare before this man and he paid me back with what I deserved? Condemnation. Rebuke. Shame.

I had proven a foolish woman too many times. This time I would wait patiently for God's timing and direction.

22 April 1775

Dear Miss Caldwell,

Please accept the enclosed package on behalf of Captain Alexander Smythe. On his sickbed, he requested I write this letter and see that it was sent to you.

My condolences,
Second Lieutenant Charles Taylor, King George III's
47th Regiment of Foot

19 APRIL 1775

My Dearest Liberty,

Another is writing this letter for me, as I lie at death's door. I could not part this world without somehow closing the separation between us. I will write in a frank manner, for time is short, and I wish to bare my heart to you in hopes you will someday forgive me.

Even as I write this I am unsure if you ever cared for me. I have made peace with that, for even if you did love me, could ever there have been two lovers more star-crossed than we? Certainly, part of what drew me to you was your vulnerability, your innocence. Yet I fell in love with you for your fire. Your defiance, even. Never a woman with her own mind had I known. You embody the American spirit that the Crown mocks. And yes—now that I know I am not long for this world, I can say I admire that.

Forgive me, dear one. Forgive me for the vast mistakes I've made. Forgive me for not being your rescuer when you needed me that day Philips exposed his vile intentions. Forgive me for selfishly trying to tear you away from the one you now love. Most of all, if ever and at all you can, forgive me for being a part of the demise of your loved ones. I pray your husband was not among those killed this day—a wretched day if ever there were.

I ask you to accept this ring as the only thing I can give to you at this time. It is a ring that has been in my family for generations—I intended to give it to the woman of my heart, and so I am. If it pains you to think of me when you look upon it, think then on who it points to. For as death nears, I can find only one strength, one consolation. The Lord is my strength, and I pray He be yours also.

When you look at this ring, think not of the wrong I have done you; think of the right that God has done you. Where I have failed to give you a promising future, I trust the Lord will most certainly prevail. This belief is the only reason I can leave this life—leave you—in peace.

Farewell, sweet Liberty. I pray when I cross into His arms, it will not seem so very long until we will meet again.

Yours forever,
Alexander

I hid the ring away in a chest of drawers, beneath the depths of James's old swaddling clothes. I mourned Alexander without show, my tears falling on my feathered pillow at night. I clung to his words, to his last effort to give me comfort in a God I couldn't help but lean on. For where else could I turn in those days?

And yet, wretch though I was, I felt a strange freedom in receiving Alexander's letter. In the moments before I read it, I had expected to feel some lingering devotion, but my heart had grown wiser, truer. I did not need Alexander's absolution to set me free. On the contrary, receiving it allowed me to set him free.

Once Hugh healed, he took on the chores of both his and his brother's homesteads. After sharing dinners in Cora's grief-torn house, he would often ask me to stroll with him around the green as we had done our first night together in Lexington. There, where he had fought alongside—and lost—his brother and nephew, Hugh and I began again. I did not presume 'twas a conscious decision on his part. And yet it seemed more natural—sweeter, even—than honey from the comb.

In the little spare time afforded him, Hugh helped his neighbors rebuild the many houses burned by the Regulars on their way back from Concord. And word of another victory for the Patriots came to us—Boston was under siege by the Americans! No soldier of the Crown could get in or out.

Cora gave up midwifery and refused to let the children out of her sight. Even Nathaniel, who worked alongside his uncle and who was now a man himself, could never flee too far from his mother's watchful eye.

I tended to patients as well as overseeing the running of the day-to-day chores. Meals, laundry, garden, cleaning. James by my side. He already knew how to milk the cow and gather eggs.

I had long since memorized Alexander's letter. In the days and months following, when the Patriots seized Fort Ticonderoga, when the Second Continental Congress met in Philadelphia, when war was no longer a question but a certainty, I clung to his proclamation that the Lord would be my strength as He had been Alexander's. I clung to the promise of God to give me a peace and a victory—a freedom—that passed all understanding.

JUNE 1775

The heat of a summer day baked the back of my neck as I parted weeds from the tender herbs of my garden. Though the hazy curtain of Cora's grief had lifted slightly in the past few days, she often chose to stay inside, leaving the garden work to me.

Many of the militiamen had left for Cambridge Common the day before. Rumors of a surprise attack upon the king's soldiers, of fortifications being built on Bunker Hill, flew faster than an arrow from a taut bow. I didn't think Hugh would go—his brother's family still needed him, grieving as we all were. Though Nathaniel could care for the fields, I didn't know what another death would do to this family.

As I battled with both thoughts of war and a particularly stubborn patch of crabgrass, I rolled up my sleeves and sought the shade of the barn in search of a small rake. The cow stomped her foot at my arrival. I breathed in the earthy scent of hay and manure, let the cooler air linger over the sweat on my face. I walked to the corner of the barn, where the tools shared a home with mouse droppings. Rummaging through the tools, I finally found the rake I sought, its metal cold upon my fingers.

I sensed a presence behind me before I saw its shadow upon the cow's stall. I gripped the handle of the rake, noting its worth as a weapon if need be, and turned slowly, half-expecting a stray red-coated intruder to demand shelter or food.

Instead, Hugh stood slouched at the door, the long fowler gun he used for hunting in his bloodied hands, his shirt and brown hair crusted with dirt and sweat, his right knee buckle unfastened.

I dropped the rake and went to him. "Hugh—you . . . I didn't think you would go."

I put my hand to his head, where a smear of blood marked his forehead. He didn't flinch at my touch, but I felt his gaze heavy upon me. His hands came up to touch my waist, gentle at first, then a bit more possessive. "Liberty," he breathed.

I searched those deep brown pools. His mouth trembled and I let my hand fall to his sticky, dirtied cheek.

"Liberty . . . I want joy. I am tired of regrets and grudges. I'm tired of looking at you and wishing things had been

different. I am ready—if you are—to *make* things different."
He licked his sun-cracked lips, swallowed. "You've changed.
I see a peace in you I long for. What I saw this morning—
what I took part in . . . it made me realize I don't want to
live another day without seeking joy. And when I think of
joy . . . when I think of a life worth living . . . I think of you.
Of James. Of a future and a family."

I blinked, drew in a shaky breath as I tried to comprehend
all he had said. I let my hand fall to his damp collar. "I've
missed you," I whispered.

His mouth covered mine in a needy kiss. He drank me in
with longing, and I sank into him, loneliness finding company in his safe embrace, in his insistent kisses.

He came up for breath, planted his lips on my nose. "I
know things will not be perfect. We are flawed, the both of
us, but I do believe with God's help we can make a marriage
succeed. Please, Liberty, say you'll come and live as my wife
in the house I built for you. For us."

I caught my breath, tried to wade through his intensity.
I pushed away, slightly, seeking words for what I needed to
say. "You once told me a marriage must be based on trust."

Hugh's eyes clouded, and I wondered if, in his fragile state
of mind, he wasn't yet ready to claim me and my honesty.
Perhaps he wished to remain in a safe fantasy, to move forward without looking at the past.

I felt him begin to shut down from me. His hands
dropped from where they held my waist. I wanted to pick

them up—dried blood and all—and plant them back on my middle. Ground him.

I wrapped my arms around myself instead, pressed them to my stomach. "I have not always been honest with you, Hugh. And I don't want to enter into this marriage with any more fallacies between us."

His mouth pressed into a thin line, the dry dirt on his face breaking away in pieces.

"I received news of Alexander's death not long ago. 'Twas after our talk at Buckman's. He sent me a ring that has been between us. I have it still." I allowed my words to sink in before I placed a hand on his arm. "Hugh, I meant what I said that day. I am ready to give myself to you—all of me, to you. No more looking back. I am so sorry for the hurt I've caused you. When I think of my future, I can imagine nothing better than sharing it with you. Is there any way you can forgive me, that we could mend the broken trust between us?"

"He is dead. . . ."

I looked at the ground. "Yes."

"And . . . if he were not?"

I felt peace with the honest answer I would give. "Long before I learned of his death, I knew I loved you. My heart has relinquished him entirely. Were he standing alive in this very room, I would still wish to spend the rest of my life with you."

He squinted beneath the setting sun, closed his eyes. When he opened them, he crushed me to his chest, pressed his face to the hair alongside my mobcap.

"I love you," I whispered.

He brushed his lips against my cheek. "There is nothing . . . better my ears should hear." His mouth moved toward my lips, parting them with a gentle sweetness that built in intensity. Then he was kissing me long and deep and full. There was healing in that kiss. Healing from my past, healing for my future.

I need not have worried about the intimacies of marriage reopening old wounds. Instead, when I gave myself to my husband the night we were wed, I found his closeness to be a balm to my wounded soul. With the sun long tucked in for the night and the crickets playing a melody especially for us, I shared my entire being with Hugh, finding in his arms not only pleasure and rest but freedom.

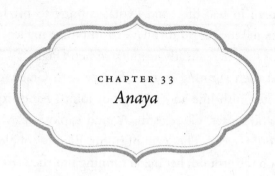

CHAPTER 33
Anaya

THE NIGHT BEFORE the Patriots' Day race brought a barrage of unsettling dreams to hover over my consciousness, picking at pieces of my memory and toying with them, drawing them out in fresh horror.

The day of the bombing and all the horrific sights and scents—mangled limbs, blood and pieces of flesh, wailing terror. A warm ring, the Old State House, red-coated soldiers firing on a mob, Brad's strong arms . . . and then all was gone, replaced by a black void of desperateness followed by flashes from my childhood with my sister.

Lydia, holding the back of my Rainbow Brite two-wheeler bicycle seat, the ribbons on the handlebars swatting my knees.

Lydia, holding my hand to kneel in front of my grandfather's casket, his skin pinched and pale—not at all like the Grampy I'd known in real life. And Lydia, coming to my hospital room to tell me they didn't have to amputate my leg after all but that they had already amputated her daughter's.

And then running in the 5K race with Grace, coming upon the finish line and raising our joined hands together, closer and closer. Closer still. A loud explosion. My hand torn from Grace's. The scent of sulfur. Bloody cobblestones. Grace on the ground, her metal running prosthesis torn from her body, Lydia across the Atlantic in the UK—

I woke, gasping for air, my body jolted upright from wet sheets. My chest heaved, the room still dark. I scrambled for the light and let it flood the room. The clock read 5:30.

As I caught my breath, I reminded myself that all of it was a dream. And yet that wasn't entirely true. Each segment held demons from my past. I couldn't pretend they were figments of my imagination, for they had all happened.

I brought my knees to my chest and buried my face in the blankets as sobs shook my body. I was scared. I was helpless. I searched, frantic, for good in place of evil but came up short.

With quivering hands, I called Brad, but after several rings it went to voice mail. My teeth chattered as I put the phone down and curled into a ball, the sheets still warm from my sweat.

"Please, God . . . help me." I thought of Grace's Jesus, of the pure light upon her face when she spoke of Him. I thought of Brad's Jesus, a companion on a dark and lonely journey. "Jesus, if You're there . . . help me." My words ended on a tremble and I lay, willing Brad to call. I didn't expect to hear from Jesus.

I stared at the phone on my nightstand and beckoned life to come to it.

Nothing.

My gaze fell to Liberty's ring beside the phone, where I had placed it when I had taken it off the night before. I thrust out an arm, grabbed the ring, and clutched it to my chest. The cold metal warmed beneath the heat of my skin, and I thought to try to summon power from the metallic elements within. But the futile thought depressed me. I needed something more real. Something bigger than myself. Something—someone—stronger than me. I dialed Brad again, eliciting the same automated response.

I clutched the ring tighter, slippery now from my grip. I loosened my hold and stared at it.

Qui fortis salutem tribute.

Victory belongs to the one who is strong.

A chill swept through me, and my body took up a shivering so intense I felt I would never be warm. I was weak. Broken. My limbs felt like slabs of concrete. I would have to call Grace and tell her I wouldn't be able to run today. I hardly had the strength to lift my head off the pillow. I was getting sick; that must be it.

The ring blurred before me. The anchor faded in and out beside the symbol of the horn.

"My anchor holds within the veil . . ."

The words we'd sung in church on Easter.

"It stands for God's strength. They put their faith in something bigger than themselves."

Brad's words.

Victory belongs to the one who is strong.

I repeated the words over and over, closed my eyes, and lulled myself into a trancelike state.

Victory belongs to the one who is strong.

I wasn't strong. I was weak. The anchor, the horn . . . God was strong.

Could He be strong enough for me? My eyes popped open at the thought.

My burden was too heavy. I needed someone to carry it for me.

Not so far away, the sound of a cannon echoed through the town. Lexington Common was no doubt alive with thousands of spectators for the reenactment. The first shots of the Revolution. The first veterans of war. Later, they'd commemorate the Battle of Concord at Old North Bridge, where Americans tasted victory for the first time. I thought of Liberty, Hugh, and Alexander. How had they been a part of that fateful day long ago?

Another cannon shot. With it, the *pop, pop, pop* I'd heard a nanosecond before my arms reached my niece, a nanosecond before the bomb threw me off my feet, ripping shrapnel through my legs. My nightmares threatened to pull me back into their steel embrace, but I shook them off, felt strength returning to my limbs.

Today, I had two options. Option A: dwell on this day from two years ago. How Grace had had both her legs, how any number of what-ifs could have changed the course of that day. Maybe by evaluating things in my head I could eventually accept the circumstances, see some sort of good in it.

Or option B: I could get up, run with Grace, leave all the pain and memories and nightmares beneath my pillow where they'd suffocate a slow death—hopefully before I came back to bed that night. I could accept that life was too wild and uncontrollable for me to waste time sitting in bed worrying about the many things that could go wrong this day.

I chose B. I heaved the covers off my body and slid my feet into fuzzy pink slippers. I showered, washing the grimy residue of my nightmares down the drain. I brewed coffee, trying to fake myself into thinking it a normal day.

The percolating coffee filled the room with an earthy vanilla scent. I heard footsteps coming up to the apartment, and I tried to wipe the sleep out of my eyes and fix my hair. A knock.

I turned and opened the door to see a bob of a ponytail beneath a child-size *Boston Strong* hat.

"Hey, Emilia."

Emilia stood with her arms folded over her chest, half-hiding a printed American flag on her sweatshirt. She stared at me, unsmiling.

"Good morning," I tried again.

She tapped her foot, kept the arms crossed. A perfect mini adult. "Well?"

"Well what?" I left the door open to pour my coffee.

"Are you gonna let me go?"

"What?" I thought I had been clear. Emilia wasn't coming. And now the little manipulator stood angry in my kitchen, her hat shouting at me. *Are you strong or not? Everyone else has moved past it. Even the double-amputees have triumphed in some way. Claimed to be stronger. What about you, Annie? Are you going to claim strong?*

Then, Brad's words from the other night. *"This isn't about you. Or me. Or even our faith—as weak or strong as it may be. Jesus is strong enough for us."*

Strong enough for me.

It sounded so easy. And what if it was? Maybe today was the day. Not because it was Patriots' Day or even two years after the bombing. Maybe it was the ancient ring on my nightstand and the history it whispered. Maybe it was the horrible, all-too-real nightmares that I couldn't shake. Maybe it was that stupid hat a little eight-year-old wore in my kitchen. Reminding me I didn't have what it took. I wasn't strong enough. I never would be.

Maybe there was an option C. Maybe God could be strong enough for me. Maybe instead of looking to Brad to be my faultless hero, I had to look to someone who actually *was* a perfect hero.

I closed my eyes, released a breath. Surrendered it all to Him. He knew the past, my struggles, my everything. I hadn't done well pulling myself up by my own bootstraps. I'd failed time and time again.

Maybe that's because I couldn't do it on my own to begin with.

Alongside the acknowledgment of my need came a foreign, sweet relief. It swept in like a honeyed balm to my spirit, like a cheery bell of freedom. A warm tear slid down my cheek, baptizing me in grace.

I felt a tug at my sleeve and I opened my eyes. Emilia tilted her head farther up than normal to peer at me from beneath the brim of her hat. "I didn't mean to make you sad, Annie. I don't need to come if you don't want me to."

I squeezed her hand, knelt down to hug her. "Of course you can come, sweetie. I'm sorry I didn't ask you sooner."

"Come on, Auntie. Half a mile more." Grace puffed the words through winded breaths. She glanced at her wristwatch. "We're at a seven-twenty pace. Let's finish strong."

Emotions bombarded my soul from every direction at the words. They were almost more than I could take. Doing this—accomplishing this—was almost more than I could take. If I dwelled too much on it, I would melt into a pile of blubbering sentiment alongside the puddles forming in the road.

I pushed it aside, focused on my feet pounding pavement alongside Grace's. Nausea welled in my belly, but I pushed onward. We neared the green and I dropped my shoulders, lengthened my stride. I searched for Brad and Emilia, Lydia, Roger, and Joel but couldn't make them out within the vast crowd of umbrellas.

We sailed past the finish line and slowed to a walk, hunched over in gasping breaths, into the crowd. I swiped a hand across my nose and Grace and I collapsed into one another's arms, wet and slick from sweat and rain.

I let the emotions take over then, as did she.

"Thank you, Grace. Thank you." For asking me to run the race. For forgiving me when I'd done the inexcusable. For helping me to glimpse a God whose power far exceeded my own.

"I love you, Auntie. I'm *so* glad you're here."

"Me too, kiddo. Me too."

And then Brad's warm, dry arms were around me, and I leaned into him, sank into the security he offered. I high-fived Emilia and Joel. Lydia and Roger hugged Grace, gave me genuine smiles, told us we'd both done wonderfully.

We walked away from the finish line to search out a place for breakfast. As we did, I pondered how normal this felt, how far away my nightmares from this morning seemed. I pondered Lydia's smile, genuine but with a piece of something missing.

Perhaps this was how it would always be from now on. We would be together, but not true sisters of the heart. We could tolerate one another, maybe even enjoy the other's presence for some time, but that closeness, that intimacy, might never be realized.

I wondered if I could live the rest of my life like that.

Then I realized I might just have to. I could only bring my repentance to the table of our relationship. Lydia would have to bring the forgiveness.

CHAPTER 34
Liberty

I rubbed my gently rounded belly as I looked at the barren building site before me atop Beacon Hill. Hugh's baby seemed to be growing well within the confines of my womb. Though the Lord had not seen fit to grant Hugh and me our own babe until James had grown and taken a wife of his own, I counted myself blessed to be able to finally give this gift to my husband.

Ignoring social niceties, Hugh placed his hand over mine and shared a knowing smile with me. I inched closer to him, thankful for the good and decent man I had shared the last twenty years with. No, we did not always agree on everything, but we chose to agree on belief in our marriage. We chose to agree on love.

From the side of the Common, coming up Beacon Hill and passing Hancock Manor, strode fifteen gleaming white horses—one for each state of the union. In their wake, they pulled a sturdy cornerstone—what would mark the foundation for the New State House.

The crowd murmured as the ceremony proceeded. Governor Samuel Adams arrived with an escort of shiny fusiliers, a container no bigger than a cigar box in his hands. I wondered if my poem was within.

I remembered the rise of his thin eyebrows as he read the poem on his last trip to Lexington. "Mrs. Gregory, when I asked you to include something that might symbolize freedom, I entertained a small relic of your brother's. I hardly thought you'd give me a poem memorializing a soldier of the Crown."

Hugh had taken my hand, squeezed his encouragement, dear man. He knew Alexander's death haunted me sometimes still, knew that this final tribute would allow me to lay my past to rest for good. In truth I had thought to bury Alexander's ring, but something stopped me at the last moment. As if prompted by the hand of God, I felt a strong urge to keep it, to hand it down to my children as a reminder that God's strength was forever available, that we weren't bound by our pasts but where we put our hope for the future.

"It is not memorializing a soldier but the bond we as humanity have. A bond where love and sacrifice can be used to purchase freedom. Please, Governor, we won our independence. My brother's blood seeped into the dirt the Old State House was built upon. Allow this to be a sort of truce with England—that we may not forget all that happened but be stronger for it. Let the New State House be a beginning for us to move forward in freedom."

Governor Adams scratched the back of his neck. "What will those of a future generation think if they ever uncover such writings?"

"They will see that despite our differing beliefs, we all long for the same things, do we not? Life, liberty, and the pursuit of happiness. And whether we are European or African or American, can we not all agree on that?"

The governor folded the poem, tucked it in the pocket of his coat. "Only because of your brother's first sacrifice do I even entertain the thought of putting this in our time capsule. I will think on it, Mrs. Gregory. That is all I promise to do."

I snapped from my reverie at the start of the fifteen-gun salute. Together, Governor Adams, Mr. Revere, and Colonel Scollay placed the metal box in the ground between two sheets of lead.

Governor Adams spoke, formally dedicating the New State House to the principles our country was built upon, which should "there be fixed, unimpaired, in full vigor, till time shall be no more."

The governor met my gaze then and gave a slight nod. I smiled my gratitude back, confident the gesture meant what I thought it to mean. My poem, my tribute to not only Alexander but to Hugh and every other human as well, would remain beneath the cornerstone of this State House for years to come.

I wondered who would find and read my poem and what, if anything, it would mean to them. I rested my fingers on the child within my womb and prayed for the future citizens of our infant country. I prayed for those who would one day read my poem, that they would glimpse my brother's precious sacrifice, my struggle with caring for a man who was the enemy, and the ultimate freedom that the Lord had brought me in the end.

CHAPTER 35
Anaya

THE BOSTON BOMBING sentencing trial began the day after Patriots' Day. I tried to ignore the news and went about my workday as best I could. My legs were tight from the race. Grace and I had planned an easy run for that evening.

I pulled up to Lydia's house already clad in workout pants. The maple beside her colonial waved new leaves at me as I climbed the steps and knocked on the door.

Lydia opened it.

"Hey." I shifted from one foot to the other. "Grace and I planned a run. . . ."

My sister opened the door wider. "Come in, Annie. Grace just called. She's running a few minutes behind. Said she needed to stay after for some help in calculus."

I entered the house, and Lydia closed the door. Strained awkwardness filled the rooms. An intense well of hatred for it erupted in my middle.

"Do you want some coffee?" Lydia walked toward the kitchen.

I really didn't want coffee before a run, but I didn't want to turn down the precious offer, either. "I'd love some."

Lydia started up the Keurig and I sat at the island, on the same stool I'd occupied the day I'd come with the potted lily not two months earlier. I thought of Grace's kind reception, of finding Brad's card, of my sister's cold greeting. How long ago it seemed.

"You two ran well yesterday." Lydia pulled down two mugs. The hum of the Keurig echoed through the kitchen.

"Your daughter's the one who pushed me. She's amazing." I clamped my mouth shut but couldn't keep it closed. If I did, we might go on like this forever. Cordial, bandying niceties, and skirting the wall that was still erected between us. "Lydia, I know you might not want to talk to me, but I can't go on like this . . . with this thing between us we both seem bent on ignoring."

"What thing?" She said it so flippantly, I wondered for half a second whether the wall between us was my imagination only. But no, behind those innocent-sounding words her defenses had risen. I could see it in the way she dumped too much sugar in the coffee cups, the way her back looked abnormally straight.

I wanted to demand she stop pretending, demand she yell

at me, curse at me, do what she had to in order to get everything out in the open.

"I found Brad's card that first day I came to visit. I'm sorry. I didn't mean to snoop. It fell out of your Bible and I went to put it back. But I recognized the logo from the ring, so I kept it."

The words flew out of my mouth, and even as I said them I wanted to take them back. Kick myself. Why, oh why did I think starting our heart-to-heart with Brad's business card was a good idea? I hadn't an inkling. Though certainly it would serve to get a rise out of her. She couldn't be so nonchalant if I brought it up.

She scooped up a mug of coffee before it was finished bubbling and hissing. The remnants dribbled into the black plastic base, settling at the rim.

I sucked in a breath. "I know I should have told you. But I just kept wondering why you didn't tell me about him. I mean, you knew I'd been looking for him. . . ."

She spun on me, and I knew that I'd finally cracked her open. "You are unbelievable."

We stared at each other and I waited for her to have her say, to vent out all her negative thoughts about me. I prayed I could stand up beneath them.

"You have the audacity to question a stupid business card I forgot about during the worst time of my life—the worst time in my family's life? I mean, it's all about you, isn't it, Annie? Things get too hard, maybe seeing your niece in a wheelchair makes you uncomfortable, so you leave, right?

Well, you know what? Love doesn't work that way." She was yelling now, her hand braced on the quartz countertop, her knuckles white. "And then to waltz back into our lives now that the worst is over . . ."

Her words condemned me, reminded me of all my failings, of the very thoughts that imprisoned me these past several months. My stomach soured as she took a breath to continue.

"I shoved that card in my Bible and forgot about it until well after you'd made your decision not to be a part of our lives. Maybe you'd asked me about your Red Sox hero now and then those first few weeks after, but do you think I heard any of that? Do you think I *cared*? For heaven's sake, my daughter was crippled, Annie. Crippled. How many times did I wish I'd been standing where she was? How many nights did I rail at God for the unfairness of it all? And where were you? Where were you, Annie, when we needed you?"

Her posture slumped. "By the time I remembered the card, you were long gone. You think I was going to go out of my way to call you after all those months of silence? After watching Grace's face light up every time the phone rang, then seeing her disappointment when she realized it wasn't you?" Her voice ended on a quiver and I thought I saw wetness at the corners of my rock-hard sister's eyes.

As much as I thought I'd been ready for this moment, I wasn't prepared. I hadn't realized the depth of Lydia's hurt, the depth of her bitterness. And who could blame her? She was right: the fault was entirely with me. Her words pinned me with fresh guilt and I wavered beneath them. I had no excuses.

I stood, but going to her was out of the question. Instead I clung to the beveled corner of the island. "Lydia, I am so, so sorry. Every day I wish I had made better choices. I—I felt so guilty about what happened to Grace. Every moment of every day I would relive that race, push myself harder, be the stronger runner I wasn't that day. I gave up during that race. And the fact remains, if I hadn't given up, if I had gone faster, we would have been out of there by the time that bomb went off."

"But we weren't, Annie. It happened. Life happens . . . bad things happen. And you don't just run away when they do happen." She raised her hand and slapped it on the counter with each word. "That's not what family does, Annie. That's not what family does!" Her hands slid off the counter, her shoulders drooped farther, and sobs trembled through her body.

As much as it hurt to hear her words, they needed to be said. They needed to be out in the open. As much as it felt like an old wound had been torn open and salt poured upon it, I felt something between us fall. As if a giant wall of bricks stood in the middle of us and after many hours of pounding my bloodied fists against the wall, one tiny, old block on the bottom crumbled.

I walked over to my sister's quaking form. I swallowed down a lump in my throat. "Lydia, I wish I could do it over. I wish I had a second chance to do the right thing." I reached out an arm but it was quickly rebuffed.

"What if Mom didn't tell you we were considering moving abroad? How long would it have taken you to come back to us? Would Grace have graduated, been off to college, gotten married?"

A warm tear slid down my own cheek. I didn't have answers to her questions, and nothing I said would make the hurt disappear. "I am so sorry, Lydia. Please, please forgive me."

"Go, Annie. Just go. I can't do this anymore."

I stood frozen. Did she really mean it? And did she mean leave for today, or leave forever? And if I did go, where would that leave us? No doubt with a bigger wall erected because we never worked through the pain.

I closed my eyes, remembered the strength that God had miraculously bestowed upon me the morning before. *Help me . . .*

I didn't get any clear answers then, but I did know one thing. If I walked out that door again, Lydia and I could never mend what was broken between us. The time was now.

"I'm not going anywhere, Lydia. Yes . . . this hurts, and yes, it's hard. For both of us. But like you said, we're family. We don't just leave. I never should have in the first place."

She looked at me through watering eyes. "You're expecting me to say it's okay, that we can go back to the way it was. And I just—I can't."

"I'm not expecting anything. Please believe me. I just want to be with you . . . to be with your family. I don't want this fakeness between us. If we're not okay—which we're not—then so be it, but let's not act like we're okay. I know I hurt you and Grace, your family. But I want to try and make it better. I want us to heal together."

She didn't say anything, just stood looking frail and wounded, the counter holding her up.

I tried again, turned so I leaned against the counter. "To tell you the truth, I don't know how Grace has forgiven me so easily. The way she talks . . . the peace she has . . . you've sure raised a great girl."

Lydia let out a small, humorless laugh. "Now that is entirely a work of God's grace." Silence enveloped the kitchen, punctuated only by the soft ticking of the grandfather clock. I inhaled the scent of hazelnut coffee, searched myself for something to say, something to open up the conversation. When nothing came, I waited.

"Grace . . . she—we—did some real searching after the bombing. Visited some churches, started praying together." Lydia licked her lips.

I didn't speak, fearful to interrupt the crack of another block in the wall.

She opened her mouth, closed it, then opened it again. "Grace changed, a lot. She became less fearful; she blossomed. I didn't get it right away. But over time . . .'"

"You got religion?"

My sister's eyes brightened, and in that split second of a moment I could see she forgot about the past, about all my sins before me.

"It's not religion—that's the whole thing, Annie. That's what I got."

I wanted to know what my sister understood that made her eyes suddenly shine like this, what my sister got that Grace also seemed to possess. Perhaps it was the same thing those early Christians hiding in the catacombs understood. Perhaps it was the same thing that Brad was trying to show me when he encouraged me to trust in God. Perhaps it was the same assurance I glimpsed yesterday morning. "Got what?"

"Grace. The work God's already done for us." She stared at me and her eyes dimmed. Her jaw dropped open.

I scrambled for words, sensing that in this moment the wall would be erected stronger than ever, or fall completely. I ran my tongue over the roof of my mouth, tried to come up with some sort of reassurance, but nothing came forth.

Lydia buried her head in her hand. "Dear Lord, help me." Her whispered words flew to me over the chirping of birds outside the window, the sound of a neighbor's car turning onto the street, radio blaring.

"What is it—what's the matter?" I reached out a hand, touched her elbow, then snatched it back.

She rubbed her eyes, let her hands fall from her face. "I can't believe I'm sitting here talking to you about all God has done to forgive me, and . . . well, you know."

She hadn't yet forgiven me. Boy, did I know. "So . . . where does that leave us?"

Lydia stared at the floor. "It leaves me a hypocrite."

"Wow, don't be so harsh on yourself."

We laughed. It served to lighten the mood a smidge.

"If I refuse to forgive you, then I guess I'm kind of spurning God's grace."

"Ouch." It made sense, though. Lydia made sense. "But, you know, I don't think forgiving is saying what I did is okay. It's not okay. I abandoned you guys when you needed me most. I think forgiving is like . . . starting over. Starting new."

I let the idea roll between us. Like the start of a small snowball, I hoped it gained visibility and appeal the longer it sank in.

My hands shook and I stuffed them inside the sleeves of my sweater. My heart pounded hard, pumping blood to my ears. I opened my mouth to speak, grasped for words that wouldn't fail, words that I had thought through. But only one question seemed appropriate. And it was risky. I might as well cut my heart out and serve it to her on a platter.

I swallowed. "Do you think we might be able to start new, Lydia? Please?"

She didn't answer, continued staring at the floor. Then, finally, "Remember when you cut one of the pigtails off my Myra Hope Cabbage Patch doll?"

I smiled. "I was playing hairdresser and I swear, the scissors just slipped. You were mad at me for months."

"I was. But do you remember the moment I decided to let it all go?"

I shook my head.

"We were on the bus and one of the older boys was picking on you. I think he had a crush on you or something, but he was being borderline cruel."

I remembered. "Brandon Kent. Biggest bully on bus number three." I sobered. "He made me cry one day, and you marched up to him like it was nothing, like he wasn't four inches taller than you." Lydia had told him off that day, and Brandon Kent never bothered me again.

"As mad as I was at you, when I saw Brandon picking on you, none of it mattered. You were my sister, and you were hurting. I forgot about Myra Hope."

I swallowed, voiced what she must be thinking. "But Grace is a lot more precious than Myra Hope."

"Yeah, she is. But God has used this mess and grown her through it. Now, maybe it's my turn." She sighed, dropped her hands. "I don't want to be mad at you forever, Annie. You're my sister. I love you. Of course I'm not saying what you did is okay. But I don't want to keep holding this thing between us. I want us to heal. I do want us to start new."

An immense burden lifted from my chest. And as I hugged her, rejoicing in the crumbling wall, I felt I truly understood mercy for the first time.

I didn't deserve it at all. In fact, I deserved the opposite. Punishment, chastisement, a life banished from my sister's family. And yet Lydia wasn't giving me what I deserved. She was giving me what I didn't.

A new beginning. Forgiveness. Love. Grace.

CHAPTER 36
Liberty

While our family survived both influenza and smallpox epidemics raging through Boston over the years, it was yellow fever that finally knocked on the door of the homestead Hugh had built for us.

I refused to send Hugh to a pest house. I sent word to Cora to keep her many, generally welcomed grandchildren away from our homestead. I also sent word to James not to visit for some time, as his father had fallen sick. The headache, backache, and fever left my husband bedridden. Not until the third day, when the yellow pallor of his skin took up residence against his normally joyful face, were my fears realized. I knew that in three days' time, I would have either a recovering husband or a dead one.

From his sweat-filled sheets, Hugh crumpled in pain, blood from his nose stanched by a small cloth. He begged me to leave him, to spare myself—to spare our unborn child.

I brewed teas of every herb known to me, reached over my bulging stomach to lift my husband's head and force the medicine down. He sputtered and spat most of it back up.

When all else failed, I ignored the midwife in me who wanted to cure all and only tried to make him more comfortable. Changing his sheets and bedpan, washing him with a cool cloth, praying with him through his delirium.

On the fifth day of his sickness, I added a log to the fire, sat down in the well-worn wood chair he'd built for us all those years ago, laid my head in my hands, and cried.

"What will I do without you? Lord, please, have mercy. Spare my husband."

A gurgling noise sounded from Hugh's throat. "I . . . love you, my . . . wife."

I ran my hand over his thinning hair, searched his red-veined eyes for evidence of the healthy man I'd fallen in love with. Mercy upon mercies, I glimpsed him. Aware, and focused on me.

"Hugh." I kissed his lips, hard, willing my love to be sufficient to spur him to life. "My joy," I whispered my nickname for him, mutual after all these years. How many times had we lain in this bed, wrapped in a physical love for one another? How many meals had we shared, just in the other room? How many prayers had we said on calloused knees on this very floor for James, for Cora and her children, for a sweet babe of our own? How many hours had we toiled in the fields just beyond this window, side by side, building a future?

He lifted a yellow hand, gestured to the stand where he kept his Bible. "In the back . . . forgive me."

I wondered if it was delirium that spoke for him, but I slid open the drawer, grabbed up the black leather Bible, the edges of the pages as yellow as my husband's skin.

I flipped to the back, found a worn envelope beside a poem I had given him on our wedding day. "This?"

He nodded. "Read."

I took a paper folded in three from the envelope and straightened it, the handwriting somehow familiar. I skimmed the signature, comprehending and not comprehending all at once, and truly not wanting to read. What did I care for that part of my life that had been long laid to rest? Why should I think on it when my husband lay on his deathbed?

"I don't see why this matters now."

Hugh shifted slightly, his head shaking back and forth, agitated. "Read."

I bit my lip, forced my eyes to the paper that held a date of more than twelve years earlier, and read.

When I finished, a tear fell past the mound of my babe onto the letter. I shook my head, grabbing for my husband's hand, letting the letter fall on the floor. "There is naught to forgive, my love. Do you think if I had known Alexander was alive, it would have changed anything for us?"

His gaze showed doubt, and it grieved my heart. "I gave you all of me on the day we married. Please, stay with me. I can't bear to be without you."

He squeezed my hand. "Liberty."

I swiped at my tears, sniffled.

"After I pass . . . after you grieve a time . . . after you bear a healthy child, I wish . . . wish for you to go to him."

Him.

I shook my head, fiercely. "You will live, Hugh. You talk nonsense; it is the fever."

His reddened eyes looked sad. "Promise me you will find him. Promise me . . . you will allow him to take care of you . . . and our child."

My jaw trembled. How could I make such an oath? How could I think beyond this day, this hour? Again, I shook my head, anger stewing in my chest. "You would send me to another in the space of a heartbeat, then?"

He struggled to push words out. "I only want . . . your well-being."

"What is well for me is you."

He slid off into sleep, but woke five minutes later in a fit of convulsions. When they finally settled, a telltale rattle of death sounded in his throat. "P—promise me . . ."

I would not be able to live with myself if I did not give him this final peace. Sobs came hard: choppy and painful, my soul begging God to spare my husband. I moved my head up and down, unwilling to utter the word *yes*.

Peace passed over Hugh's face, then. He slipped into unconsciousness. I slid under the damp covers beside him, positioned his arm around me, and huddled into the safe spot beneath his arm. I hugged his weak body to me and let my tears fall on his shirt.

When I woke the next morning, his breaths were no more.

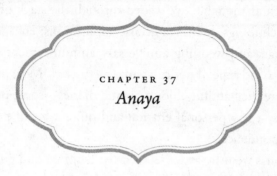

CHAPTER 37
Anaya

I RUBBED MY temples where the start of a headache formed. "Where else is there to look, Brad?"

For two weekends we'd looked for more information on Alexander Smythe or Liberty or Hugh Gregory or anything Lexington, but to no avail—online, at the archives, and now at the genealogical society.

"Why don't we look in the Lexington manuscripts they have on record from that time? Maybe we'll find something here, even if there's nothing on the people we're looking for."

I shrugged, thinking to appease him. "Sure. Whatever you think."

We asked a reference librarian to point us in the right direction and tried not to be overwhelmed by the amount of material she gave us.

Back at the table, we waded through the stack of newspaper clippings; marriage license applications; engagement, marriage, and wedding anniversary announcements; legal, divorce, and funeral notices; and society news. Most interesting were the handful of journals and diaries—some business ledgers, a few personal entries, and quite a bit of personal correspondence.

Hours went by as we learned the comings and goings of late-eighteenth-century Lexington, Brad and I exchanging pieces of our discoveries. My headache eased as I felt myself drawn in by a people who longed for liberty, a people who were willing to sacrifice for the Cause of freedom.

Brad slid an opened book toward me. "Look, the journal of Reverend Jonas Clark. It mentions Hugh Gregory."

I scanned the entry. "From October 1783."

The entry recorded a sort of inner battle for Reverend Clark. It stated that an English spy by the name of William Richards had been discovered in Lexington by Hugh Gregory. Mr. Gregory had received a letter from a British deserter informing him of the actions of a Dr. William Richards during the Revolutionary War. Hugh Gregory had reported the findings to Reverend Clark, though he seemed reluctant to do so, fearing that it may cast his wife in a bad light.

My pulse sped up at the mention of Liberty. The entry ended with Jonas Clark determining he would send the information of the spy on to Samuel Adams but leave the personal details surrounding the find between himself and Hugh.

The letter Hugh Gregory received, which incriminated William Richards, was carefully copied in Jonas Clark's journal following the entry. We read.

24 SEPTEMBER 1783

Dear Mr. Gregory,

I write this knowing you may not read a word and knowing it may be a sin to so much as think to send this letter. And yet my heart cannot rest until I know for certain that Miss Caldwell (Mrs. Gregory) is cared for.

I grabbed Brad's arm as I continued reading.

Now that the war is at an end, I can say that Lexington was home of a British spy, gone by the name of a Dr. William Richards. I received much of my information from him.

From him I learned that you were the one to strike me that April morning. From him I learned that you were the one to wed Liberty. With sincerest gratitude I wish to thank you for taking care of her. Forgive me; I realize it is not my place and terribly presumptuous, and yet all I ask is one letter—one sentence—stating the

*welfare of Liberty and that of her son. I do not believe I
will ever stop feeling responsible for them, and if that be
a sin, may God forgive me.*

*I have settled in the mountains of New Hampshire,
not feeling a need to return to the mother country
when my time to serve the king had ended. Some
call me a deserter. And while I cannot call myself an
American, I believe I could live with the title "British
American."*

*May I allay your fears in stating I never plan to
make contact with Liberty. I respect her desires and her
deep love for you. 'Tis why I have let her think me dead
these passing years.*

*One letter, one sentence, is all I ask. Then I will
breathe easy and continue to depend on God to put your
wife from my mind. His strength will hold me fast, as
always.*

Sincerely and not without shame,

Alexander Smith

Brad traced the name written at the end of the letter with his finger. "Whoa."

"I can't believe it." I traced the signature. "Alexander Smythe, Liberty's soldier. But the British archives said he died at Lexington."

"Apparently he kept the fact that he didn't from the Crown all those years. Probably by changing the spelling of his last name."

"Unbelievable," I whispered. "He did love her, and if we go by the poem, I think we can assume the feeling was mutual."

Brad nodded. "Must have been hard for Hugh to receive such a letter . . . harder still to know what to do with the information."

I pulled at my bottom lip. "He was a Patriot through and through, though he must have been torn over delivering this into Reverend Clark's hands."

"He felt it was his duty to continue to protect his country. But it seems he and Reverend Clark were close. He probably never felt that his friend would betray his wife by making the information public."

I agreed. "Perhaps Hugh and Liberty's connection to Jonas Clark and Sam Adams has something to do with the poem in the time capsule."

"Remember, her brother was one of the first casualties of the revolution. That alone could have been reason enough for Governor Adams to include it."

We sat in silence as we read the letter over again. I sat up slightly to cross my leg underneath me, my palms sweaty from the excitement of the find. "So Hugh wounded Alexander at Lexington. Crazy."

"Talk about a love triangle. But there it is—our story of the ring, or part of it anyway."

"Alexander settled in America. I wonder how much of that had to do with Liberty. . . ."

I stuck my finger through the ring around my neck, the

despair of the story settling in. Perhaps the happy ending of the ring's story would have to be mine. Maybe Liberty and Alexander never did get a happy ending. "I wonder if Liberty and Alexander ever saw one another again. . . ."

Brad shook his head. "Strange that Alexander chose not to return to his home country. He would have been a hero, wounded in the first battle of the war." He shrugged. "Maybe they did meet again."

I pointed to the last line of Alexander's letter. *His strength will hold me fast.*

"I like that. It ties into the ring, too. You know, depending on God to control this uncontrollable life."

I thought of the morning of the race, how the ring had helped me see the very thing Alexander spoke of. I leaned over, planted a kiss on Brad's lips.

"What was that for?"

"For giving me the ring that day. For letting me share in this journey."

He trailed a finger along the inside of my arm. "Believe me, Annie, it is entirely my pleasure."

We continued reading the reverend's journals. Most of the entries included excitement over a newly birthed America, concerns for his flock, prayers for his wife and children. Hugh and Liberty were mentioned several times.

James Gregory has taken a wife of his own from Concord. A finer man one could not know.

It is with great gladness that we learn that Hugh and Liberty Gregory will be expecting a babe this year. They have reminded me of Abraham and Sarah in their patient waiting.

With a heavy heart, I must report that I have conducted the funeral of my good friend and faithful member, Hugh Gregory, who died of yellow fever weeks before his wife was to give birth. I only pray mother and child remain well.

"Oh, poor things." Liberty's pain came across to me from the simple words on the page. What would it mean for her to be a single mother in this new land?

We continued reading, learned that Michael Gregory was born to Liberty healthy and well.

I swallowed a lump in my throat. "After all those years of being wed, Hugh never even got to meet his son."

The journal entries came to an abrupt stop soon after the announcement of the birth of Michael Gregory. It appeared we would get no more answers from Jonas Clark.

"We should look for another marriage announcement to see if Liberty married again. We never did a search this late in the eighteenth century."

"Do you think she could have found Alexander?"

Brad wiggled a pointer finger in the crook of my elbow. "Chances are next to nothing that Liberty and Alexander got together again after all those years. There's too much against them—he's a deserter, she ran with the Patriots. Say they did know one another around the time of the Boston Massacre . . . by the time Hugh died, more than twenty-five years had gone by. Surely Alexander wed within that time too. And what about poor Hugh? The guy sounds like a good man. I'm not sure Liberty would be so quick to betray his memory by marrying a Regular. That would have been heavy stuff back then."

I mulled over Brad's words. "But none of this explains one thing."

"What?"

"Why Alexander's ring was the object handed down generation after generation. Why I'm the one holding it here, now, in 2015."

CHAPTER 38
Liberty

In my grief, I ignored the letter on the ground. I left it there while I cleaned Hugh's body for burial, while I washed the sheets and laid him out, while the weeks passed after my husband lay in the ground.

I walked aimlessly over the hard planks of the floor during that time, my footsteps echoing in the rooms. The hearth, once giving warmth and light, too often felt chilly. The phantom laughter of James and a much-younger Hugh as one clunked down his king sideways, admitting defeat in chess, haunted me. The canning of preserves, smattered stains on clothes and aprons, candles softly wavering in the night. A gentle kiss, a tender moment, a family to love.

Cora helped deliver my child, and as Hugh and I had already decided, I named our newborn after Hugh's nephew who had died that horrible day on the green all those years earlier. James and his wife came for two days to help with the chores. When all left, I doted on my babe, who resembled Hugh in every way possible—from the dimple on his chin to his slightly oversize ears.

When Michael turned three months old, I faced the stark reality that I could not plant and care for the house and a newborn by myself. Even Cora, who had plenty of children to help her and made a decent amount of money midwifing, had taken a husband after her mourning time.

I finally picked up Alexander's letter to Hugh, which had nestled itself under the bed I'd shared with my husband, dust collecting in its folds. I read it over, wondered at the Brit's audacity to write my husband, wondered at his audacity to allow me to think him dead.

Truth be told, I'd done fairly well not dwelling on Alexander. A few times during the early part of our marriage, I'd dreamed of him, leaving me to fight off images of him in my mind's eye for days. But the Lord would help me push him aside and cling to life. To Hugh.

I can honestly say I had no regrets over our twenty years together.

Now, though, I had bound myself with a promise. A promise I wasn't certain I could keep. I hadn't seen Alexander in twenty years. Why should I think he had not taken a wife since his last letter? Why should I think he would even want to wed me and care for my fatherless son? This was not like all those years ago. I was no longer a spry, lovely girl with supple skin and smooth curves. He no longer had need to feel responsible for me.

In the end, I chose to write him, only to keep my promise to Hugh.

8 May 1796

Dear Mr. Smith,

I write this letter reluctant to make a fool of myself. It has been many years. I hope all is well with you and your family.

I must make clear my reasons for writing. I write only to fulfill a promise to my husband, made on his deathbed this past harvest. I expect nothing from you and find nothing to forgive in any false notions of our past. I am in fact very happy to hear you are alive and well, and practically an American, I would say! My new babe, Michael, was born beneath the American flag.

This ring has traveled a circuit between us more times than I care to count. And so it is with a humble heart that once more, I give it back to you. Please, give it to your wife, or perhaps one of your children.

If you should happen to have none, then perhaps it will find its way back to me one day soon. As you have written in a previous letter to my husband, He will hold us fast. I am trusting in this, no matter the outcome of this post. Thank you, Alexander, for sharing your faith with me in that final letter. Thank you for pointing me to a strength I could never possess myself.

Warmly,
Liberty Gregory

CHAPTER 39
Anaya

THE SUN'S DESCENT behind the genealogical society reminded us that our time would soon be cut short once again. Brad and I ran a few searches for Liberty, limiting the time frame to the 1790s.

Nothing.

"Maybe search Jonas Clark? If Liberty got married again, he would have likely performed the wedding."

"That would be in the church records, though. Probably not here." Brad typed in Reverend Clark's name, along with our target time period. "We'll give it a try, anyway."

Three results came up under Jonas Clark's name, but no church records. The first result was a Sons of the American

Revolution membership application. The second, a newspaper extract that looked to pronounce his death, and the last—another newspaper extract from the *Columbian Centinel*. The catalog pointed us to the microfilm floor.

Brad and I made copies of Jonas Clark's entries, gathered our things, and took the elevator to the fourth floor of the society. We signed in, grabbed the correct microfilm from the back wall, and put the film in the machine and scrolled to the correct file number.

I didn't expect to find anything having to do with Liberty, but my heart trembled at the promising black-and-white headline. It was a newspaper article from the *Columbian Centinel*, titled *Governor Adams Attends Wedding of Regular*.

My mouth grew dry as I sensed we were about to find the rest of our answers. The rest of Liberty's story. Brad put an arm around me, holding me up as we read the article.

In one of the last events of his governorship, Governor Samuel Adams surprised the state of Massachusetts by attending a rather untraditional wedding in Lexington last week. The groom was a former soldier of the Crown. Alexander Smith became a resident of the state of New Hampshire shortly after the end of the war. He and his bride, Liberty Gregory, have both survived the death of spouses. While they knew one another at the time of Britain's occupation of Boston, it was not until last year that they reunited. Mr. Smith told the

Centinel that in marrying his first love, he had been the recipient of God's tremendous grace. "This is a second chance, a new beginning for Mrs. Gregory—Mrs. Smith, rather—and I."

Liberty Gregory is the sister of James Caldwell, one of the first casualties of the war, who perished in the Boston Massacre. She told me that it was her late husband's wish that she seek Mr. Smith out after his death. It is worth noting that Hugh Gregory was an avid Patriot, one of the men who stood their ground at Lexington in April 1775.

When the *Centinel* questioned the governor in his reason for attending such an unorthodox wedding, he replied as such: "The Sons and Daughters of Liberty have fought the good fight for our freedom. We have won that fight. As Mrs. Smith can attest, and as I agree, it is time we lay down old grudges and begin anew. In this day, in this marriage, I see not only two hearts united but a symbol of two countries that must continue to seek peace. Both Mr. and Mrs. Smith have borne tremendous loss. It is time to move forward together, in freedom."

The groom bestowed upon his wife a gift of a signet ring after the nuptials, which were performed by Mrs. Smith's late husband's dear friend Reverend Jonas Clark. Mrs. Smith shewed much emotion over the present. Though neither bride nor groom would divulge its history, the significance of the ring—and this day—will surely not soon be forgotten by those in attendance.

I wiped tears from my eyes as I finished out the article. I couldn't be certain, but I thought I caught a couple sniffles from Brad also.

"That. Is. Amazing." He shoved his hands in his pockets and stared at the image still lighting up the machine.

We stood, read the article over once more, and then again, soaking up every bit of the precious story we'd spent months looking for.

"They found each other. They got their happy ending." I clutched Liberty's ring in my palm.

"And we found the full story."

"Liberty must have given Michael the ring because in a lot of ways, Alexander *was* Michael's father. Michael never knew Hugh, but he would have considered Alexander his father."

We stood in silence for another moment before Brad spoke. "I like what Alexander said about new beginnings."

I nodded. It reminded me of my conversation with Lydia, of the glimpse of grace she'd shown me. My heart threatened to bubble over at the reminder, at the mercy given to Alexander and Liberty, and even Hugh all those years earlier.

We downloaded the article onto the flash drive and left the society.

I swung my hand in Brad's. "You know, I'm going to miss this. Playing detective with you. Coming here. It brought us together. Liberty and Alexander and the ring brought us together."

Brad gave me a sly smile. "I'm thinking I'm actually going to continue some of this. Find out more about the ancestors we traced to Liberty." He jiggled my hand in his. "Maybe you could find out some about your family."

"That might be something Lydia and I could bond over." I squeezed his hand. "We had another good talk the other day, actually. And they finally made a decision about the UK. They're staying."

I recalled the intense relief that swept over me when Lydia had told me her and Roger's choice. The way she welcomed my embrace after sharing the news.

Brad smiled. "I'm glad for you two."

We walked in silence for another minute before he spoke. "Funny, but I'll bet Liberty and Alexander never would have guessed their ring would have such a big role in our lives too."

I smiled. "We never would have gotten together if it weren't for that ring."

"Or the bombing."

I looked over at him. "You're the best thing to come out of that day, Bradford Kilroy."

He groaned. "I never should have put my full name on that card." We laughed and he stopped us from walking by pulling me close, lowering his mouth to mine. His fingers trailed down my arms. I breathed in that earthy scent of woods and spice, remembered our journey that began two years ago all over again. He kissed me deeply and fully, right there on the streets of Boston. When we parted, he took my hand and continued to lead me down Newbury Street.

"Ready to go back to your apartment and snuggle in with a movie?"

"Only if you're ready to venture out from *Rocky*."

When we reached Clarendon Street, I tugged his hand. "Actually, I was wondering if you're up for one more adventure."

"Sure . . ."

"Would you take me to the finish line?"

My question hung in the air. I'd surprised him. I could tell by the way his jaw hung loose, the way he blinked. "Really? You sure you're ready?"

"No. No, I'm not sure at all. But I'm tired of doing things out of fear. I didn't want to run that 5K with Grace, Brad. I even almost chickened out that morning. But I kind of rested in the fact that I'm not strong. That Jesus can be strong for me." I shrugged. "I get what Alexander was talking about—about God holding him fast. I think He's holding me, too."

He was looking at me so intently, I felt heat rising to my face. I looked away, but he chucked my chin and steered my gaze toward him. "I love you, Anaya."

I didn't miss the intentional use of my first name. Completely free. Maybe by the end of this walk I would feel I finally lived up to my name.

Together we turned left on Clarendon and then, a block later, right on Boylston Street. I clutched Brad's hand, felt my heart pumping blood to my limbs. I kept my gaze focused on the ground in front of me. We passed Copley Square on our left. An older man with a stack of newspapers under his arm greeted us and asked if we'd like to buy a paper.

Brad answered something, but I couldn't grasp his words. For just ahead, painted on the Boylston Street pavement, was the blue and yellow finish line. My knees weakened and I felt the pinch in the back of my calf more acutely than I had in weeks. I focused on the bold letters, the unicorn logo of the Boston Athletic Association that called to mind the unicorn atop the Old State House.

I stood on the red stone cobbles of the sidewalk, breathed in the scents of fried food and car exhaust. Brad didn't question when I continued up the street until I'd reached the spot of the first explosion—the spot where Lydia and Grace stood, cheering me on.

Memories threatened to break me. But for some reason here, with Brad and all I'd been through the past several weeks with him, Lydia, Grace, Liberty, and even God, I felt protected, safe.

His strength will hold me fast.

The cobblestones were scrubbed clean of the stains of blood. No sulfur haze marred the air. People went about their day in business suits and skirts, jeans and backpacks.

I was a different person than I'd been two years ago. And although I couldn't say I was glad the bombing occurred, I felt it had changed me for the better. I knew how to love better, how to receive forgiveness and accept it from myself.

I thought of Liberty and her ring. How precious the

symbol of God's strength and love had been to her in order for her to hand down the ring to Hugh's son. And because she had given it to her son, I could now bask in its legacy.

I took Brad's hand and gave a sharp nod to him, as if to say I was all set. I'd faced the place of my nightmares and conquered. I even thought about asking Grace if she'd like to try and run the marathon with me next year.

We walked back toward the Common and a calm contentment settled over me.

The reason runners love the finish line so much is what it symbolizes. That thick, painted line on the pavement means you can stop running. Stop pushing your body into further pain. Stop proving you have what it takes to make it.

The work is finished.

You are free.

EPILOGUE
Anaya

The muscles in my legs burned from the last twenty-six miles as my feet pounded the pavement on Boylston Street, keeping in rhythm with Grace's steady pace. Ahead, the blue-and-yellow finish line called to me.

"You ready to finish strong?" Through huffing breaths, Grace asked the question she'd asked at the end of every grueling workout we'd been through together the past eight months.

I heard Brad and Lydia shouting encouragement to us. I spotted them, little Emilia in her *Boston Strong* hat beside them.

Memories tugged at me. Sounds and scents of old threatened to resurrect havoc on what I intended to be victory.

Victory.

I had a new definition of *victory* this year. And a new definition of *strong*.

I might not be Boston Strong. Or even Annie Strong. I lacked too much, both in myself and my ability.

But God Strong? That I trusted. He could do any work He had in mind through me.

And I was convinced this was one such thing He wanted accomplished.

In sync with Grace, I raced past the spot where I had gone to hug her three years earlier. The wind swept my face, chilling the sweat on my brow. We picked up our pace, stretching our legs, dropping our arms, lengthening our strides.

It felt like flying.

Freedom.

Grace grasped my hand and lifted it high as we sailed over the finish line together. We slowed to a walk to catch our breath, and I slung a sweaty arm over her. When she hugged me back, tears glistened on her shining face.

I understood. This was victory in so many different ways.

We grabbed a water and a medal and meandered through the crowd to find Brad, Emilia, Lydia, Roger, and Joel. My sister got to us first, hugging us both at the same time, her voice quaking. "I'm so proud of you two."

I whispered back that I was proud of her, too. This was her victory as much as ours. Being here—bringing Joel—these were things she did out of faith instead of fear.

When Lydia pulled away, Brad swept me up in his arms, twirled me around, and pressed a kiss to my salty lips. "I love you."

"I love you." I hugged him, pressed my face to the Red Sox sweatshirt I'd found comfort in three years ago.

As much as that day had caused immeasurable pain, the fact remained that the two best things in my life had come from it. I sank into Brad's strong arms, marveling at the journey we'd been on together. Falling in love, finding faith.

An insatiable stirring of hope filled my chest. I'd been given a gift. A new beginning, a new story. My past had been wiped clean by grace.

And because of that, I could finally claim strength.

HISTORICAL NOTE

THE FIRST BOSTON MARATHON was run on April 19, 1897, setting the precedent that the oldest continuously running marathon in America would be run on Patriots' Day, a holiday commemorating the start of the American Revolution, which is recognized only in Massachusetts and Maine.

While the Battle of Lexington officially began the Revolutionary War, the five men who died in the Boston Massacre are considered some of the first casualties for the Cause of American independence. James Caldwell, a young sailor who died the night of March 5, 1770, was said to have no known family. Therefore, Liberty Caldwell is entirely fictitious.

The Massachusetts State House time capsule, buried by Governor Samuel Adams, Paul Revere, and William Scollay in 1795, was unearthed for a short time in 1855, and then more recently in December 2014. It was opened at Boston's Museum of Fine Arts a month later and put on display from March 11, 2015 to April 22, 2015. The time capsule contained coins, newspapers, a medal with the likeness of George Washington, and a silver plaque believed to be Paul Revere's work. Liberty's poem is also, of course, fictitious.

While I have tried to stay true to the real-life historical characters and their beliefs, I cannot presume I did so perfectly. Therefore, any fault is completely my own. Nevertheless, I hope I have honored the fathers of our country within the pages of this story.

ABOUT THE AUTHOR

HEIDI CHIAVAROLI is a writer, runner, and grace-clinger who could spend hours exploring Boston's Freedom Trail. She writes women's fiction and won the 2014 ACFW Genesis contest in the historical category. She makes her home in Massachusetts with her husband, two sons, and Howie, her standard poodle. Visit her online at heidichiavaroli.com.

DISCUSSION QUESTIONS

1. Both Annie and Lydia feel strongly that Annie abandoned her family after the bombing. What were Annie's reasons? What other choices could she have made?

2. Liberty found herself in a difficult situation—alone with no support system. Did she betray her principles by working for the British Army? What were her other options?

3. Describe Annie's connection to the ring. Would you call it a healthy or unhealthy connection?

4. Eighteenth-century Patriots like Liberty's brother, James, were willing to give their lives to combat British injustices. Have you ever strongly supported a Cause? What was it? How were you involved? Did people in your life support you? Question you? Oppose you?

5. How did Annie and Brad's history at the bombing affect their relationship? Did they successfully move past that?

How did they discover the real individuals underneath the mysterious figures from their memories?

6. After Liberty is assaulted, she's inclined to place some of the fault on herself, thinking her antagonism was partly to blame. This continues to be a serious issue in our time as well. Have you known anyone who was a victim, yet claimed some (or all) of the blame? What can we do—as individuals or as a society—to protect the vulnerable and afflicted?

7. Brad experienced the terrors and tragedies of war. How did his connection to Christ affect his view of those experiences? Read 2 Corinthians 1:3-4. What is God's intention for believers' struggles?

8. Hugh Gregory comes to love Liberty, overlooking the obstacles between them. How is this like God's love for us? How is it different?

9. Brad and Annie are eager to learn the history behind the poem and the ring. Are you connected to your own family history? Are there any mysteries you wish you could solve?

10. Through the course of the book, Liberty falls in love with two men. As you read, did you perceive a clear right choice or wrong choice for her? Have you ever been conflicted between two choices that both seemed right to you? How did you decide?

11. Annie and Lydia both have to learn about forgiveness before they can mend their relationship. Discuss Grace, Lydia, and Annie's different approaches to the dysfunction in their family. How do you respond when people have wounded you? Read Jesus' parable in Matthew 18:21-35. How do these verses apply to the characters in *Freedom's Ring*?

12. Liberty and Annie both feel the need for strength greater than what they inherently possess. When have you needed God's strength? How have those experiences affected your relationship with God?